I'm Losing You

(Book Four in the Stafford Brothers Series)

Chicki Brown

http://sisterscribbler.blogspot.com

Please Note

This is a work of fiction. Names, characters, places, and incidents either are the product of the author's imagination or are used fictitiously, and any resemblance to actual persons, living or dead, business establishments, events or locales is entirely coincidental.

The scanning, uploading, and distributing of this book via the Internet or via any other means without the permission of the copyright owner are illegal and punishable by law. Please purchase only authorized electronic editions, and do not participate in or encourage electronic piracy of copyrighted materials. Your support of the author's rights is appreciated.

What people are saying about the Stafford Brothers series...

"Chicki Brown's ***Don't Stop Till You Get Enough***, book three in her Stafford Brothers series, is a story that I read without stopping until I'd gotten to the end. There's nothing more exciting than tossing the hero into hot–and really, really hot–water at the beginning of a story. The character, Greg Stafford, is written with a real touch that leaves the reader empathetic to his dilemma and mind-set. At the polar opposite, in profession and upbringing, is Rhani Drake, who sets the tone for the battle of wills.

With introspection, humor and cautionary lessons, the romantic journey never strays into boredom or the other state of *meh*. Chicki Brown provides a well-rounded story that is a fun, enjoyable read and a pleasure to recommend for the top of the to-be-read pile." **– Michelle Monkou, USAToday**

"I just finished **Don't Stop Till You Get Enough** (The Stafford Brothers Book 3) and gave it 5 stars. "Don't Stop Till You Get Enough" definitely lived up to its title. Greg and Rhani's story is a must read for anyone who loves reading about destined love. I've had a couple of Chicki Brown books in my TBR list for a minute, but hadn't had the time to read them because they kept getting pushed back each time I would '...One Click' a new book. Boy did I ever realize how huge of a mistake that's been. I downloaded "Don't Stop Till You Get Enough" so that I could participate in an upcoming chat. To say that the book was very intriguing and exceptionally written would be an understatement. I can't wait to dive into the first two books of this and whatever else Chicki has to offer. Summer 2015 can't come soon enough for the release of the fourth book in the series, "I'm Losing You". If you haven't had a chance to read "Don't Stop Till You Get Enough", don't sleep on 'One Clicking' it! You will not be disappointed." **—Tina V. Young**

"I absolutely LOVE the Stafford Brothers series...these are books I'll read over and over. Can't wait for the next one!**—Reader JLT**

"This family series is right up there with the likes of the Westmorelands (Brenda Jackson), the Graysons (The late Francis Ray) and the Wolf Pack (Maureen Smith). Get the first one and settle back, enjoy the ride from the ATL to Vegas to Nigeria."**—Amazon review**

Acknowledgements

Marcia Vaughan-Matthews, my "northeast promo coordinator" for the fashion show details. I wanted to get them right, and I knew I could trust you to give me the real deal.

Estella Robinson and the members of the Critters Vineyard for beta reading. I know how busy everyone is, and the time you spent is greatly appreciated.

Renee Luke of Cover Me Book Covers for another awesome cover. Thank you for making me look good. Everyone loves your work!

And, most of all, to my readers. You have made my dream of becoming a popular author come true. None of this would be possible without you Thank you!

I'm Losing You

Chapter One

*R*amona Stafford peered at her image in the mirror. She was supposed to be getting ready for another fundraising meeting, but at the moment she couldn't gather enough energy or interest to put on her makeup.

"There isn't enough concealer in the world to hide the bags under my eyes," she mumbled at her reflection. "And getting rid of the redness will be a major project."

Her pride had kept her from crying in front of Vic, but once he'd left the house, she sat at the built-in vanity table in the spacious master bathroom and let the tears flow.

"I don't want those women to spend the evening guessing why I've been crying. They would just love that. The best thing to do is walk into the meeting with a smile, clear eyes and full makeup."

It hadn't taken her long to find out that doctors' wives could be the most jealous, critical people on Earth. Everything seemed to be a game of one-upmanship–who had the biggest house, drove the nicest car or had their children enrolled in the best school. A couple of them already disliked her for a variety of reasons. Some simply because her husband held a higher position than theirs did. Others because she still rocked her former Miss Georgia appearance–tall, slender with long, thick hair and a natural fashion sense. And a few because Vic was so handsome he made their husbands look like Lil Wayne.

"If they discover Vic and I are having issues, it'll cause more talk than Bruce Jenner's sex change." Gossip within the black medical community in Atlanta, which was smaller than most people on the outside realized, spread like wildfire. "Oh, God, I'm talking to myself."

Of all the wives in this particular fundraising group that worked to raise money for childhood cancer research, the only one she considered a friend was Daphine Weber. Her husband, Marv, was Vic's closest buddy other than his brother, Jesse. But she didn't even want Daphine to know what was going on between Vic and her.

Every day she regretted encouraging him to take the offer to become chief of surgery two years ago. At the time it seemed like a blessing, but their life was turning out to be just the opposite. Yes, the job came with a half-million-dollar salary, but it had also taken him away from the family. No amount of money in the world could compensate for that. Tonight they'd had another run-in before he left for his meeting.

"Can I talk to you before you go?"

His shoulders slumped. "Can't it wait until morning? My meeting starts at seven."

"So does mine, and I have to pick the boys up early in the morning in case your mother has plans."

Vic eased down onto one of the kitchen stools as though his whole body ached. "What's going on?"

"I miss you, Vic."

His heavy brows drew together. "What are you talking about, baby?"

"I'm lonely, Vic. You're never around, and when you are, you're too tired or too distracted to even notice I'm in the room."

He stared at her for a long moment without any response then groaned. "Mona, we're not kids anymore, and we're way past the infatuation stage. I know you have nothing to occupy your time, and that was your choice, but I'm overwhelmed."

"Which is exactly the problem. You have no time for me or the boys. Are we just supposed to sit around and pretend you're no longer in our lives?"

"If I wasn't in your lives, we wouldn't be having this conversation in a two-million-dollar house. How do you think all of this," he waved a hand in the air, "is being paid for?"

For the next few minutes, he went into what had become his standard lecture about being under scrutiny as not only the youngest but first black chief of surgery in the history of Atlanta's largest medical center—in the entire South for that matter. It wasn't as though she didn't understand the importance of his job. In fact, she was wildly proud of his status, but most of the time she wished he would go back to just being a surgeon. Surgeons were the elite of the medical community, but that hadn't been enough for him. Vic followed in his namesake's footsteps, and now he'd surpassed the professional status his father had reached. Sometimes his ambition actually frightened her.

"When is it going to stop? Do you have to become Surgeon General of the United States before you're satisfied?"

Vic rubbed the back of his neck and glowered at her. "Now you're just being ridiculous! You wanted me to take this job, remember? That was before this house and the Bentley."

"I didn't ask you for the car or the jewelry." She dragged in a long, frustrated breath, and spoke through clenched teeth trying not to lose it. "You bought those things for me, because you felt guilty."

"Guilty?" He rose to his full height and leaned over her. "What the hell do I have to feel guilty about?"

Mona looked up at him without blinking. "Abandoning your family so you could be the king of your hospital."

"You wanted me to be king. Or have you forgotten?"

"You're not being fair, Vic. I saw how desperately you wanted the position, and I did what I was supposed to do. I supported your

decision to go for it." She ran her fingers through her long hair that brushed her shoulder blades. "I never dreamed our lives or you would change so much."

How could such a brilliant man be so stupid? Why couldn't he see the negative turn their life had taken? He used to notice how she looked every day, but over the past two years, his interest in her had gradually waned. And it wasn't because she'd let herself go. For God's sake, the hours she spent in the gym were more for him than herself. No woman could love a man more than she loved Vic. They had been together for fifteen years, married for twelve, and at one time, he'd only had eyes for her. Now his new love–his hospital–had taken her place. He nurtured her, protected her, bragged about her, and spent endless hours thinking about how to make her better–the things he used to do for his wife. Nothing could be more painful than having your husband obsessed with another love.

The two of them hadn't been together in the same room long enough to have a real conversation in two weeks. She yearned for the times when he used to share everything with her. One of those conversations came back to her mind as clearly as though it had been yesterday.

"Hi, baby, are you sleeping?"

She rubbed the sleep from her eyes and propped herself up against the headboard, smiling at the sound of his voice. "It's okay. Are you off for the night?"

"No, I have to work a double shift. I'm on my way to the On Call room to try and catch a nap, but I just had to tell you what happened a little while ago." The excitement in his tone was almost tangible.

At the time, he was an intern doing grunt work for the residents, but he was eager to learn everything possible about medicine first-hand. She loved hearing about every detail of his days and nights on the job.

"A couple of hours ago the EMTs brought in a guy with a

screwdriver sticking out of the top of his head. It was the wildest thing I've ever seen, baby. He was alert and talking as though nothing had even happened. He kept telling the surgeon on duty to just yank it out, but the doctor made it clear he couldn't do that without possibly doing further damage. They had to run a head CT before they could figure out what to do. Well, to make a long story short, I got to observe the surgery from the gallery. It was amazing. I wish you could've been here to see it."

"No thank you! I probably would've passed out cold just from the sight. I'm glad you got to watch the surgery, though. You're going to be a great surgeon, Vic. It's where your heart is, and you get so geeked up when you witness that kind of thing."

"You have so much faith in me." The love echoing behind his words made her heart swell.

"Of course, I do. I love you."

"I love you too, baby, and when we get married and I get done with this program, I'm going to make sure you live like a queen."

She chuckled. *"Being Mrs. Vic Stafford will be enough for me. Go get some sleep before you collapse."*

"I will. Talk to you later."

Often they stayed up late into the night talking on the phone, and he asked questions about her burgeoning modeling career as though he was sincerely interested. She treasured the closeness and affection they had once shared. After listening to the women she associated with talk about their relationships, she realized just how unique and powerful it had been. Vic's studies and then his internship and residency put him under constant pressure. Yet when they were together, his super-serious demeanor softened. He laughed more and was able to relax.

After the wedding, once they moved into their own apartment, one of the things that brought her the most joy was lying in bed listening to his amazing stories about the inner workings of the hospital. She felt his thrill at being able to save lives. So often she stroked his long fingers thinking she couldn't have been prouder of his God-given talent.

Now, if they talked at all, it was about mundane, necessary things before he drifted into a work-induced coma. When he was conscious, hospital business constantly occupied his mind. He traveled to conferences, conventions and symposiums, and his schedule usually didn't allow him to accompany her to fundraising events or sit with her in the bleachers at the boys' football games. He'd become little more than a ghost in their own home.

Mona hunched over, folded her arms across her stomach, and rested her head on the vanity table. The moan she uttered sounded dismal to her own ears. She couldn't go to the meeting feeling this way. Everyone would take one look at her and know her heart was broken. Recently she'd decided to start going out with the ladies following their meetings. All they did was have a few drinks, watch the crowd and flirt with the bartender every now and then. In the past she'd refused, because she felt it wasn't right to leave Vic and the boys while she sat in a cocktail lounge with a group of women who, for whatever reasons, didn't want to go home. Now she understood her coiffed and manicured associates' reasons firsthand. By no means could she call them friends, and she wondered what their individual marital situations were, her mother's words came to mind.

"Vic's going to be a doctor one day, and a doctor's wife can't be frumpy or out of shape. Your hair and makeup should always be perfect. Your clothes should be the best quality you can afford until he starts buying them for you." Her mother had drilled it into her head as soon as she found out they were engaged. Mona could practically quote her word for word.

Whenever she voiced her discouragement with the situation, her mother quickly pointed out, "You have to stop being ungrateful, Mona. After all, you have everything most women would die for."

"Mama, have you forgotten when I married Vic he was as broke as MC Hammer. I married him because I *loved* him!" Her mother's canned response was, "You knew he would be somebody important one day. You don't have to work, and he leaves the daily finances up to you. What more do you want?"

Yes, Vic made the financial decisions, because he knew more about those things, and he always did so with the best for the family in mind. Having money was wonderful, and he had always been extremely generous. But did women like her mother actually believe that sharing money could take the place of sharing intimacy, in or out of the bed?

At first she thought she imagined it, but she clearly heard the words her mother had spoken to her before one of the biggest pageants she'd ever entered. She'd had the flu, complete with low-grade fever, stomach cramps and body aches. All she wanted to do was stay in bed with the covers pulled over her head, but her mother reminded her of the five-thousand-dollar scholarship grand prize, which was on the line. *Push through it, Ramona. Breathe deeply and smile. Nobody will ever know.*

She'd done it that day and this evening as well. When she walked into the restaurant meeting room an hour later, she greeted everyone with a wide smile and a wave. "Good evening, ladies! I hope you're ready to get this done quickly, so we can have a few cocktails in the lounge."

"Ooh, look at Ramona dressed and ready to do some socializing tonight," one of the women said, her gaze running from Mona's topknot to her Blahnik-clad feet.

"Well, Vic is at a meeting tonight, so I might as well." She took the empty chair at the head of the table. "Let's get started."

Vic Stafford pulled into the circular driveway of his home at ten forty-five p.m. Today had been the worst day he'd ever had at the hospital, thanks to a gruesome tour bus accident on Interstate 75. The fifty passengers on the bus and twelve occupants of other vehicles involved in the crash had been divided up between his hospital and Grady, since they were the only level one trauma centers in the Atlanta metropolitan area. According to the EMTs and State Patrol officers who were the first to arrive at the scene, the bus driver apparently mistook the exit lane at Northside Drive off I-75 as part of the carpool lane. He came up over Northside and continued over the side of the overpass. The bus traveled over a two-and-a-half-foot tall concrete barrier, leaving it intact, and through the middle of the overpass, crashing onto the interstate below.

As chief of surgery, Vic had to pull in every staff member on call in order to handle the volume and even performed two of the surgeries himself, something he rarely did anymore. When he'd left for the night, six of the accident victims had died, which considering the horrific nature of the crash, was a miracle. Five remained in critical condition, and twenty were lucid and being evaluated for broken bones and other non-life threatening issues.

He was drained from the emotion and pace of the night, and when he gazed up, every window in the sprawling eight-thousand-square-foot house was dark. Not even the flickering light from a TV screen or the glow of a computer screen. Usually he had to go into the boys' rooms and make them power down their iPads or game console when he came in at night. Where were they?

Before he left this morning, Mona had mentioned a

meeting with one of her fundraising groups. He hadn't really paid much attention, but he thought she'd surely be home by now. As if his work-related stress wasn't enough to push him over the edge, the changes he'd seen in her only added to his emotional anxiety. Their communication had deteriorated to only the necessary conversations about their sons, the house, and the daily finances. They had strayed so far from the long talks they used to have in the early years of their relationship. Back then, she'd been his sounding board, his confidante and his best friend. And she blamed him for the loss of that closeness.

Vic drove around to the side of the house. Even the guest house where Maite, their live-in housekeeper, stayed was completely dark. He hit the button for the garage door opener and entered the house through the kitchen. After he loosened his tie, he walked into the room Mona called his *man cave* and poured himself a scotch at the wet bar.

Even though he wasn't performing as many surgeries as he once had, ever since he'd been appointed chief, his hours had increased. Now he dealt with a myriad of daily administrative issues. A day never went by when he didn't consider stepping down and going back to just being a surgeon. But the position carried with it clout, great perks he hadn't gotten as a staff doctor and a more than a half-million-dollar-a-year salary. When he'd simply been Dr. Stafford, he and Mona owned a nice home, but once he became *the Chief*, they upgraded to this house, which contained three thousand more square feet, had an Olympic-size pool, wine cellar, home gym and guest house.

Now it seemed she was never home long enough to enjoy the home she said she loved. For the past few months, the evenings she spent with the ladies were getting later, and she never offered an explanation of the reason why. He'd ignored her behavior long enough. Tonight he would confront her. His anger built as he sipped his drink. He knew good and damn well these meetings to raise money for their favorite causes didn't run this long. If she wasn't asleep when he came in, she wasn't home at all. Vic didn't appreciate his boys spending so much time with Maite or at his parents' house.

He gazed up at the sloping double staircase that appeared to be as tall as Stone Mountain. Too tired to climb to the second floor, he trudged back to the foyer, removed his shoes and eased his weary body onto one of the bottom steps to wait for his wife to come home. After he drained his glass and set it on the shiny wood, he rested his head back against the wall and drifted off to sleep until the sound of her heels clacking loudly on the marble floor woke him.

"Where have you been?"

She jumped. "Oh, my God, Vic! You scared me half to death. What are you doing sitting here in the dark?"

"Where have you been?" he repeated, spacing his words.

She flicked the light switch on the wall which illuminated the chandelier hanging in the center of the twenty-foot ceiling. "I told you I had a meeting."

"Where are the boys?"

"With Mama and Daddy," she said, meaning his parents. "Mama said they could spend the night, since I told her I'd probably be late. Why are you asking me all of these questions?"

He checked out her appearance. Mona had a lot of clothes, but he'd never seen the outfit she wore tonight—a short, sleeveless dress with a keyhole back. Not exactly attire for a meeting with a bunch of doctors' wives. "Was there anybody else I know at the meeting?"

She looked toward the ceiling for a second then her voice grew louder. "Are you serious? You're really going to question me like I'm a teenager breaking curfew?" Jerky hand movements punctuated her words.

"Tell me who else was there," he insisted, his voice still calm.

"Why does it matter to you?" she asked, sounding tired and disinterested.

"You're not dressed like you've been to a business meeting. And you don't smell like it either. You've been drinking."

"Don't be ridiculous. Our meetings aren't like corporate meetings. We don't have a dress code. I'm not a child," she said, her voice brimming with indignity. "Why are you suddenly interested in where I've been or what I'm doing?"

"You're my wife. I have a right to know where you've been hanging out."

"*Hanging out*? Please, Vic! We go out for drinks after our meetings now." She flipped her long, auburn hair over one shoulder, turned on her five-inch heels and stormed up the staircase.

He watched her long, shapely legs–very much exposed beneath the short dress–cross the foyer and climb the opposite side of the double staircase as though she didn't even want to pass too close to him. Even after twelve years of marriage, she still had the power to excite him. Ramona Cox-Stafford was the most beautiful woman he'd ever met. People often said her creamy complexion and luxurious hair reminded them of singer Chanté Moore, and he'd always been proud to say she was his wife.

Unfortunately, exhaustion had outpaced his passion lately. He didn't often think about it, except at times like this, when he wanted to grab her, take her into the bedroom and spend the rest of the night making her scream his name the way she used to. That hadn't happened in a while. Quite a while. Just how long he couldn't recall.

He always remembered the first time he saw her. Fifteen

years ago, he'd been a guest at a pool party given by one of his fellow med students. She walked into the back yard wearing a bikini with a sarong wrapped around her hips, looking like a Victoria's Secret model. As soon as they were introduced, a mutual spark ignited between them and had been burning ever since.

Until recently.

His brothers often teased him about spoiling her, and it was true. He loved her. She'd been a great wife and mother. She'd helped him study for his Board exams as if she'd been a paid tutor. During his internship she always made sure he ate; something he often ignored. Sometimes she showed up at the hospital with take-out from his favorite restaurants, so he didn't have to eat cafeteria food. Even though she wasn't a great cook, the girl had a skill for ordering the best takeout in the city, and she often brought meals to the little apartment he shared with his roommate.

When he was under stress, he had the bad habit of closing everything else out except the task at hand. In addition to taking care of his nutritional needs, she became an expert at getting him to lighten up. One of her favorite phrases was, "You are too serious for your own good. Remember to breathe and smile every now and then. You're not a robot."

She discreetly bragged about his accomplishments whenever they were out with friends, which made him feel like a king. From the moment they began dating, he knew Mona only had eyes for him, a lowly intern at the time who owned nothing but a used car and the clothes on his back. So whatever request she made of him, he'd given her, because she deserved it. For her last birthday, he'd surprised her with the Bentley. Trinkets made with chocolate diamonds, her favorite, filled her jewelry box, and her closet overflowed with top designer ensembles. What more could she ask for? Sadly, he knew the answer, but he pushed it into the recesses of his mind.

When he eventually mustered enough strength to climb the stairs to the bedroom, Vic wondered how long he had been sitting there. Maybe he'd fallen asleep again and hadn't realized it. Mona was already in bed with a scarf tied around her head and her back turned away from the door when he entered. He knew she wasn't asleep already, but talking to her when she was in a mood like this was out of the question. Without a word, he crossed the room and went into the bathroom to wash his face and hands and brush his teeth. On the way out, he grabbed a pair of lounge pants from his chest of drawers then eased under the covers so they were back to back.

Chapter Two

*T*he next morning, Vic showered, dressed and dragged himself down to the kitchen. He made a cup of coffee, and while it brewed, he contemplated what he needed to do once he got to the hospital. The sound of footsteps shuffling down the hall drew his attention to the doorway. Mona sauntered in thumbing through the latest issue of *Vogue*.

"Hey, baby." He came up beside her and kissed her cheek as though they hadn't locked horns last night. "What are you doing up?"

"You're working *another* Saturday?"

"Yeah, the Board needs a report for their meeting next week. I couldn't get it done with everything else going on." He reached for a travel mug from the cabinet and popped another K-cup into the brewer.

"Hmph," she grunted and turned to leave. "I never imagined this job would take you away as often as it has, and you obviously see no reason to adjust your schedule for us. I've had enough of this, Vic. If I'm not important enough to you, I will find a way to *keep myself occupied*."

Vic uttered a scornful laugh. "Right. Like you're going to get a job."

"When I got pregnant with Trey," she replied in a low tortured voice, "you were the one who said I should stay home and take care of him."

"That was twelve years ago, Mona! Less than two years later, you announced you were pregnant again."

She slumped down onto a stool and gaped at him. "Are you saying I got pregnant so I wouldn't have to work?"

He glared back at her. "I never said you *had* to work, but why all of a sudden have you become so clingy?"

She shriveled a little at his expression. "Clingy? So I'm being clingy, because I want my husband to spend some time with me and his kids? The only reason you noticed me last night was because you've suddenly become suspicious. Two years of begging you to go back to being a husband to me and a father to the boys is my limit. Thirty-seven is too young to become a medical widow. You've ignored me long enough, Vic."

When the ready light came on, he poured his coffee and stirred in cream and sugar. "I'm sorry for what I said last night. I didn't mean to hurt your feelings. I was tired and I needed to get a few hours of sleep." Her words had cut him, and he knew she was right.

"You said exactly what you meant."

When he looked up to respond, she was gone. He could've gone after her, but he was in no mood for another argument. Instead, he entered the garage from the kitchen and left the house, welcoming the silence inside the soundproof cabin of his S600. The traffic surrounding him while he drove to work faded into a blur as he recounted last night's scene with his wife. Was he treating her like a child or were his suspicions justified? After all the years they'd been married, he should've been able to trust her, but due to the changes in her schedule, wardrobe and attitude, he questioned every move she made. And after her behavior last month at the barbeque, he didn't put anything past her.

They had all been at his parents' house for the annual July Fourth celebration. As usual, his mother hired a DJ and a crew to install a dance floor in the yard. All was going well, and they were having a good time until Mona got on the floor with his baby brother, Nick. He still hadn't recovered from the shock of her showing out the way she had. It was bad enough she'd come dressed like a twenty year old, but when she got on the dance floor with Nick and danced like a stripper at Magic City, he'd lost it.

Mona never behaved so unseemly before. It all started after a benefit she had worked hard on—one he'd been too busy to attend. Vic brushed the last thought aside. After being a doctor's wife for so many years, she surely understood his responsibilities. Or was he expecting too much from her?

As he neared the hospital, he made a quick decision. He knew if anyone saw him, they would surely find reason to pull him aside in order to ask his opinion on one thing or another. To avoid being spotted in the hospital cafeteria, he went through the drive-in at Dunkin' Donuts and bought another coffee, a breakfast sandwich and a Boston cream donut. As he drove into the hospital garage and pulled into his reserved parking space, he tried to focus his thoughts on the project awaiting him upstairs. Unfortunately, last night's scene with Mona monopolized his thoughts. She'd avoided giving him any straight answers. She had her faults, but lying had never been one of them. Mona always told him the truth, even if she knew her answer would upset him. Why in God's name would she start now? Almost involuntarily he reached for his cell and dialed Marvin Weber, his closest friend and colleague. Marv's wife, Daphine, worked with Mona on both of her fundraising committees. If anyone knew what she was up to, Daphine would.

"Marv, it's Vic. Are you in the hospital today?"

"No, man. In fact, I'm on my way out to breakfast with the family. What's up?"

"Is Daphine right there with you?"

"No, she's upstairs getting dressed. Is something

wrong?"

"Did she have a meeting last night?"

"Nope, not last night. Why?"

Vic didn't want to reveal his suspicions about his wife just yet, not even to his best friend. "I thought I remembered Mona saying something about it."

"So why don't you call her, man?"

"Eh, it's not important. Enjoy your breakfast, and tell Daphine I said hello. Thanks." Vic shoved the phone back in his pocket.

Maybe you're blowing this whole thing out of proportion. Perhaps he'd talk to Jesse about it later.

He scratched his head and reached for a thick folder his assistant had compiled filled with information he needed to complete his report to the Board. After Vic popped the spout of the plastic top on his coffee and took a big bite of the sausage and egg sandwich, he settled in to work.

The only thing disrupting his concentration was an urgent need to go to the men's room. He hadn't even noticed several hours had gone by. These were the times he wished for a bathroom in his office. As soon as he stepped out into the hallway, one of the surgeons spotted him.

"Dr. Stafford, I was hoping you'd be here today. I really need a consult on a patient."

"Well, I'm not really here. Isn't Dr. Monodee working today?"

"Yes, but he's in surgery right now."

Vic exhaled a heavy sigh. "All right. What've you got?" he said, following the other doctor down the long hallway of the surgical floor. What difference did it make anyhow? He hadn't told Mona what time he'd be home, and she hadn't asked. All he wanted to do was finish putting together his notes so his assistant could type them up on Monday morning before the Board meeting.

The consultation went from a mere discussion with the surgeon to a hands-on examination of the patient in question and a second discussion. On the way back to his office, one of the nurses waylaid him with a question. By the time he returned, he'd lost an hour. If he buckled down and concentrated on the matter at hand, he might be able to get out of there in another two hours.

His estimate turned out to be optimistic, since it was nearly two o'clock by the time he closed the folders. Instead of going home, he dialed his brother, Jesse. "Hey, what're you up to?"

"Nothing much. I'm on call, so I can't go far. Where are you?"

"Just leaving the hospital. I had to catch up on some paperwork. Can I stop by? I need to run something by you."

"Sure. Did you eat lunch?"

Vic laughed.

"Yeah, that's what I thought. Cyd just fixed us something. She and the kids can go ahead and eat. I'll wait for you to get here."

"I'm on my way." Vic gave his handwritten notes a quick scan, stapled the lined sheets together and placed them in the center of his assistant's desk as he locked the office and left.

Jesse answered the door of the expansive brick house and let him in and preceded him to the dining room table. Most of the time he and his brother sat outside on the deck overlooking the pool, but the early-August Atlanta weather was so stifling, inhaling the air felt like breathing steam. Until their younger brother Greg was born, it had been just the two of them, and being two years apart, they had attended the same schools and worked together for a while in their father's practice years ago. Until recently he and Jesse were the only brothers who were married and their relationship had always been easy.

Two plates covered with plastic wrap, two tall glasses filled with ice and a pitcher sat in the center of the table. He took a seat, and Jesse slid one of the plates in his direction. "Nothing fancy, man. It's only turkey sandwiches, some leftover potato salad Cyd made on Sunday and sweet tea."

"I *love* Cyd's potato salad. Where is she anyway?"

"Upstairs washing the girls' hair, which is a real project, so we won't see her for a while."

Both men unwrapped the plates, bowed their heads and offered a silent blessing. Jesse filled both glasses with tea then sat back in his chair and studied his older brother. "What's on your mind?"

Vic bit into his sandwich and chewed, giving himself time to think of how to finally reveal to Jesse what was going on in his home. "Last night," he began slowly. "I got home after eleven, and the house was dark. In my gut I had a feeling something wasn't right. Mona had mentioned a fundraising meeting, but when she goes to those things, she's always home by nine o'clock." He stopped and took a forkful of potato salad.

"Maybe they just ran late. Why are you making a big deal of it?"

"This isn't the first time it's happened, and she was wearing a little short dress like she was going out for the drinks not a meeting." Vic drew a long breath. "And she'd been drinking."

"Hey, you know the ladies get their drink on sometimes," Jesse continued, playing devil's advocate.

"I know, but she and Daphine work in the same

groups, and Marv said she was home last night."

Jesse leaned forward and his olive gaze zeroed in on Vic. "What are you saying, man? Do you think Mona is creepin' on you?"

"I don't know what I think. She's been so cold lately. I tried to talk to her when she finally came in, but she refused."

His brother stroked his unshaven chin. "The family *has* noticed a difference in her lately, but Mona's always been devoted to you. I can't believe she'd do that."

"Yeah, well I don't want to believe it either, but she's been staying out later after every meeting. Trey and Julian spend more time with Mama and Maite than they do with their own mother."

"I think you're exaggerating a bit. Does she have any new friends?"

"If she does, she hasn't mentioned them to me."

"I hate to say this, but if you really think she's hiding something, you can always have her followed."

Vic grimaced at the suggestion. "We've always trusted each other. That's kind of hitting below the belt, don't you think?"

"Has she given you any other choice?"

He shook his head. "I know I've been busy since I took this job, but she seemed to be as happy as I was about it…at the beginning. All she does now is complain about my hours and how she's tired of being alone."

"And you think she's not alone anymore." Jesse phrased it as a statement not a question.

Vic nodded.

"Then you need to be sure of what she's up to before

you confront her." Jesse rose from the table. "I'll be right back."

Now that he was alone, Vic dropped his head into his hands and groaned. All of the time he was in medical school, during his internship and residency, Mona had been right beside him. Now, when they had everything they had dreamed of back then, she'd left his side, and he didn't think he could survive without her.

Jesse returned and handed him a business card. "This is the firm I used when we had the theft problem at Dad's practice. They do business and personal investigations, and they were excellent. I got to know the owner pretty well. You can tell him I sent you."

For a few moments, Vic stared down at the card then he slipped it into his pocket. "I need to think about this before I do anything." He let out a rush of air, dreading his next step. "It's time for me to go home. Tell Cyd I said hi and thanks for lunch."

♥♥♥♥

While Vic was at the hospital, Mona went to pick up Trey and Julian to save her mother-in-law from making the trip.

"I just made a fresh pot of coffee. The boys are downstairs watching a movie. Sit and have a cup with me." Vic's mother always made it impossible to simply run in, say thank you and run out.

"Oh, Mama, I promised the boys we'd have lunch then do something special today, since they're going back to school next week."

"I just fixed them breakfast not too long ago. Sit and talk to me for a few minutes." She set two of her pretty china cups and saucers on the table.

Mona reluctantly pulled out a chair and busied herself with adding cream and sweetener to her cup.

"How are things with you and Vic?" Her mother-in-law asked once she joined her at the table.

"The same," she said without looking up from her cup. "He's too busy for me and the boys."

"Have you tried talking to him about how you feel?"

"Too many times. He thinks I'm ungrateful and being overly-dramatic. All he gives me is the *have you forgotten I'm the first black and the youngest chief of surgery the hospital has ever had?* speech. I'm not asking him to step down, but I'm tired of hearing it."

"I'm worried about you two. Victor and I went through a couple of similar stages, once while he was doing his residency and again when he started in private practice. Thankfully, we worked it out. Have you considered talking to someone about what's going on?"

"You mean someone like a shrink?" Mona asked in a tight voice.

"Not necessarily a shrink, but a person who's trained to listen."

Ramona gaped at the older woman whom she loved deeply. "I'm not the one who needs counseling, Mama! He just brushes me off like what I think and feel are unimportant. I have nothing against counseling, but I refuse to go alone."

Mrs. Stafford placed a hand atop hers. "Honey, being married is hard. Being married to a doctor is hard. Being married to a black doctor with a prominent position is even harder. You need to talk to someone." She patted Mona's hand. "I have a thought. What about calling Rhani? I know she's no longer practicing, but she was trained for this. And since she's in New York, none of your friends or associates know her."

It sounded like a good idea, but she refused to budge

on her stance. "I'm not going to counseling without Vic. If he wants to stay married to me, he needs to put forth some effort. I think he just doesn't care." She finished her coffee, rose and went to the door leading downstairs to the theatre. "Trey, Julian, are you ready to go? Make sure you turn everything off before you come up."

"Do you want me to talk to him?" her mother-in-law asked with a downcast expression that tugged at Ramona's heart.

"No. Vic knows what he needs to do. He just won't do it."

The boys raced up the stairs into the kitchen, and the eight year old hugged her around the waist. "Hi, Mom. You look nice." He offered her the sweet smile she missed seeing from her older son. Soon to be thirteen, he now thought he was too cool to express his feelings for his mother.

"Thank you." She glanced down at her Black Girls Rock tee-shirt, skinny jeans and sandals. This was about as dressed down as she ever got, but she assumed he meant she looked stylish. "Do you guys have all your stuff together?"

"Yup," Trey answered.

Looking at them, she felt a twinge of an emotion she couldn't quite put her finger on. Her sons were both so handsome. Trey, whose name was actually Victor Stafford, III, was the image of his father. He had the same square jaw, heavy wild eyebrows framing deep-set hazel eyes and a sprinkling of freckles across his nose. He even insisted on keeping his hair cut close like Vic's.

Julian was a combination of Vic and her. A mass of brown curls he'd had since he was an infant still framed his always smiling face. Of the two, he was the mama's boy, and she thanked God he wasn't yet ashamed to love on her in front of others. It was the only love she received these days.

"Thank Grandma for letting you stay last night, and take your bags out to the car."

Once Trey and Julian were outside, Mona said, "Don't worry about us. We'll be okay."

"I hope so. Give some thought to what I said about Rhani."

Ramona bent down to kiss her. "I will. Love you, Mama. Thanks for keeping them."

"Okay, guys, where do you want to eat?" she asked as they pulled out of the driveway.

"Is Dad home?" Julian asked, with a hopeful note in his voice.

She swallowed and pasted on a smile. "I don't know, baby. He had to go into the hospital this morning. He wasn't back when I left."

"Oh." His optimistic expression disappeared. "Can we go to Sky Zone?"

She groaned inwardly. "All the way up in Roswell?"

"Pleeease, Mom."

"Trey, do you want to go there?"

"Okay."

"All right then. It'll take a while to get up there, so why don't we talk about school. Are you ready to go back?"

"Pretty much," Trey answered. "This summer has been boring."

"Yeah, it was boring."

"I'm sorry we didn't get to take a vacation this year, but your dad's been so busy. He says he couldn't take a whole week away from the hospital."

Both boys attended the same private STEM school,

which emphasized science, technology, engineering and math. The tuition ran close to twelve thousand dollars a year for each of them. Thankfully, they were good students and never complained about not going to public school.

While her sons played dodge ball on the trampolines, dove into a pit filled with ten thousand blue and orange foam cubes, and flew ten feet in the air from trampoline launch pads to dunk basketballs, she entertained herself on her iPad. They seemed so engrossed in their play, she decided to move to the cafe and call Daphine. "Hey, girl. What's on your calendar for today?"

"I just came from getting a mani/pedi, and I'm about to go see if I can find a gown for the masquerade ball. We only have a few weeks, you know."

She lowered her body into one of the plastic chairs "Don't remind me. It's hard for me to get excited," Ramona said, whispering so the other parents in the cafe couldn't hear what she was saying. "Because Vic won't be coming. He'll be in Dallas attending some kind of meeting on Friday, and he won't be back until Saturday afternoon."

"So. You can still come and have a good time. After all the work we did on this event, you *have* to be there, Ramona."

"I know, but everyone will be coupled off. I despise being the one who's always alone."

"Everybody understands why you're unescorted, because they know who Vic is."

"I suppose. Where are you going for the dress?" she asked, changing the subject.

"*Morgan Kylee* first. If they don't have anything, then I'll try *Jeffrey* in Phipps. Do you have yours yet?"

"No. Trying to drum up some enthusiasm over the event hasn't been working."

"Come on, Ramona. You practically put this event together single-handedly."

"I've been doing just about everything single-handedly lately, and it's become really tedious."

"Where are you now? Can you meet me at *Morgan Kylee*? I'll help you find something fabulous."

Ramona chuckled. "I'm sitting on a hard plastic chair in the snack bar at *SkyZone*. Julian and Trey are in one of the other rooms acting like maniacs. There's no one to stay with them, anyway. Vic's mother kept them last night, and I gave Maite the night off so she could start her weekend early. She went to visit family in Florida. I'll find a gown. Maybe I'll try *Celebrity* on Paces."

The friends talked for a few minutes about the kids returning to school before they ended the call, and Ramona re-entered the play area to search for her sons.

"You two must be hungry by now. Where do you want to eat?"

"Here!" Julian answered with a broad smile as though he were speaking of Wolfgang Puck's.

"Oh, Julian," she whined.

"Mom, you promised we could eat anywhere we wanted."

She wanted to kick herself for putting that out into the universe. "You're right. I did," she confessed with a sigh. "Okay, let's see what they have."

Once they had ordered their food, Mona thought about the upcoming masquerade ball and picked over her greasy hot wings while the boys chattered on about what was going on in their world. She hadn't really been listening until she heard Julian say, "Suppose she's not in your class this year?"

Trey frowned at his younger brother. "Well, she'll still

be in the same school."

"Who is this you're talking about?" she asked, noticing how Trey's gaze immediately dropped to the paper tray holding his hot dog and fries.

"Nobody," he mumbled.

"Come on, tell me. Is there a girl in your class that you like?"

Trey looked "Yeah…umm…she was in my class last year."

Ramona tried hard not to appear shocked by his admission. After all, he would be knee-deep in puberty soon, so an interest in the opposite sex was to be expected. "What's so special about this girl, and what's her name?"

"Her name is Megan, and she's *white*," her youngest eagerly volunteered.

"And how do you know all of this, Julian?" she asked, again struggling to keep her expression blank.

"You need to shut up!" Trey snapped. "See why I don't tell you anything. You have a big mouth!"

She took a sip of her bottled water to cool the hot sauce burning her lips and to give herself a moment to consider how to respond. "Don't yell at your brother, Trey. Why don't you want me to know you like her? Is it because she's white?"

He hung his head then slowly gazed up at her from beneath the long-lash-fringed green eyes he'd inherited from his father's side of the family. "No…maybe, kinda."

"Why, Trey? You know we're not prejudiced like that."

"I never hear anybody talk about it."

"You mean dating a white girl?"

"Yes."

"Well, I know for a fact Uncle Marc and Uncle Greg have both dated women who weren't black."

His eyes widened slightly. "Really? And Grandma and Granddad didn't have a problem with it?"

"I don't think so, but why don't you ask Dad how they felt?"

Trey winced. "He doesn't have time to talk about stuff like that."

Her heart squeezed. "How do you know? Did you ask him?"

He bowed his head and mumbled. "I'm always asleep when he gets home at night, and I only see him for a couple of minutes in the morning, but he's always in a hurry to get to the hospital."

"I know, but that's probably because he doesn't know you want to talk about something important. When he gets home, I'll let him know you need to chat."

"Men don't *chat*, Mom," Trey said with a touch of laughter in his voice.

"Oh, I'm sorry." She grinned back at him.

"And what about you, Julian? Is there a girl you like?"

"I hate girls," he groused. "They're real pains."

She sighed, thankful her second-born was still her baby. "They're not pains. They're just different."

Once they finished eating, she squired them back out to the car. Trey asked her to change the radio station to one of the Atlanta Top 40 stations, which she never listened to. While he and his baby brother sang to songs she didn't recognize, she thought about her sons. The way things were at home now, it was almost as though she were raising them alone. Trey had gotten right to the core of the problem. Vic was never around for them, and with Trey soon to become a teen, having a man to confide in was paramount. All the way home, she mused on how handsome her sons were, and how it wouldn't be long before the little girls started calling, texting, Instagramming and sending them Kik messages. If they weren't already. She shuddered at the thought.

Her mother-in-law had done an incredible job of raising her sons to not rely on their looks but rather on their intelligence as they grew into men. Ramona had no idea how to do that. Beauty ranked number one on her mother's list of most desirable traits. She needed to have a sit-down with Vic's mother to find out how she'd accomplished such a feat.

"Daddy's home," she said when she saw Vic's car parked in the driveway. I need to talk to him first before you two jump on him. Go upstairs and wash your hands with the pink soap, okay? I hate to think of all the germs you picked up playing in that place. "

"Vic, are you down here?" Mona called out when they entered the house. Trey and Julian raced up the stairs to the second floor.

"You don't need to yell. I'm right here." He appeared in the open door of his man cave. "Have you decided to tell me where you were last night?"

"We don't have time to discuss it right now." She looked past him and saw several files spread out on the black leather sofa behind him. "Trey needs you to have the talk with him."

He squinted. "What talk?"

She shoved her hands on her hips and inclined her head as though speaking to a mental defective.

"Oh, *that* talk. Did he ask you something?"

"Not exactly. Julian let it slip that Trey likes a girl at school. A white girl. I think he wants to know if it's okay."

A rare smile graced his face, which was lined with exhaustion. "Okay to like a girl, or okay to like a white girl?"

"Both, I think. He needs to discuss it with a man. Do you have time to talk to him now? I see you're working."

"Why are you talking to me like I'm a stranger?"

"Because you are," she replied bitterly.

He squeezed his eyes shut for a moment then said, "Of course I have time."

"Just don't get all clinical with him, okay?"

"We need to talk about last night."

"There's nothing to talk about."

He pinned her with a cold stare. "I disagree."

"Ssh! Here they come." Mona passed the boys in the hall as she left the room. She really wanted to hang around and eavesdrop but knew it would be wrong, so she went upstairs to the bedroom and sat on the end of the bed. After she removed her sandals, and pulled on her favorite soft slippers, her gaze slowly drifted around the master suite. As she studied it with a critical eye, she realized it no longer had a calm, relaxing atmosphere. Today, the all-white room with its minimalist decor seemed stark and cold. It needed something alive in it–a tree and some plants. Although she knew adding greenery wouldn't solve the problem, she made a mental note to ask the owner of the landscaping company that maintained the yard if he could take care of it the next time they came.

A few minutes later, she heard footsteps, and Julian appeared in the doorway. "Dad said he had to talk to Trey. Is he in trouble?"

"No, honey, he's not in any trouble. He wanted to talk to Daddy about something in private."

Julian shrugged. "Can I swim for a while?"

"Sure. Just take a towel and dry off before you come back inside. Maite will kill you if you get water stains all over the floors."

He raced off to his bedroom seeming not to give the pow-wow between his brother and his father a second thought. She, on the other hand, looked forward to the end of their discussion with trepidation. Vic wasn't going to drop the issue of last night, so she needed to stand up to him. If he insisted on putting her on the shelf because he was too busy but thought she should respond as to her whereabouts–as if he cared–he had another think coming.

Chapter Three

*V*ic rested a hand on Trey's shoulder when he came into the room with his head down and his shoulders slumped. "What's up, man? Mom said you want to talk about something."

"Yeah, I guess," he answered without looking his father in the eye.

"Well, whatever it is, you don't have to feel uncomfortable about it." Vic sat on the black leather sofa and patted the cushion beside him. "Sit down. Let's talk."

His first born flopped down next to him and poked his lips out before he finally spoke. "We're going back to school next week. Last year there was this girl…and she…" He exhaled a frustrated sound.

"Do you like her?"

Trey nodded with a hint of a smile.

"Does she like you?"

"She said she thought I was nice, and she was always looking at me in class."

"She likes you. So, what's the problem?"

The way Trey rubbed his palms up and down his thighs told Vic just how nervous he was. "It's okay, man. Just talk."

"She's white, Dad."

Vic smiled, knowing he needed to incorporate the *real world* talk into the respect/safe sex conversation. "You know what, buddy? I don't think there would be a problem with you liking her. What's her name, by the way?"

"Megan."

"Megan might really like you, but you need to know how her parents feel about her being friends with a black boy."

"How would I find out?" he asked, finally looking at his father for the first time since he entered the room.

"Just ask her. If she says something like she has no idea or they don't have to find out, then you know there's a problem."

"Mom said Uncle Marc and Uncle Greg dated white girls, and Grandma and Granddad didn't have a problem with it."

"They were older than you at the time, and I wouldn't exactly say Grandma and Granddad didn't have a problem with it. Granddad was worried about other people retaliating against them because they were with girls who weren't black."

"But that was a long time ago."

Vic knew exactly what his son was thinking "It wasn't *that* long ago, and times haven't changed that much. People can still be hateful when it comes to race. It doesn't matter how light-skinned you are or how much money you have, you *are* and always will be a black man."

Trey chuckled.

"I'm serious, Trey. Having a black president uncovered just how a lot of white people *really* feel about us, and we have to be careful in public situations. You're too young to go out on dates or anything, but you need to find out how Megan's parents feel." Vic figured it was best to set the ground rules now.

"I know, but our friends only go to the mall or the arcade."

"Mom and I don't have a problem with it, but there are some things you should know before we allow you to go."

"What kind of things?"

"Things like the right way to treat a young lady. It means showing respect for her and never putting your hands on her or yelling at her." Vic's own words plucked his conscience. Here he was giving his son advice he himself needed to heed, but things had deteriorated between Mona and him to the point where all they seemed to do was yell at each other.

"You mean I can't even hold her hand?"

Momentarily confused, Vic frowned until it dawned on him. "No, I mean don't push her around or hit her, even if you're just playing."

Trey looked horrified. "I'd *never* do anything like that, Dad!"

"I hope not. It also means you never do things to a girl that she doesn't like. Don't touch her inappropriately, and if she doesn't want to kiss you, don't try to make her. You can go to jail for that."

Vic wanted to laugh at Trey's embarrassed expression. He concluded the safe sex talk wasn't even necessary right now, but he needed to get a feel for exactly where his son was emotionally. "When you were around her, did you want to touch her?"

From the way Trey hung his head and a blush crept up the back of his neck, Vic knew he should delve a little deeper. "Have you?"

"Nope. I...I didn't know what to do."

"Well, it depends on the circumstances–you know–

whether you're alone or with a bunch of people. Just don't rush it. You're only twelve, man."

"I'm going to be thirteen in a few months."

"I know, but it's too young to be thinking about this stuff. Take my word for it. You'll be dealing with women for the rest of your life. Do you want to ask me anything?"

"No." Trey's gaze dropped to the floor.

He slapped his son on the back. "Whenever you need to talk, just let me know, okay?"

"Okay. Thanks, Dad."

Vic grinned as he watched his son leave the room looking as though a weight had been lifted off his shoulders. Trey didn't have a clue how simple his life was at the moment. He had no job, no debt, no board of directors to answer to, and no wife to pacify. And with that thought, Vic left the room which represented his peaceful place and made his way toward the bedroom.

"How'd it go?" Mona asked when he entered the room where she was sitting on the bed thumbing through a magazine.

"All right. The sex talk would be premature. He cringed when I mentioned kissing." Vic chuckled. "I just warned him about not getting too physical with her."

"Well, if anybody knows about not getting physical, it's you," she said in a snarky tone.

He reached behind him and slammed the bedroom door. "All right, Mona. I've had it with you! You have a hell of a lot of nerve throwing that in my face. No, I haven't been in the mood to get physical with you in a while. You have no idea what it means to work until you're so tired you can't even see straight or to be under so much pressure you think you might snap any second."

"No, I don't, Vic, but *you* were the one who didn't want me to work." She laid the magazine on the bed. "You wanted to be able to say I was a housewife, you provided for me, and all I had to do was take care of you and your kids. That was all *your* idea. Don't throw it in *my* face now."

"I'm not talking about you having a *job*. I expected you to support me and back me up when things got tough."

"And I didn't expect you to put me aside like I was no longer important when you became a *big shot*."

He stepped closer and stared down at her. "Are you screwing somebody else?"

Mona flipped her hair over her shoulder then uttered a harsh laugh. "You say somebody *else*, as though you mean in addition to you. You haven't touched me in months, Vic. It makes me wonder if *you're* screwing somebody."

He threw his hands in the air and glanced at the ceiling. "For God's sake! When would I have the time? You've lost your mind."

"I used to be first in your life." Her voice was soft now, and she stared out the window. "And I felt important to you."

"I've said this before. If you had something to occupy your time, you wouldn't even notice when I'm not around."

"Really? So *that's* your solution?"

"Baby, you have to admit you have more time on your hands than anybody needs."

She gaped at him. "You're right, Vic. You're absolutely right. I need to find something to do, so you don't have to waste your precious time being bothered with me."

He massaged the growing tightness in the back of his neck. "You know that's not what I meant."

"No?" She stood and stepped closer. "What did you

mean then?"

"I just think you'd be happier if you had something of your own."

"I thought I had *you*," she mumbled as she removed her slippers and slid her feet back into her sandals. "I always thought you wanted me close to you. Boy, was I deceived." Mona turned and snatched her purse from the bed. "Fine. Get your sons something for dinner. I'm going out."

"Where are you going?" he said to her retreating back. "Mona!"

"Like you give a damn." She almost ran down the stairs and out the front door.

Thankfully, Trey and Julian were in their rooms and didn't hear this latest confrontation. Here it was his first weekend off in a month, and he'd just driven her out of the house. He hadn't meant to hurt her, and when he'd suggested she find something to do, he hadn't meant it facetiously. She didn't understand, and he couldn't seem to make her. He missed her, but he was caught between a rock and hard place—between a demanding wife and an even more demanding job. Both were pulling at him so unmercifully he felt like a Puritan nailed to a pillory in the town square. Every passing day stretched him to the point where he thought for sure he would split in two.

The worst part was he didn't understand what was happening to him. Being chief of surgery was something he'd dreamed of for nearly twenty years. The money the hospital paid him made it possible to have the lifestyle he and Mona had fantasized about when he was in medical school. But the stress, fatigue and travel were robbing him of the simple pleasures he'd once enjoyed.

He missed the incredible sex he and Mona always had. She had a wanton, irrepressible nature and did whatever he suggested without hesitation. Not like some women who capitulated to their man's pressure and reluctantly acquiesced. She seemed to really enjoy it. One of his favorite memories was of the time he took her down to Savannah for the weekend. They had been married about two years, and hadn't been away together since their honeymoon. He'd reserved a hotel room overlooking the beach at Tybee Island. And it was a good thing, because they never made it onto the actual beach. They only left the room to go out for meals. The rest of the time they made love on every available surface in the room and even out on the terrace after sunset.

Vic missed the sex and knew the change was his fault. Even when he was doing his internship/residency, he remembered being dog tired, but it never stopped him from wanting her. Sure, he was older now, but his health was excellent and couldn't be blamed for the fatigue and flagging libido. It had to be the stress. Serving as chief was about obligation. Each patient on the surgical floor–his floor–was his patient, even if he wasn't the one doing the cutting. The knife stopped with him when the surgery didn't go well. It was his responsibility to face a family and tell them his staff had done everything possible to save their loved one. He couldn't help but get absorbed in seeing to the needs of patients' families. And because he'd accepted the burden of looking after other people's families, he'd sacrificed his own. His only goal had been to become the best at his job and give his family everything they wanted or needed, and his plan had backfired. Had he allowed his desire for status and power to ruin the best thing in his life? Mona had been his partner, lover, friend, and soulmate for the last fifteen years. Could he have been wrong in assuming she was strong enough to be the wife of a successful man? He was losing his wife. Maybe he'd already lost her. That prospect put fear in him like nothing else could. A crushing sensation in his chest prevented him from moving from where he stood at the top of the staircase.

"Dad, are you okay?" Trey's voice snapped him out of

his contemplation. Vic hadn't even heard him come out of his room, but his son was staring up at him with panic in his eyes. Vic dragged in a deep breath and then answered, "Yeah, buddy, I'm fine."

"Why are you holding your chest?"

"Uh, it's just heartburn," Vic said, thinking quickly. "Guess I shouldn't have eaten Maite's leftover empanadas so late last night." He laughed, hoping to reassure Trey he was all right. "How about I call for pizza and then we can watch a couple of movies?"

"Really? Julian!" he called to his brother. "Dad's getting pizza and we're gonna watch movies!" The way Trey's face lit up made Vic feel lower than a slug. He'd been so absent his son thought sharing pizza and a movie with his own father was cause for celebration.

"Yeah. What do you guys want on the pizza?"

Once they'd decided on the toppings, Vic called in the order. "Let's go in the cave. Do you guys know how to get those Amazon Instant Videos on the smart TV?"

Julian stared at him as though he couldn't believe his father was so dense. "It's easy."

Ramona had bought the TV for him for Father's Day, but he hadn't had the time to figure out how to make it work. They also had a smart TV in the den, so he assumed this was how his sons had developed their technical skill. "Can you show me how to do it?"

Trey looked up at him and grinned. "Sure, Dad. Come on, we'll teach you."

In the time it took for the pizza to arrive, his sons had given him a crash course in how to order movies directly to the television. After he paid the delivery man, Vic carried the boxes into the room, set them on the floor and sent the boys to the kitchen to get plates, glasses and ice for their sodas.

"Mom doesn't want us to eat in here," Julian said, eyeing the boxes sitting on the off-white carpet. "We're supposed to eat in the kitchen."

"Mom had somewhere to go," Vic explained. "And this is *my* room, so let's pray and eat. I'm hungry."

Both boys beamed, as though they were getting away with a major crime. Each of them claimed a spot on one of the leather sofas, and they devoured two large pies and two liters of soda. Vic tried his best to get into the film, which was about a group of intergalactic humans, mutants and talking animals who were forced to work together to stop a fanatical warrior from taking control of the universe. But just being able to relax put him into an instant coma. The next thing he knew, Trey was standing over him jiggling his arm.

"Dad, the movies are over. You slept through both of them."

Vic raised his head, rubbed his eyes and groaned. "Oh, guys I'm sorry. I was wiped out."

"It's okay," Julian said. "We had fun anyway. Can we do this again?"

"Sounds like a good idea, man." He smiled at his youngest son. "You two need to take your showers. We have church in the morning." He and his brother, Jesse still attended their parents' church where they were raised.

"You're not working tomorrow? Is Mom coming too?" Trey asked. "She didn't go with us last time."

"I'm off unless there's an emergency. I don't know if your mom's going. You'll have to ask her when she gets in. All right, hit the showers, and I'll clean up the mess in here." His sons left the room, and he closed the empty pizza boxes and scooped up the soda bottles. For a minute he thought about calling Mona, but she wasn't going to tell him where she was, so he changed his mind. After he had disposed of all the evidence of their eating outside of the kitchen, he climbed the stairs and turned on the bedroom television. Before he stretched out across the bed, he pulled out his wallet and removed the business card Jesse had given him. He studied the writing on the card for a few moments, and then returned it to his wallet. If Mona had no plausible explanation for where she'd been tonight, he would place the call on Monday morning.

Mona got into the car and hit the button to put the top down. She snatched her hair up into a ponytail and secured it with one of the elastic hair ties from the emergency makeup bag she kept in the glove box. It probably would've made more sense to leave the convertible top up and put the air on, but she felt as though steam was pouring from the top of her head. The breeze might help to clear her head.

Hadn't Vic made it clear? The answer to their problem wasn't for him to make more room for her in his schedule. No, he wanted her to busy herself, so he wouldn't have to be burdened with her. The idea disturbed her deeply, because they had always shared everything. Even when he was an intern putting in eighty-hour weeks, she had been his sounding board. He'd included her in what was going on in his life. Their best times were when he confided in her after they had made love and lay in each other's arms. Yes, he had given her all kinds of material things, but they weren't what mattered most to her.

Maybe he was simply tired of her. After all, they had been married for more than a decade, but she'd followed her mother's advice and done everything humanly possible to keep herself as close to how she looked on their wedding day. Granted, after two pregnancies she'd put on about fifteen pounds, and her body wasn't as tight as it was when they met. But it was close. His brother, Charles had even given her a minor tummy tuck and a breast lift before he'd closed his plastic surgery practice. What more could she do?

Quite possibly he'd gotten bored with her. He worked with professional women who had degrees and could relate to him intellectually, which she couldn't do, but it never seemed to bother him before. As she drove with no idea where she was going, visions of her husband engaged in stimulating conversation with different women at work raced through her mind. Her intention when she'd gotten into the car was not to visit her mother, but when she finally realized it, she was turning onto her street in Decatur. She'd been driving for a half hour. When she parked in the driveway, Mona sat for a moment asking herself why she was there. Of all the people in the world, she knew what her mother would have to say, but there wasn't anyone else she could talk to about her current situation. She didn't want to mention anything to Daphine until she knew for sure exactly what was happening with Vic.

"Hi, Ma," she said when the older woman opened the front door with widened eyes.

"Ramona, what are you doing here?"

She stepped around her mother and into the living room of the cozy brick bungalow. "Gee, thanks for the warm welcome."

"Stop it! You know I'm happy to see you. It's just rare for you to come by on the weekend." Cecily Cox or Cee Cee, as her friends called her, eyed her daughter with a skeptical squint. "So…what's wrong?"

Mona headed down the wide wood slats of the hallway into the kitchen. "Why does there have to be something wrong? Do you have any coffee?"

"Of course I have coffee. You bought me the brewer, remember?" Mona approached the coffeemaker as though she were on a mission. After she chose a flavor from one of the boxes on the counter, she opened the lid, inserted the K cup, impatiently closed the cover and pressed brew.

"Don't tell me nothing's bothering you. I can tell by the way you slammed that lid. Sit down and talk, girl." Her mother pulled out a chair at the table.

Mona slumped down onto the seat. "It's Vic. I think he's tired of me."

"Why on earth would you think that?"

"He's so wrapped up in his job, it's almost like he doesn't even see me anymore."

"Impossible! You're just as gorgeous as you were the day you walked down the aisle."

"That's just it. I think he's lost interest in me. He keeps telling me I need to find something to occupy my time."

Her mother reared back in her chair. "You have a house, two sons to take care of and your volunteer work. I would think that's enough to keep any woman occupied."

"Well…I don't really take care of the house, Maite does. We have a cleaning service, a landscaping company and someone else to take care of the pool. I think what he means is I need to get a job."

"A job!" Her mother looked stricken. "Ridiculous. Why in the world do you need to work?" The epitome of the pageant mom, Cecily Cox had raised her daughter to be a beauty queen, a woman who would be put on a pedestal by a successful man. And she had achieved her goal.

"He didn't come right out and say it, but it's what I believe he meant. Vic works around smart, educated women all day, and then he comes home to me. All I know how to do is walk a runway and smile."

"And I suppose that's my fault."

"I didn't say that. Why do you always read something into everything I say?"

"You have a bachelor's degree, and you were crowned Miss Georgia, for God's sake!"

"And both of those equate to absolutely nothing in the real world," she said, knowing her mother had only sent her to college to find a suitable husband. And her mother's plan had worked.

She gave Mona a confused look. "Didn't he tell you from the beginning he wanted you to stay home with Trey and Julian?"

"Yes, but I guess he figures they've both been in school all day for years now."

"So what are you saying?"

"I don't know. All I know is I'm not willing to let Vic put me on the shelf as though I don't matter anymore."

"Ramona, Vic is a good man, and you have to do everything you can to keep him. Are you?"

Her hair swished as she tossed her head back and forth in frustration. "I know he's a good man, but I don't know what else I can do. We don't talk the way we used to. Now he seems to want to keep everything to himself."

"Well, if you don't want to lose him, you'd better find out what he needs and start doing it."

"Don't you think I would, if I knew what it was he wanted? And did it ever occur to you that maybe he needs to start doing something? Vic has always been perfect in your mind. Well, guess what? He isn't."

"I never said he was perfect, but he's as close to it as I've ever seen. No matter what you need to do to get his interest back, do it."

The clock above the sink said it was only six o'clock, but Mona needed to escape from the unspoken accusations. She cringed at the idea of going home. The last thing she wanted to do was get into another disagreement with Vic, so she kissed her mother goodbye and headed to *Cakes and Ale.* If she went to a restaurant, she could waste a couple of hours, and since she wasn't dressed up for dinner as she normally would've been, this was a perfect spot. By the time she got home, hopefully Vic would be asleep.

Women who went out to dinner or a movie alone had always seemed a little pathetic to her. It was as though they were advertising their loneliness to the world. Until now, she'd never found herself in this position. Once inside the casual, yet pricey eatery, she asked the hostess for a corner table and ordered a glass of wine instead of an appetizer and the pork loin with polenta and savoy cabbage as her entree.

The entire time she lingered over her meal, the advice of the two women she loved and respected kept replaying in her head. She tended to give more credence to Vic's mother's advice, because she'd been through it herself. Her mother was looking at everything from the outside, and she tended to glamorize it all. By the time she finished eating, Mona had come to a conclusion. Everything she'd done so far had failed to get Vic's attention, but knowing her husband as well as she did, there was one thing that would make him take notice of her once again. It was risky, but nothing else had worked thus far. Just like his patients who coded on the operating table, he needed to be shocked back to life.

The following Friday, while Vic was in Chicago at a convention, Mona stood in the Astor Ballroom of the St. Regis hotel in Buckhead wearing an ivory and gold gown that matched the room's regal décor. Tonight marked the culmination of numerous meetings and planning sessions. She and her committee had pulled it off–the city's biggest masquerade ball to raise money for childhood cancer. Invitations had gone out to the wealthiest patrons of the hospital and many others who were known for their generous giving to Atlanta charitable organizations. Judging by the number of tuxedoed, sequined and masked bodies filling the ballroom, the majority of them had made good on their RSVPs.

Thrilled with the turnout, Mona spent the early part of the evening strategically making her way through the crowd. She greeted the guests she already knew and introduced herself to those she had never met. As committee chairperson, she was expected to keep a high profile and cajole those who had already paid a thousand dollars per ticket to give an additional donation. For the past few years, she had been doing this, and she excelled at it. After she delivered a heartfelt welcome to the crowd, she introduced the first of a succession of guest speakers and left the stage.

The man had been watching her for about an hour. She'd noticed his eyes following her before he made his way across the ballroom. From that distance she hadn't been able to tell his age, but as he got closer she realized he was young, probably only in his late twenties.

When he got close enough, he said, "Ramona Stafford?"

He obviously knew her, and she hated not calling people by their names. She just couldn't place him. "Yes. I'm sorry, have we met?"

"Unfortunately not. May I ask you a personal question?"

Her eyes widened. "It depends."

"How tall are you without the heels?"

"Five nine," she answered, smiling and meeting him eye to eye. In her stilettos, she stood over six feet tall and towered over every other woman in the room.

Although he couldn't see her whole face due to the

elaborate feather mask she wore, he said,

"You're stunning." He extended his hand, and she marveled at its size and the stark contrast of their skin as it engulfed hers. "Rayvon Patterson. Can I get you a drink?"

The way his gaze slowly traveled down her body sent a tingle simmering beneath her skin. A tingle she hadn't felt in a long time. It had been ages since anyone looked at her that way. "A Cosmopolitan, thank you."

"Don't move, Ramona. I'll be right back."

She watched as he moved across the room and headed to the bar in what she could only think of as a glide. He had to be at least six-foot-three. His movements were graceful, and his muscles flexed beneath the black designer suit that fit his big body like a custom-made glove. And he was as different from Vic as he could possibly be—big, muscular, as dark as a panther and quite good looking. She wondered what he did for a living.

Rayvon returned, placed the rosy cocktail into her hand and answered her unspoken question.

"This is my first big event since I relocated to Atlanta. I'm the new point guard for the Hawks," he said with a proud smile that seemed to glow against his smooth onyx skin.

"I should've known you were an athlete."

"Why?"

"You move like one. Point guard, huh? So you're the floor general, the play-maker."

His eyes widened. "You know basketball?"

"I cheered for my college basketball team all four years."

"I can see you being a cheerleader." He stared at the three-carat diamond and matching band on her left hand when she raised the glass to her lips. "You're married?"

"Yes, and I have two sons."

"What a shame," he said, giving her yet another appreciative head-to-toe scan.

"Why?"

"I was hoping we could be friends."

"Married people can't have friends, Rayvon?" All of the reasons why she shouldn't take this any further buzzed in her head like a swarm of angry bees, but what harm could a little flirtation do?

He grinned. "How can I get in touch with you?"

Mona opened her Marc Jacobs clutch and handed him the personal business card she gave to new acquaintances at networking events and social gatherings. "Call me."

When she turned to walk away, Ramona plucked a flute of champagne from a tray carried by one of the roving waiters and traded it for the now empty Cosmopolitan glass. Her hands were shaking.

She moved through the crowd making sure to spend a few moments chatting with those whose pockets she hoped to empty on behalf of the charity. About twenty minutes later, her phone rang. She moved into the hallway to take the call, but realized the number wasn't familiar.

"You said to call you. Did I wait long enough?" the deep voice said with a chuckle behind his words.

"Rayvon? Where are you?"

"Upstairs on the balcony. Look to your left."

Mona scanned the railing above her head. He was looking down at her with his tantalizing smile, and the tingle returned.

"Will you have a drink with me?"

She thought twice before answering. "Are you here for the children, or just to be seen?"

"Both," he answered honestly. "But I wrote out a check before I got here tonight. Meet me at the bar, and I'll put it right into your hand."

"You are very determined, aren't you?"

"No doubt. I'm on my way down. What are you drinking?"

"Sparkling water," Mona said as she moved through the packed room. "I think I've had enough tonight."

Chapter Four

Vic had to be in Chicago to speak at the American College of Surgeons Clinical Congress. Mona had the big fundraiser she'd been working on for the past few months. It was an unfortunate coincidence the two events happened to be scheduled for the same weekend. He left the house on Wednesday morning with his bag packed because he planned to go to the airport directly from the hospital for a three o'clock flight. When he left the house that morning, she'd kissed him goodbye and wished him a safe trip. He'd expected her to make a stink about him not being home to escort her to the masquerade ball, yet she didn't say a word. Perhaps he'd finally gotten through to her. Yet, the sudden turnaround in her attitude gave him the distinct feeling something ominous was brewing.

Ever since the night Mona left him with the boys, the atmosphere at home had been peaceful. When she'd returned that night, and he'd asked her where she had been, she looked him straight in the eye and said she'd gone to her mother's house and then to Cake & Ale for dinner. The dinner part seemed a bit strange, since she had never been one to entertain herself in public. But because her facial and body language gave no hint that she was lying, he decided to hold off on calling the private investigator, a move, which in his opinion, was too extreme.

Vic hated traveling, and when the flight landed at O'Hare, all he wanted to do was check in at the hotel and rest for an hour or two before he had to attend the last seminar of the night. He stayed at the O'Hare Hilton whenever he had business in Chicago. The No-Fly Zone, sound proof windows, blackout drapes and Serenity beds always helped him to relax and have a good night's sleep. After he washed his hands and set the alarm on his phone to wake him in two hours, he stretched out on the bed and closed his eyes, but he couldn't sleep. His mind was too preoccupied with questions about what was going on with his wife. He should've been happy when she didn't say anything about him not being able to attend the masquerade ball, but it struck him as strange. Lately, Mona never missed an opportunity to remind him of how he was failing her and his sons. If he were in another line of work, he could say, *when things slow down I'll take some time off.* But things never slowed down at a hospital. Not really.

He lay there mulling over what had happened between them in the past couple of weeks, and finally gave up on getting a quick nap. After he took a brief shower, he changed into a set of clean clothes and made his way downstairs to one of the smaller meeting rooms to sit in on a class, Non-Technical Skills for Surgeons in the Operating Room. A couple of familiar faces greeted him when he entered, and once the class ended, a group of them decided to have dinner together downstairs in The Gaslight Club.

The well-known restaurant offered live music, fine dining and class. The décor was reminiscent of the Roaring 20s and served the finest prime, aged steaks, chops and fresh seafood. The doctors indulged in single malt scotch, bourbons, and cognac served by the Gaslight Girls. Vic appreciated being able to unwind with colleagues in a pressure-free atmosphere. Once the conversation changed from a recap of the class, the topics transitioned easily from medicine to golf, boating, and women. It took him a little while to realize he might have been the only one who didn't notice the attractive women at the bar who seemed focused on the nine men seated together lingering over their after-dinner drinks and coffee.

An attractive blonde made sure she caught his eye several times. Vic supposed she could be a pro, but he doubted it, because she didn't make an effort to approach him. Doctors often had groupies just like musicians and athletes. Some were working girls who hoped to make good money for a couple of nights. Others were average women who hoped to hook a doctor. They came to these conventions and meetings and made their presence known at the restaurants and bars where the conventioneers relaxed after the business of the day.

One by one, his companions left the table and drifted over to where the women congregated at the bar. Vic momentarily questioned the wisdom of socializing with a single woman, and then he brushed it off. There was nothing wrong with having an innocent conversation. Besides, it had been ages since he'd socialized with any women who weren't colleagues or the wives of other doctors with whom he worked. He took his glass, eased onto the stool next to her and, even though he was pretty confident he knew the answer, he asked, "Are you attending the conference?"

She tucked her hair behind one ear, smiled and met his gaze. "No, I just stopped by for a drink after work. What kind of conference is it?"

There was no need to get technical. "Medical." He extended his hand. "Vic. And you are?"

"Heather." She gazed at the name tag pinned to his lapel then down at his left hand, but she didn't say anything about the platinum wedding band. Judging by her trim figure and youthful complexion, she appeared to be in her late twenties.

"Where are you from?" Heather asked, her blue gaze settling on his face as though she were sincerely interested.

They studied each other for a long moment before he broke their gaze suddenly feeling the attraction to her was out of place. Inwardly cursing the stirring in his groin, he concentrated his attention instead on the liquid he swirled around in his glass. "Atlanta. And you?"

"I live here in Chicago. Never been to Atlanta, but I've heard it's really nice."

"Yes, if you like heat and traffic." Vic chuckled. He could tell she wasn't a pro, because she was a little too shy. He'd been to enough conventions to know the professionals were more aggressive. Pretty by the typical American standard of blonde, blue eyes and slender figure, Heather was nowhere near as beautiful as Mona. Why was it he thought about his wife when they were apart, but when they were together they grated on each other like sandpaper? Having a conversation with a woman without any strife or hot button issues was refreshing. Heather seemed like a nice woman who was probably hoping to meet a nice single man. If he wanted to turn this into a hook-up, he could. In spite of his physical attraction to her, a one-night stand wasn't what he wanted or needed. After an hour or so, they said goodnight. Neither one suggested they meet again.

Vic took the elevator to his room and clicked on the TV then checked his watch and fished his phone from his pocket. Mona had her benefit ball tonight, so Trey and Julian were with Maite. He'd made it his habit whenever he was traveling, and it wasn't too late to call them and say goodnight. After he spoke to each of his sons, he stripped down to his underwear and turned down the linens. He propped himself up with all of the pillows behind his head and proceeded to hit the remote until he found something he wanted to watch. Since he worked all the time, he hadn't really watched television in a couple of years. A movie briefly caught his attention, but thoughts of the woman in the bar distracted him.

Ever since he and Mona got married, he'd never had a roaming eye. Hell, he always had the most beautiful woman in the room, so there was no need to look elsewhere. So, why tonight? He and his brothers often joked about the attention they received from women when they were out in public. It had been that way since they were in middle school. Thanks to the constant warnings and instructions from their parents, most of them had learned how to handle it. Even Greg, who at one time had been unable to resist the constant temptation when it came to strange women, had overcome his weakness once he met Rhani, the woman who became his wife. He'd been arrested for having sex in public, which sparked a stint in therapy. Vic had never experienced that kind of weakness. From the day he met Ramona Cox, he'd only had eyes for her.

It made no sense to him that after all the years they'd been together, and after all the financial hardship they had been through, they would start having problems now. They lived in their dream house, and their sons were no longer babies. Perhaps his brothers were right. He'd spoiled Mona terribly, and she wasn't satisfied unless she had his undivided time, attention and funds. But wasn't that what your wife was supposed to expect? And why had he been so interested in sharing a drink with Heather? These questions plagued him until he couldn't keep his eyes open and allowed sleep to take over.

Sometime during the night, Vic awoke in the middle of a dream. It had been decades since he'd had a dream that had awakened him on the verge of an orgasm. Sweating and panting, he wasn't totally conscious, but he did what came naturally. With his eyes squeezed shut, he grasped his erect penis in a tight fist and stroked hard and fast. Unsure of whether he was awake or still in the midst of the dream, visions of Mona with her thick hair billowing around her head and her long legs spread to receive him was all that appeared behind his closed lids. As he worked himself to a climax, scenes from the past sped through his subconscious like a music video directed by Spike Jonze. Flashes of their first sexual encounter came back to him as though they were in real time. From their first time fifteen years ago, she had always been so ready for him. It hadn't mattered to her whether they were in a hallway during a party or in his parents' pool while they were away on vacation. Mona always made him feel like a sex god. Vic grabbed a handful of tissues from the box next to the bed and groaned as his release came, then he relaxed into the pillow, physically relieved but emotionally empty. He lay there listening to the soft whirring of the air conditioner trying to recall the last time he'd resorted to self-gratification. As far as he could remember, it had been when Mona was pregnant with Julian. She'd had some complications in the last trimester, and her doctor put a moratorium on their sex life until after the delivery. Back then it was necessary, but now his only reason was because of the emotional distance between him and his wife. It was his fault, but it wasn't intentional. It just happened while he was trying to deal with the pressures of the job. Somehow he needed to fix the situation, but before he'd left home, he'd insulted her. He hadn't meant to, but in his effort to get his point across, he'd hurt her feelings. The way she responded to him before he left, made it clear she was beyond furious. Mona usually screamed and threw things when she was mad, but when she withdrew into silence and plastered on a phony beauty queen smile, he knew it was serious.

Staying awake and meditating on the growing tension between them served no purpose. He needed to get some sleep, so he would be in halfway decent shape in the morning to teach a course.

The morning began on a good note with a packed room for his class called *Measure Twice, Cut Once: Advanced Health Systems Engineering for Surgeons*. He had prepared for this last week, and he hoped to give the attendees what they'd come for. As it went with most seminars, most of the participants were younger doctors. Older physicians tended to believe they knew everything there was to know and relied on tried and true methods. They weren't too keen on learning new procedures.

The ninety minutes went by faster than he had anticipated and ended with him receiving a round of applause from the enthusiastic attendees. Being considered an authority on certain surgical disciplines was surely a feather in his cap. Maintaining a visible presence also helped his reputation. Afterwards, Vic and a few of his colleagues, none of whom he knew personally, grabbed a quick lunch of paninis and salads at Caffe Mercato in the hotel then dispersed to attend a full afternoon of sessions. He considered calling Mona to ask how the benefit went last night, but immediately had second thoughts. They needed to talk about the conversation they'd had before he left, which couldn't be done over the phone.

By the time the day ended, he'd garnered some critical information and learned about a new surgical technique, but he was mentally drained. Some of the doctors had plans to hit the Magnificent Mile to check out the nightlife, but Vic wasn't up for it. Instead he chose to have dinner in Andiamo, the hotel's Italian restaurant. When he entered, he saw Heather sitting alone at the bar. She didn't see him at first, and his immediate instinct was to simply take a seat without acknowledging her, but that was ridiculous. There wouldn't be any harm in asking if she was waiting on a date. Their conversation last night had been friendly and upbeat, and God only knew how much he could use a little pleasant and positive interaction with a woman.

"Heather." He came up behind her. "It looks like we had the same idea. Are you waiting for someone?"

She glanced up at him, with a surprised smile. "Vic, we meet again. No, I'm not expecting anyone. Just stopped in for a drink. Please, have a seat," she said, indicating the stool next to her.

"Well, I was planning to have dinner. Would you like to join me?"

Her smile widened. "Yes, I'd like that."

Vic took her hand to help her dismount the stool. She was only about five-foot-five, and while seated, her feet didn't reach the floor. He inhaled as he got a whiff of her perfume, a light fragrance with a refreshing hint of lemon, and reminded himself of what he'd told Trey about white women. It didn't take much to put a brother in a bad light when seen in public with them. The hostess sat them at a table with a high-back booth on one side, which gave it an intimate feel–more intimate than he would've preferred.

"My colleagues wanted to investigate the clubs tonight, and I wasn't in the mood." Vic's gaze ran over her. She was well-dressed, wore just the right amount of makeup and exposed only a peek of cleavage beneath a feminine ruffled-neck blouse. "I hope you don't take this the wrong way, but if you were hoping to meet someone tonight, I don't want to block that."

Her blue gaze dropped to his left hand then she studied him as though she were trying to figure him out. "I *have* met someone." She smiled. "Let's order dinner."

"Why did you decide to become a doctor, Vic?"

"My father, my two uncles and two of my brothers are doctors." He smiled at the way her eyebrows lifted.

"So you're carrying on a family tradition then?"

"I guess you could say that. It's all I ever wanted to do. A couple of my brothers say they felt pressured to go into medicine, but I didn't feel any pressure. I admired my father and the good work he was able to do for his patients."

Heather seemed fascinated to hear that he came from a

family of physicians. She leaned forward and twisted a lock of her hair around her index finger. "That says a lot about him and what kind of man he is. I grew up in a small town in Arkansas and never knew any professional African-Americans."

Vic marveled at how easily they communicated. It felt like a second date as he devoured his house salad, New York sirloin, mashed potatoes and a glass of Zinfandel. When he mentioned his mother had been a teacher, they talked at length about Heather's job as an elementary school teacher.

She suggested they split the chocolate fudge cake topped with whipped cream and raspberry coulis, and he ordered after-dinner cocktails. She had been nursing a drink when he came in, and by the way she giggled and kept touching his arm, he thought she was a little buzzed. But when their dessert arrived, and she dipped a spoon into the rich treat and raised it to his lips, he was certain his pretty companion was now tipsy.

"Come on, taste it," she said, drawing her words out lazily and locking her seductive gaze with his.

Vic parted his lips enough for her to insert the spoon then closed them and savored the rich fruity chocolate flavor. Actually, he used the brief moment to consider what he might say when he opened them. "I'm married, Heather," he said, choosing to go the direct route.

"So," she said, holding his gaze, refilling the spoon and bringing it to his mouth again.

The whole scene was so seductive, and his body responded against his will. Reluctantly, he received the second spoonful then, when he opened his mouth to continue explaining why this little rendezvous was improper, she filled it with her tongue. As much as he knew he should've resisted, he didn't, and he responded with matching enthusiasm. A moment later, he literally pushed her away.

"Are you driving tonight?"

Her eyes filled with expectation. "No. What do you have in mind?"

Vic swallowed and took a deep breath hoping to slow his breathing. "You're a little buzzed. I'm going to get you a cab. I enjoyed dinner." He rose, grabbed the check and dropped a fast kiss on her lips. "Good night, Heather." Once he paid the check, he asked the bartender to call a taxi for her and didn't look back as he left the restaurant.

♥♥♥♥

Once the opening addresses were done and Mona made her initial appeal for donations, the band got the crowd onto the dance floor with covers of the latest hip-hop and R&B hits. She loved seeing people enjoying events she'd planned and knew the better time they had, the wider they would open their wallets.

Surprised and pleased by Rayvon's call, she made her way through the tables to the bar. When she saw him walking toward her waving a piece of paper between his long fingers, she smiled.

He stopped when there were only inches between them, which required her to look up into his face. "I'm a man of my word," he said, placing the check firmly in her palm.

Mona blatantly examined the amount, and her jaw dropped, which made him laugh. With a pleased smile, she hooked her arm through his and signaled the bartender. "Rayvon, let me buy you a drink." They both chuckled, knowing the event was open bar. "What'll you have?"

He ordered a Zombie. "Are you sure you don't want a drink? If you're worried about getting home safely, I have a car coming to pick me up. I'd be happy to drop you off."

Mona laughed to herself. What would she look like coming home in the wee hours of the morning semi-inebriated with a gorgeous young athlete? "No thanks, sparkling water will be fine."

He relayed her request to the bartender. Rayvon brought his questioning gaze back to her face and studied her as though he were standing in a museum admiring a work of art. "You are such a beautiful woman, Ramona. Did you ever do any modeling?"

"Yes, briefly. My focus—or I should say my mother's focus—was on pageants."

"The reason you carry yourself like a queen." He grinned and, when he placed his large hand on her bare back, a shiver ran through her. "Let's move away from the bar. It's too congested here." He steered her toward an empty table, pulled out one of the white chairs draped in a sheer cover and waited for her to sit.

"Thank you. It's been a while since I competed, though."

"What titles did you win?"

"The last one was Miss Georgia, and I also took part in the Miss America Pageant the following year."

"What year?"

Mona hesitated to answer but rethought her reluctance. What difference did it make if he knew her age? She looked better than most women ten years her junior. "Nineteen ninety-seven."

His eyes rounded then narrowed. "How old were you, five?"

66

Flattered, she laughed and said, "You have to be at least eighteen to enter the pageant." If he could count, he'd figure it out.

Just then one of the photographers Mona had hired to record the event stopped them and began snapping a succession of shots. Since the two of them were used to posing for the camera, they immediately assumed the position to make sure they wouldn't come out looking crazy. Rayvon slipped his arm around her waist and flashed his dazzling grin. A minute later, another photographer Mona didn't recognize positioned himself in front of them and did the same. Once the picture-taking was done, Rayvon signaled a roving waiter and took two glasses of champagne from his tray.

"Is your husband here tonight?" he asked nonchalantly as they sat at their table.

"No. He's out of town attending a conference."

"Does he usually let you come to these things alone?" Rayvon asked with a curious squint.

"He's extremely busy," Mona said as casually as she could manage.

He smiled. "He *must* be to leave a fine woman like you all by herself. Does he travel a lot?"

Goose bumps popped up on her arms at the way his gaze ran over her body. "Too much for my taste," Mona replied, realizing she sounded snippier than she'd intended. "He's the chief of surgery of the largest hospital in Atlanta. It comes with the job."

"You don't sound too pleased, though." It was obvious he was fishing for information, but she didn't take it as being nosy. As a matter of fact, she kind of liked the expedition.

"I'm not, but there's nothing I can do about it."

Rayvon angled his body closer and zeroed his rich umber gaze on her face. "If I had a woman like you, I'd never leave her all by herself." His voice, deep and sensual, sent a ripple of awareness through her.

"And how would you imagine doing that?"

"I'd make sure she was so content, she wouldn't want to go anywhere without me." Mona shivered when he ran the back of his index finger over her cheek, down her neck to her bare shoulder. It seemed like ages since Vic had touched her like that. She took a deep breath in an effort to slow the pounding of her heart against her rib cage.

Well, he'd left no doubt in her mind about his intentions, but she wasn't sure how to respond. It had been more than fifteen years since she'd had any romantic or sexual contact with a man other than Vic. She didn't want to give Rayvon the wrong idea, but she felt as though she was floating on a cloud from the attention and compliments he lavished on her.

"Let's dance," he suggested, pulling her up by the hand after they'd sat silently for a little while watching the action on the dance floor.

Visions of the last time she'd danced before a crowd instantly rushed to her mind. The July Fourth barbeque was the last time she tried to get Vic's attention, and she had gone about it the wrong way. All she wanted was to tempt her husband into joining her, only it backfired on her. Instead, Vic watched her from the sidelines until he exploded from embarrassment over the sexy twerk she'd done with his baby brother. He'd bellowed at her and stormed out of the yard. Her mother-in-law had quickly intervened and taken her inside for a probing heart-to-heart chat. This time she kept it as sedate as possible yet allowed Rayvon to see that she could move.

The photographers appeared to be intent on

documenting Rayvon's every move. Mona assumed their interest was because he was the new face of the Hawks. And a beautiful face it was. She watched him work his impressive body to the music then shook the thought out of her head when the song ended. She had no business entertaining sensual thoughts about this young man.

"I think I should get back to my duties. I *am* the hostess, you know." She stood and smoothed the skirt of her gown with moist palms.

"I understand. I'll let you get back to your responsibilities."

When she turned to head toward the podium, he took her hand. "I'll be calling you this week."

Everything in her head said their whole conversation was inappropriate, but the fluttering in her stomach made her want more. "I look forward to it." She crossed the room, and didn't look back, but she would've bet her Bentley he was watching her every move.

She spent all day Saturday with Trey and Julian shopping for clothes and going to the game store to buy some kind of video game both boys assured her they would die without. The afternoon ended with lunch at their favorite pizza restaurant. As usual, Julian was the one to ask about his father's return.

"When is Dad coming home?" he inquired with a long string of cheese dangling from his bottom lip.

"Wipe your mouth. He said he'd be back tomorrow afternoon. By the time we get home from church, the day will be half over anyway."

"I hope he gets here early."

"Why?" The question came out before she realized how it must have sounded to her sons.

"So he can play Emperor's Pursuit with us."

"Julian, you know Daddy is going to be tired from traveling. He might not be in the mood to play video games."

Her baby boy gave a confident grin and said, "I know how to make him."

"Oh, really?"

"I look really sad, and I tell him I've been waiting for *three days* for him to come home to play with me."

Mona offered him a weak smile and wondered why the same tactic no longer worked for her. When she looked sad, he'd tell her she was being overly dramatic. She couldn't remember the last time she and Vic played at anything. All of their interaction was necessary, serious and recently combative.

Vic returned from Chicago late Sunday afternoon. Trey and Julian were watching a movie in the den, and they didn't hear him come in. She and Daphine had a lunch date the next day, and Mona was upstairs in her closet trying to select an outfit to wear. He entered the bedroom, called out her name and startled her. She slapped a hand to her heart, looked down and saw him standing in the door of the lower level of her two-story wardrobe room, the one his brothers constantly chided her about.

"Vic! You have to stop sneaking up on me like that!" Normally, he would have kissed her when he came home from a trip, but he didn't, so she made no attempt to move or look up from where she stood searching through her sundresses.

"I didn't mean to scare you. I called you from the bottom of the steps. What are up to?"

"Trying to decide what to wear to lunch with Daphine tomorrow. How was your flight?" she asked, not because she really cared but because she thought she should.

"It was okay." He hesitated for a moment. "So, were you the belle of the ball Friday night?"

"Of course." A flash of memory brought the heat of Rayvon's hand on her back so vividly she almost reached back to touch the spot. The memory prevented her from making eye-to-eye contact with her husband. "We surpassed our donation requests by thirty percent." She said without looking in his direction, with the distinct feeling he also avoided looking at her.

Vic pushed his hands into his pockets and glanced at the floor. "Congratulations."

"How did your class go?"

"Good. No one had any complaints." He walked out, left her in the closet alone and went back down the stairs to the master bedroom.

Mona frowned. It wasn't just her imagination. He'd avoided looking her in the eye. What was that all about?

Chapter Five

Wow, that was the most awkward conversation they'd had in months. As far as Vic could recall, it was also the first time he'd returned from a trip and they hadn't greeted each other with a kiss. He entered the bedroom, walked over to the windows overlooking the pool and stared down at the shimmering reflections coming from the water. All he could think of was the kiss he'd shared with Heather and how their tongues had engaged in a chocolate-flavored tango before he pulled away. It hadn't been a spectacular kiss, but the sheer illicitness of their contact made it seem like it could've won a movie award. His guilt had kept him from looking in his wife's face. Not that she seemed eager to even speak to him. He had left town without undoing the hurt he'd caused her before he left. Mona was right. When they got married, he'd insisted she become a stay-at-home mom and raise his children. Whatever she was at this season in their marriage was his doing. Fifteen years ago, all he wanted was a beautiful woman who took good care of herself, him and his children. And it was exactly what he'd gotten. Why wasn't it enough for him now? She only wanted what she'd had all along, and his career had changed everything. He turned from the window, pulled his shirt over his head and unzipped his pants and stepped out of them on his way into the bathroom. He stretched under the hot water from the six heads hitting his travel-weary body, he thought about how to fix the mess they were in. This coming weekend he had no meetings or travel on his schedule. If his mother agreed to let the boys stay over, he could make reservations for dinner and an overnight stay at one of the city's nicest hotels. A major apology needed a major setup.

A few days later, Vic sat behind his desk engrossed in preparing for a meeting with the staff surgeons when Marv knocked on his door.

"Have you seen this?" he asked, holding a magazine.

He looked up. "No. What is it?"

"This month's issue of *Jezebel*."

"Not exactly my preferred reading, man, but Mona reads it sometimes."

"I don't think she's anxious to show you this issue."

Vic removed his glasses and closed the file he was reading. "Why?"

Marv crossed the office and put the open magazine atop the folder in the center of the desk. "Do you know this guy?"

He glanced down at the picture of a tall, dark-skinned man with his arm around Mona's waist. In another shot, the man, who appeared to be in his twenties, was leaning against her so their shoulders touched, and he appeared to be whispering in her ear. Vic studied the photos, and it took a few moments for him to come up with a response. After he swallowed and took a deep breath, he closed the magazine and slid it back toward his friend as though he wasn't in the least bit curious. "Nah, never seen him before, but Mona knows a lot of people I don't, because she goes to so many of these events." He gritted his teeth and kept his expression blank.

Who the hell is this guy with his hands on my wife? Vic wanted to hit something, but kept his fists balled up beneath the desk. Obviously, Mona and her companion hadn't posed for these shots. The photographer had captured them unaware for these candid moments. He gritted his teeth and smiled at his friend and colleague. "I'll need to swing by the store on the way home and pick up a copy for her."

Marv picked up the magazine and frowned as though Vic had sprouted a third eye. "Okay, I'm headed out for lunch. Can you afford to leave for an hour?"

"Not today. I have to get this report together before the surgical staff meeting tomorrow."

"Just thought I'd ask. Check you later."

Vic contemplated what he'd just seen for a few minutes, and then buzzed his assistant. "Shondell, are you going out for lunch today or to the cafeteria?"

"I was thinking about going out. Do you want me to pick you up some lunch?"

"No, I'll probably go downstairs, but could you stop at a store that sells magazines and get me the new issue of Jezebel magazine? You can take an extra thirty minutes."

"You read Jezebel?" she asked with an incredulous lilt to her voice.

"No, but my wife does. It's for her. Come in before you leave, and I'll give you some cash."

Ninety minutes later, after Shondell had taken advantage of every available second, she returned and knocked on his closed door. Anytime she was away from her desk and wasn't there to run interference for him, he kept his office door shut.

"Come in," he said to her gentle knock.

She entered carrying a flat brown bag, placed it on the corner of his desk. When she got ready to hand him the change from the ten-dollar bill he'd given her, he waved her off. "Thanks. Mona will appreciate it."

"No problem." Her lopsided smile gave him the

impression she had taken the time to scan through the periodical and knew why he wanted it.

"You can close the door. I'll be going downstairs for a sandwich in a few minutes." He had only given the photos a cursory scan when Marv showed them to him, and he wanted to study them more closely. Mona looked spectacular in the form-fitting, backless gown, which had most likely cost him two grand. The cost of the dress wasn't what made his jaw tight. He literally felt his blood pressure climb at the expression on the face of the man sitting with her. As Vic scanned the captions beneath each shot, he discovered who he was—Rayvon Patterson, new point guard for the Hawks. His body language appeared confident. Although he couldn't see the player's face because of the mask he wore, the curve of his mouth indicated a cocky smile. Judging by his general physical appearance, he couldn't be more than twenty-two or twenty-three, and he seemed completely enamored with Mona. She knew how to take professional pictures and her gaze was directed at the camera, while Patterson's was glued to her face. *The way his used to be.* What the hell was wrong with him? Mona was just as sexy and alluring as she'd always been. Why on earth was it getting harder for him to shift from work mode to focus on her when he got home?

The rest of the afternoon went by quickly after he'd been pulled from his office for consultations with two of his attendings. When he was finally in the car leaving the hospital garage, he remembered his father had mentioned he needed to talk about something. Vic promised he would stop by on the way home. Of course he remained elusive. It was his way of guaranteeing that his sons showed up when he summoned them. Vic arrived to find Charles', Nick's and Jesse's cars already parked in the driveway. They were all sitting in the family room at the back of the house with a drink in hand when he walked in.

"What's going on?"

Nick glanced up from his laptop and gave him a nod. "We're wondering the same thing. Daddy asked me to bring my computer so I could Skype Marc and Greg."

"Where's Mama?" he asked glancing through the pass-through window into the kitchen.

"She's at a meeting tonight, and I figured it was a good time to get you boys together." He looked to see if Nick had anything on the screen then eased into his massage recliner. "Let me know when you get them on the line."

Vic went to the bar in the corner and poured himself a Scotch on the rocks.

"Got 'em," Nick announced. "Hey, man. Hold for a minute, so I can get Greg on the screen then I'll turn you around so Daddy can do his thing."

When he spun the computer around so the screen faced their father, the older man began. "I don't know if you boys know it, but your mother's sixty-fifth birthday is coming up on the seventeenth of October. The raised eyebrows told Vic he wasn't the only one who wasn't aware this was a landmark birthday for his mother. "Since she's the one who always takes care of the celebrations in this family, I want to surprise her with a big bash in her honor." Murmurs of agreement filled the room. Lillian Stafford was the closest thing to a saint as far as her sons were concerned, and they were up for anything that would make her happy. "I think I'll tell her I'm taking her somewhere special, and then everyone can be there when we arrive."

"Sounds great, Daddy," Marc said from the screen. "Where did you have in mind?"

"That's what I'm leaving to you boys. Since the seventeenth is a Saturday, we need to have the party that night, and I need *all* of you to be there," the elder man directed into the laptop with the blue-green gaze his sons had inherited from him. "If you have something scheduled, cancel it."

Greg shook his head, knowing the comment was aimed at him and Marc, the two who had chosen to move away from Atlanta. "We'll be there, Daddy."

"Us too," Marc agreed. "Gianne will be thrilled to get all dressed up for a party."

"Good. Now, do any of you have suggestions for a venue?"

"How many guests are we talking about?" Charles asked.

"A couple of hundred, I guess. Adanna, Mona and Cydney will probably know best."

"Mona's fundraising committee held an affair at the St. Regis last weekend. The ballroom looks pretty fancysomeplace Mama would like."

"All right. Can I count on you to go check it out and make a reservation if everything is suitable?"

Vic had no doubt that asking his wife to handle a chore for his family was out of the question at the moment. Maybe he could bribe Shondell into checking it out for him. "Sure."

"Two months is short notice for such a popular site, Daddy," Greg chimed in. "We should come up with a second choice in case it's already booked."

"I'll ask Adanna for some ideas," Charles offered. "She's done a few fundraisers for the foundation, and she knows some of the nicer places around town."

"The other thing is, we need to come up with a gift from the family that will knock your mother's socks off." His father's cheeks puffed into a smile and his eyes narrow into slits. "We need to wow her."

"We'll come up with something," Jesse said as he rose and swallowed the remainder of the liquid in his glass. "I have to get moving. Cyd needs me to pick up some diapers."

Marc laughed from the screen. "Daddy duty never ends, man. It was good seeing you."

Jesse waved goodbye over his shoulder as he left the room.

Greg logged off by saying, "I'll pick Rhani's brain for gift ideas. Talk to you soon," and then he was gone.

Nick turned off the computer and stashed it back into the black bag he carried everywhere he went from the day he started college. He turned to Vic and whispered, "Meet me in the library. I need to talk to you about something."

He rose, picked up his glass and watched his baby brother retreat down the hall, curious about what he didn't want the rest of them to hear.

"Daddy, I'll see if I can get Mona to come up with some ideas. She'll probably call you in the next few days." Volunteering Mona's participation was stupid, since she didn't even want to speak to him.

When he entered the room lined with books, which had belonged to his parents and all of his brothers, Nick was sitting on the edge of the desk holding a folded newspaper. Vic closed the door. "What do you want to show me? Are you in some kind of trouble?"

"No, but you might be." He opened the paper and handed it to Vic. "Turn to page nineteen."

Vic looked at the front page and frowned. "Rolling Out? I doubt there's anything in there I'd want to read?"

His brother crossed his arms and waited while he thumbed through the pages then froze when he saw the pictures. When he flicked on the green banker's lamp sitting on the table, he wished he hadn't. The local entertainment/news tabloid had a center spread of events around the city from the previous weekend. The chain on the lamp swung wildly when he slammed his hand on the table seeing the shots of Mona and Patterson dancing together. In one he had his hands on her hips, and in the other hers were clasped around his neck. These were worse than the Jezebel photos. Vic cursed, folded the paper and shoved it under his arm.

"Did you know about this?"

"Yeah, a friend of mine showed me pictures in Jezebel magazine this afternoon."

"Are you and Mona all right?"

Vic snorted and searched for words to explain to Nick what was going on in his marriage and, at the same time, imagining how photos of Heather and him in Chicago would've looked. He let out a loud sigh. "We're having some issues right now."

"What's she thinking? He's younger than I am." Nick sounded dumbfounded.

Vic's eyes stretched. "That's the only thing you have a problem with?"

"No, but it just seems out of character for Mona. Is she seeing him?"

"I don't know. Please don't mention this to Mama or Daddy, okay?"

"Don't worry. They won't hear it from me, but you know Mama's had a subscription to Jezebel for as long as I can remember."

Nick was right. Vic recalled seeing the publication on the cocktail table in his parents' house. "Oh, hell. Let me get out of here before Mama comes home. Thanks for showing me these. Tell the rest of them I said goodnight." He slipped out of the front door unnoticed and got into his car with volcanoes erupting behind his eyelids, wanting nothing more than to destroy this punk who had the barefaced boldness to put his hands on another man's wife. *His* wife. The steering wheel suffered the brunt of his anger as he pounded it several times.

Beneath the anger, he was tormented by conflicting emotions. Seeing Mona receive the obvious attention of another man filled him with rage, but his anger was clearly unjustified, considering he'd done the same thing. In fact, what he'd done was even more intimate. Confronting her would make him a hypocrite. If there was one thing he despised, it was a man who pretended to have virtues he didn't actually possess, and he was that man at the moment.

While he drove the short distance home, he decided how he would bring up the matter. The Bentley was sitting in its usual spot beside the fountain when he pulled up to the house and made sure he grabbed the magazine and newspaper as he exited his car. The sound of some hip-hop song playing in the distance when he entered the house told him Trey was upstairs in his bedroom. Most likely Julian was playing a video game or reading in his room. He didn't see or hear any evidence of Mona being on the first floor. Rather than announce himself, Vic took the stairs to the master bedroom two at a time. Mona's voice drifted out into the hall. He pushed the partially shut door open wide. She was on the phone, so he sat on the edge of their bed, removed his shoes and tie then waited for her to finish the call. She glanced his way but didn't acknowledge his presence.

"How's Rayvon?" he asked as soon as she put the phone down on the arm of the chair where she was sitting. He felt a wave of satisfaction when her face blanched.

"What?" Her lashes flew up and her posture straightened.

"Rayvon, Mona. What's he been up to since your *date* last Friday?"

"He…I…uh…" she stammered, running her fingers through her hair seemingly in shock. "It wasn't a date."

"How long have you known him?" Vic asked softly, struggling to maintain his composure.

"I don't know him. I just met him at the ball."

"Really? You just met him, and you let him put his hands all over you?" He grunted and let his gaze linger on her face for a long moment then threw the publications across the bed in her direction. Mona stared down at the magazine and newspaper as if they were explosives that might detonate if she touched them.

"Vic, please." She held her palm up. "You're getting to be such an old fart. All we were doing was dancing."

He flipped open the glossy Jezebel issue to the page where the new hoops hopeful appeared to be caressing her neck and turned it around so she could see it from where she stood. "That's bullshit."

❤❤❤❤

Vic's bluntness momentarily astounded her. She picked up the magazine first, studied the pictures and tried to ignore the way his eyes bore into her. The newspaper shots were a bit more revealing than those in Jezebel, and she was surprised Rolling Out even covered the event. Their coverage usually leaned more toward entertainment, popular culture and fashion. Someone had obviously run to him eager to spread some gossip, because he didn't read either of those publications.

"Have you forgotten I asked you to escort me months ago, but you were too busy, as usual? Rayvon kept me company during the evening. No harm done."

They locked gazes and neither refused to look away until he said, "You're lying."

"How dare you! Ask anyone who was there. I arrived at the ball alone, and I left alone, but the fact that you don't believe me says a whole lot, Vic. I never wanted to do these events. I did them for you. After I've devoted all my time to helping you and making you look good, this is the thanks I get?"

"Well, it's not like you have anything better to do."

"Why do you keep bringing that up?"

He uttered a harsh, cynical laugh. "Because there's a lot of truth in the old saying, *an idle mind is the devil's workshop.*"

"You've lost it, Vic." She grabbed her purse and headed for the door. "I'm not listening to this anymore."

"Come on, Mona, why won't you talk to me? Isn't that what you've been begging for? Don't you want to have that heart-to-heart?"

His snide tone made her angrier. "Not like this! This isn't a conversation. You're grilling me like I'm some kind of criminal."

"You're not the only one who caught somebody's eye last weekend." He sent her a furtive smile then picked up the remote and turned on the TV, effectively dismissing her.

He'd met someone while he was in Chicago. And he was using it as a weapon against her. She'd done nothing wrong. Nothing more than dance with a fine-looking man. What had he done?

Hearing him say those words felt like a hot lance piercing her heart. The idea of her husband with another woman made her sick, but she maintained her poise and kept her expression even. She refused to allow him to see how much it hurt. "Good for you, Vic."

Mona stood at the top of the stairs with the peculiar feeling that this house, with its many rooms, wasn't big enough for the two of them. She stormed down the stairs, locked herself in the den and dropped down onto one of the sofas. What had happened to her marriage? Maybe her mother-in-law had the right idea. She needed to talk to someone–someone she could trust to keep her confidence. Greg's wife would be a good choice. She wasn't in Atlanta, so she didn't meet with Mama or the other sisters-in-law for coffee every week. Rhani had been a psychotherapist by trade before she lost her license for getting personally involved with Greg, who was her client at the time. Mona had only been in her presence a few times, but she liked her openness and how she had handled herself with the family. The Staffords could be intimidating at times, and assimilating into the family took confidence and strength. Rhani had even had the gumption to opt out of a typical huge Stafford wedding. Instead, she and Greg got married on the beach in Hawaii with only a handful of their closest friends, her brother and his brother, Charles present. Of course, after Mama got over the initial shock and disappointment of learning they had eloped, she threw them a reception for the record books.

After she turned on the TV, Mona reclined on the sofa and contemplated where she stood with Vic. Since they married, she had always been at his side, going along with whatever he felt was best for the family and for his career. She had done everything possible to present a united front within their social circle and the Atlanta medical community. Although none of it seemed particularly distasteful to her, she hadn't always been gung-ho about attending events for causes she hadn't even been familiar with before marrying a doctor. Once Vic became more prominent in his field, he had to be more concerned about his image, and so did she. Looking the part was never a problem, but feigning interest in things she didn't even understand wasn't as easy as it looked. She was no dummy. She'd earned a B.A. degree, but often when she researched and studied the conditions and diseases which were the focus of different organizations, a lot of it went right over her head. Thankfully, she'd pulled it off, though, and she'd done it all for Vic, the man she'd loved with every fiber of her being. As her memory drifted back to their early years together, she recalled how compatible their temperaments and sexual appetites were. No one would've believed what an uninhibited lover he was. All of that abandon had disappeared under the stress of his new position. It seemed as though all he could think about were patients, their families, budgets and board meetings. He'd always been serious, but the job had robbed him of the free spirit that once simmered just beneath his intent, deliberate exterior.

Mona swiped at the tears she hadn't realized were dripping down her face onto the black and white chevron pillows beneath her head. Before she knew it, the trickling tears turned to full-fledged sobs. She cried as though someone had died, and perhaps a death *was* on the horizon. She and Vic had been together for fifteen years, twice as long as most of the marriages in their circle. Maybe it had come to its inevitable end. Finally, jerking upright, she mentally slapped herself. *What is wrong with me? I will not allow Vic to turn me into a miserable, desperate housewife.*

Almost as if she'd summoned it to the television screen, a commercial caught her attention. While the announcer spoke, Mona absorbed his every word, and it was almost as though a light turned on inside her head. She'd probably seen this advertisement many times, and never paid attention to it. But this time the images on the screen seemed to come to life before her eyes.

As soon as it ended, she reached inside her purse for her phone and pulled up the web site it gave on Google. She saved the phone number on the web site and closed the browser. It was too late to call the number now. She would have to wait until tomorrow morning. Instead, she called

Greg.

"Greg Stafford," he answered, taking her by surprise. She had been ready to leave a message on his voicemail.

"Oh, hi, Greg. It's Mona. I didn't expect you to answer."

"Hey girl! What's new with you?"

"Nothing much," she lied. "I need to get in touch with your wife." She chuckled. "That still sounds strange to me."

"What, saying *my wife*?"

"Yes. I still can't believe you're a married man."

"Best move I ever made."

"I'm happy for you." She truly was, but her words sounded hollow nevertheless. "Can you give me her cell number?"

"Sure." He recited the digits and waited until she saved them into her phone.

"What's the best time to get her?"

Greg chuckled. "Now that she's self-employed, she can communicate any time, as long as she's not in a meeting."

"Sounds like you're happy about it," Mona said, noting the contentment in his voice.

"I am. It was rough at first, when they took her license. She had to adjust from being a practicing therapist to more of an overall mentor, but I believe it's really where her heart was to begin with."

"You're proud of what she does, aren't you?"

"Incredibly proud. My wife is one awesome woman."

Newlyweds. That was her first thought, but she knew it was more than that, and she blinked back tears at the obvious pride Greg felt for his new bride's accomplishments.

Other than giving him two sons and keeping her figure, Vic had never been able to say the same thing about her.

"Well, I need to ask Mrs. Awesome a question. Is it too late to call her now?"

"No, baby. She's not even home yet. She's been with the contractors at the building she found to house her program."

"That's good to hear; I'm glad everything is moving right along. Thanks a lot, Greg."

"You're welcome. Tell Vic I said hi."

Mona ended the call and stared at the phone for a long moment before she clicked into the contact list and selected Rhani's number. Before it had a chance to ring, she hit the end call button. What would she say? Instead she looked up the number she'd taken from the television commercial, took a deep breath and placed the call. By the time the call ended, she had an appointment. The prospect struck fear in her heart, but it was a choice she needed to make.

No sooner had she put the phone back in her purse, it rang with the call she knew was coming sooner or later. "Daphine! I've been meaning to call you."

"Sure you have," she said with a snarky laugh. "We were both so busy during the ball; I didn't even get a chance to speak to you. Judging from the pictures, though, you didn't need any companionship."

Mona snickered. "And exactly what do you mean?"

"Please, Ramona. This basketball player apparently monopolized your attention for most of the evening, and I can't say I blame you, girl. He is one fine chocolate man."

"I think we need to chat. Can you meet me at Zen Tea tomorrow?"

"I *love* that place," Daphine gushed.

"I know. I have to drop the boys off at Dynamo for their last swimming lessons at ten. I'll see you at Zen at ten-fifteen."

Mona made sure the boys showered and got ready for bed before she returned to the master bedroom where Vic was watching TV. He didn't say a word to her while she searched through her dresser for something to sleep in, but she felt his gaze on her. If only Maite wasn't occupying the pool house, she'd go out there and spend the night. He obviously wasn't leaving their bedroom. Once she chose an unsexy baseball-style nightshirt and retrieved a tube of make-up remover from the bathroom, she went down the hall to one of the guestrooms. No one had slept in the room since houseguests visited last year.

Mona undressed, removed her make-up and crawled into the bed. Sometime later, after she'd given up on squeezing her eyes shut and trying to make sleep come, she sensed she was no longer alone. When she turned over and blinked, she saw Vic standing just inside the doorway, his tall form just barely illuminated by the light from the hall. She cringed. Was he actually coming to continue their argument? God, she was still livid from their earlier confrontation. Rather, he surprised her when he wordlessly moved toward the bed, pulled back the covers and slid in beside her without a word.

"Vic, this isn't–" she started to protest until he pulled her into his arms and his mouth came down on hers in a punishing kiss. As much as she wanted to refuse, the force of his kiss and the urgent hardness pressed against her stomach rendered her incapable. It had been months since he'd made love to her, and she couldn't resist him. She didn't want to resist him. The satin smoothness of his skin and the fragrance of his signature cologne, combined with a scent which was uniquely Vic, never failed to arouse her. Her hands roamed over his shoulders and back of their own accord. When they reached the elastic waistband of his briefs, her anger over his questions about Rayvon melted away. He moaned when she slipped her fingers under the band and ran her hands over the firmness of his butt then rolled onto his side and undid the buttons down the front of her nightshirt. Automatically, she rose up so he could get it over her shoulders and arms. As soon as he tossed it onto the floor, his mouth left a searing trail of kisses down her neck and finally to her breasts where he lingered.

Damn him! He knew what she loved and what made her crazy. The sound of him sucking at her nipples sent an automatic signal to her legs to open wide. No matter how wildly she wriggled her hips, he angled his body away from her so his erection pressed against her thigh and not where she wanted it most.

Finally, he tested her readiness with two of his long expert fingers then growled against her ear, "You're so wet, you can't tell me you don't want this."

Cursing herself for her weakness, all she could do was purr and mimic the movement of his fingers with her hips. It felt so good, and it had been so long since they had been together. She closed her eyes and imagined her body floating on the wave of rhythm he'd created. When he raised his body above her and lifted one of her legs onto his shoulder, it was clear he wasn't getting ready to be gentle. He plunged into her in one hard stroke, going so deep she uttered a loud gasp and hooked her other leg behind his. For a moment, the force of his strokes shocked her. With each one, he sank into her then withdrew almost all the way. Her hips lifted off the mattress to keep him from leaving her body. Rough lovemaking wasn't typical for him, but it excited her so much, she dug her nails into his shoulders and surrendered to his passion.

Every time she tried to kiss him, he pulled back, and when he sensed she was on the verge of climax, he withdrew and took his time changing their position. Finally, after he'd done this three or four times, he flipped her over, wedged a pillow under her hips and pinned her hands against the mattress so she couldn't move from beneath him. In all the years they'd been together, Mona couldn't ever remember him being so aggressive. He was so hard he didn't even need to guide himself into her. Doing it this way put him at the perfect angle to hit her spot. Vic knew her body so well. A few short minutes later, his name filled the room as she screamed her release. In a few seconds, he uttered a roar unlike anything she'd ever heard from him. Thankfully, the boys' rooms were at the opposite end of the floor.

When it was all over, Vic didn't pull her back against him so they could spoon the way they used to. He fumbled around on the floor with one arm for his briefs then sat up and pulled them on. He got up and glared down at her with such a cold look in his eyes it sent a chill down her back. "He'll never be able to make you scream like that." He walked out leaving her body still quivering and her mouth unable to form any comprehensible words.

In the morning, when she woke, she turned over and winced. Vic had left his mark on her body. Her leg muscles ached, which wasn't an easy accomplishment considering she did a thirty-minute session on the elliptical trainer three times a week. She hadn't experienced the soreness between them since the early days of their marriage, but it wasn't exactly unpleasant. What happened last night still had her confused, but one thing she did understand: Vic had made sure she'd remember it. Their sex life had changed since he'd taken the new job. Physically it was still good. Vic kept himself in good shape and still had the stamina he'd had when they got married, but what had changed was the emotional connection. They always looked into each other's eyes when they made love. Now she tended to keep her eyes closed and concentrated on how it felt. Or perhaps she wanted to avoid seeing the distraction in his—a distance which told her he wasn't fully present. Like the old song by the O'Jays said, *Your body's here with me, but your mind is on the other side of town.*

She left the guest room and refused to peek into the master bedroom to see if he was still there. It was still early, so she looked in on her sons then minced down the staircase and followed the aromas coming from the kitchen. Maite was busy fixing breakfast softly singing a song in Spanish.

"Good morning," Mona said as she poured herself a cup of coffee and eased down onto a stool at the center island hoping the housekeeper didn't notice her difficulty sitting. "Did Vic leave already?"

"Good morning," Maite said, not looking up from the eggs she was scrambling. "Yes, he left about a half-hour ago."

"Hmm." Mona absentmindedly spooned some stevia and milk into her cup. "I was sleeping so hard, I didn't even hear him get up." Maite didn't need to know she and Vic had slept in separate bedrooms for the second time in a month. "The boys are still asleep. They have their last swimming lesson today, and I have to meet Daphine Weber at ten, so will you please get them up and make sure they're ready by nine?"

"On my way."

Silence enveloped her as she watched Maite leave the kitchen and brought back thoughts of last night. Vic hadn't treated her like that in all the years they'd been married. The rough way he'd made love to her was exciting, a bit scary, and some warped thing inside her loved every second of it. Her ambivalence over the fact that he thought she was fooling around with Ray was the problem. On one hand, she wanted to make him jealous. On the other, it struck fear in her heart that he might get so angry he'd do something drastic in response. When she thought about it, though, his anger and jealousy were what had turned him into a sex machine. Perhaps a little bit of jealousy wasn't a bad thing after all.

Chapter Six

Vic intentionally arrived at the hospital early, because he wanted to get out of the house before Mona woke up. She would surely question his behavior, and he didn't want to talk about it. Last night was the best sex they'd had in a year, and it disturbed him that it had resulted from anger. After seeing those pictures, he wanted to strangle her, but when he joined her in the guestroom, everything he did seemed to arouse them both. It really hadn't been his intention. In spite of the fact that Patterson was younger, fitter and wealthier than he was, he wanted to remind Mona that she belonged to him and him alone.

On the way to his office, he stopped in the cafeteria for breakfast to take to his office. Before his trip to Chicago, he'd been oblivious to female attention at work. Most often, his mind was preoccupied with hospital business, and he didn't even notice the admiring looks from female staff members. This morning, while he got his large coffee and apple Danish, he didn't miss a couple of them who made it a point to catch his eye and greet him.

"Good morning, Chief," one of the surgical nurses, a bubbly redhead, said with a flirty smile he considered a little too cheerful for eight o'clock in the morning.

"Hi, Doctor Stafford." The administrative assistant to the Chief of Staff greeted him. "How are you today?"

He smiled at his boss's assistant. "I'll be better once I get this caffeine in my system. How about you?"

"I'm great." She focused on his face and held his gaze for a long moment. "Got a busy day ahead with the visiting doctors from Japan. I guess I'll see you later."

"Right. Eleven o'clock. See you then." Vic paid for his food and left the dining hall more aware than he'd ever been of the female attention. His brothers always teased him about being "the serious one." From his freshman year in college until his graduation from medical school, his goal had been to excel at his studies. Unlike Marc, Greg and even Charles, who'd always found time to study as well as party and date, Vic had been single minded. His interest in dating ended when one of his buddies introduced him to Mona at a pool party during his first year in med school. It didn't take them long to become exclusive, and eighteen months later, they were married. The epitome of beauty and sexiness to him, Mona had more than satisfied him. It never occurred to him that perhaps marrying in their early twenties had been a mistake until now.

It was still early, and his assistant hadn't arrived yet, so he could eat his breakfast in peace while things were still quiet. He entered his office, closed the door and retrieved the business card Jesse had given him from his wallet. If one more person asked him about the photos of Mona and Patterson, he'd probably lose it. Since she refused to be straight with him, he was determined to get to the bottom of the issue, but having her followed just didn't sit right with him. He studied the business card, which listed twenty years of experience and being specialists in infidelity investigations. *What if I had him followed instead of her?*

He drummed his fingers on the desk then looked at the clock. It was probably too early to call now. But if he called before the office opened, he could simply leave a voicemail message stating what he needed and they could return the call. He dialed, and voicemail picked up.

"Good morning, this is Vic Stafford. I was referred to

your firm by my brother, Dr. Jesse Stafford. The reason for my call is to find out how you handle infidelity investigations. You can reach me anytime on my cell." He recited the phone number and clicked off the call, chewing on his bottom lip. Going this route wasn't how he preferred to handle the problem, but since Mona refused to engage in a rational conversation, she left him no other choice.

One of his attendings called him for a consultation, and he was in the middle of examining the patient when the return call came. He let it go into voicemail and didn't listen to the message until he returned to the privacy of his office.

"Mr. Stafford, this is Doug McClendon from Superior Investigations. I'd like to sit down with you at your convenience at a location of your choosing. Let me know, and thank Jesse for the referral. I look forward to meeting you."

Vic pulled up his schedule on the computer then hit Return Call. While he waited for someone to answer, he decided it would be best for him to go to McClendon's office. It was too risky that someone at the hospital might recognize the private investigator. A woman answered and instructed him to hold.

"Mr. Stafford. Thanks for calling me back. I take it you want to meet."

"Yes, I could come to your office. Do you have a spot on your calendar tomorrow or the day after?"

"Could you make it at three o'clock tomorrow?"

Vic gazed at his schedule on the screen. "Looks good. Do you need anything from me?"

"Photos would be helpful."

"Oh, I have those," Vic answered cynically.

"Good. I'll see you at three tomorrow afternoon."

"Shondell, I need to run an errand, and I'll be gone for about ninety minutes," he told his assistant the next day. "Don't call me unless it's an emergency."

It took about twenty minutes to drive to McClendon's office in a high-rise in Buckhead. By the time he parked, grabbed the magazine and newspaper from the back seat and walked into the building, he was wiping rivulets of sweat from his face and neck. It wasn't just the low nineties temperature but more so his trepidation over what he was about to do that caused his clothes to stick to his body. He used the elevator ride up to the twenty-seventh floor to compose himself. By the time the chime sounded and the doors opened, he'd shrugged his suit jacket back on and readjusted his tie.

A pleasant receptionist greeted him when he entered the small, well-appointed suite occupied by Superior Investigations. "Mr. McClendon will be with you in a moment. May I offer you a bottle of water? It's brutal out there."

"Yes, thank you." Vic took a seat, twisted the cap and guzzled the chilled liquid. Just as he considered turning around and giving up on the idea of hiring an investigator, a man entered the waiting area with his hand outstretched.

"Mr. Stafford, sorry for the wait. I couldn't get off a phone call."

"No problem." Vic grasped the hand of the man, thinking he was entirely too nerdy looking to be a P.I. He had to put a check on his Hollywood-influenced image of the hardboiled sleuth like Samuel L. Jackson or Richard Roundtree as John Shaft.

Vic didn't come to terms with his reason for being there until McClendon closed the door to his office, and he settled into a comfortable upholstered chair. Now that he had, he needed to act on his decision.

"On the phone you said you needed an infidelity investigation. Why do you believe this is necessary?"

"My wife has been acting suspiciously for the past few months. I ignored it until recently when these came out." He opened both publications to the pages he'd folded down.

McClendon studied the photos for a moment then sat back in his chair and began a litany of questions he'd most likely asked dozens of times. "How long have you been married, Mr. Stafford?"

"Vic. Fifteen years."

"Is this the first instance of questionable conduct in those fifteen years?"

"Yes. Mona's never given me any reason to doubt her faithfulness until now."

"Are these photos the only basis for your suspicions?"

"No. Her general behavior has changed. She's become somewhat of an exhibitionist lately."

"Please don't take offense to my asking this, but are you certain she isn't having any mental or emotional issues?"

"I ask myself the same question every day," Vic answered with a bitter laugh. "No, it's nothing like that, but it's not her I want investigated. It's him. I want to know if he sees her again, where and when."

Vic's phone vibrated in his pocket, and he ignored it. McClendon's attention returned to the pictures. This time he read the captions and pursed his lips. "If he's a professional athlete, he has a busy schedule and travels a lot. It would be virtually impossible for me to trail him everywhere. It would be a lot more efficient to keep an eye on your wife."

"Are you certain she'd have no idea she's being watched?"

"I've been in this business for twenty-two years, Vic, and I've never been identified or exposed by the subject of an investigation."

Once more, his phone vibrated. Vic blew out a long breath. "Okay, go ahead."

"Have you checked her cell phone for any calls to or from Patterson?"

Checking her phone should have been the first thing to come to his mind, but it hadn't occurred to him. "No, I haven't, but I will."

"Would you prefer a weekly report or monthly?"

"Weekly. I need to stay on top of what she's doing."

McClendon asked Vic a few more questions, discussed his fees, and then Vic left. He checked his phone as he headed back to his car, lost in his thoughts and feeling unsettled about paying someone to spy on his wife. It was a 911 call from the hospital. He hit the redial and waited. Shondell answered.

"I'm sorry for paging you twice, Dr. Stafford, but Dr. Sternhagen has been trying to find you. It seems an incident on our floor needs your immediate attention. He wants to see you in his office ASAP."

If the Chief of Staff wanted him, it had to be urgent. "He didn't say what it was about?"

"No, but he sounded disturbed."

"All right, I'm on my way back. Can you transfer me?"

"Right away. Hold on."

"Sternhagen," Vic's boss answered.

"Bill, it's Vic Stafford. Shondell said you've been trying to reach me. I'm in my car right now."

"Finally. Yes, Vic, we have a situation that we need to

address right away. We'll be in my conference room when you get back and can discuss it then."

"I'll be there in twenty." Vic ended the call, curious as to what the secrecy was about. Bill appeared to not want to talk about it over the phone, which in itself seemed strange. Probably a staff issue. He called Shondell back to let her know he'd be in the chief's office, turned the car toward GA-400 and pushed the speed limit all the way.

Several other people already occupied the conference room next to the chief's office when Vic walked in. He recognized the two doctors from the Infectious Disease unit, but the woman was unfamiliar to him.

"Dr. Stafford," Bill Sternhagen addressed him when he entered the office. "This is Evangeline Cardenas from the CDC. You know everyone else."

Vic offered a cordial smile. "What's going on?"

"It looks as though we have a case of CRE on the surgical floor."

Vic's jaw dropped at the mention of the bacteria, Carbapenem-Resistant Enterobacteriaceae, known as CRE, which were named for their ability to fight off antibiotics– the last means of warfare in the medical arsenal. These bacteria had materialized almost solely in hospitals and nursing homes, and attacked the most fragile patients. "What's the patient's name, and whose case is it?"

"A fifty-seven-year-old male named Chauncey Higgins. He's Dr. Jhaveri's patient."

Jhaveri was one of Vic's residents. "Why wasn't I made aware of this?"

"That's what we're trying to determine. Jhaveri is in surgery right now, but I've paged him 911. Here's what we know so far." The chief tapped his iPad a few times. "The patient was admitted twelve days ago for an aortic dissection.

Dr. Jhaveri detected the infection last week, and prescribed three different antibiotics over the past five days, none of which were effective. The infection has continued to progress. The worst part is it seems there's another possible case. A twenty-three-year-old female admitted by Dr. Schmidt for a total knee replacement as a result of a severe sports injury. She's developed a lung infection and has a persistent cough and chills."

"Instances like this should've been reported to me immediately," Vic said, fuming. This oversight by his staff made him look as though he didn't know what was going on in his own department.

"I'll deal with Jhaveri and Schmidt when they get here," the chief reassured him, seeming to sense Vic's tension. "The only way you'll know what's happening on the surgical floor is if the staff informs you. You can't be everywhere at once."

A few minutes later, the two doctors in question entered the room, and Vic listened intently as Dr. Sternhagen interrogated them on the details of the cases. When he'd gotten the facts he wanted, he said, "I'm sure I don't have to remind you that CREs can exhibit a myriad of symptoms, anything from pneumonia to intestinal and urinary tract infections. The death rate among CRE patients can be as high as forty percent, much worse than MRSA or C-Diff. I'm counting on you to keep Dr. Stafford and myself apprised of the status of these two patients and any others you might be concerned about." He then turned to Vic. "We need to call an emergency meeting today for the surgical staff to inform them of how critical the situation is."

They adjourned, and Vic left the conference room feeling a major headache working at the base of his neck. His day had begun on a sour note after the hot yet angry encounter he'd had with Mona last night. No one could convince him she wasn't having an affair with the new Hawks player. Nonetheless, he was still unsettled by his decision to have her watched. Now he had this hospital issue on his hands and the horrible feeling these two cases weren't the end. If so, he was in for some long days and nights.

Vic returned to his office and instructed Shondell to arrange the emergency meeting for his entire surgical staff at the end of the current shift. She paged those who weren't working the current shift and left voicemails for those she couldn't reach with a short message containing the details.

Two hours later, the available surgical staff congregated in another conference room noisily awaiting word on why they had been called together. Once Vic explained the situation, he told them, "Thankfully, this hospital has the lab capability to identify CRE and the resources to effectively screen and isolate patients carrying these potent virile organisms. We'll see if there is any commonality among the infected patients and work with the CDC to pinpoint the source, if possible. Every patient on the floor *must* be tested and a copy of the results delivered to my office as soon as the results are obtained."

Before he closed the ten-minute meeting, one of the nurses said, "Dr. Stafford, we might have a possible third case. It looks as though Mrs. Burns in 643 has developed a bladder infection in the past twenty-four hours."

Vic closed his eyes and rubbed them. "Who is assigned to her during this shift?"

"I am," another nurse spoke up.

"I want her tested stat and tell the lab I said to put a rush on it."

He thanked the staff, dismissed them, and then walked back to his office with Shondell.

"This is really bad, isn't it?" she asked.

"I hate to say it, but it looks like we might have an outbreak on our hands. If we do, it'll be necessary to contact every patient who was admitted on the floor within the last two weeks and tell them they need to be tested immediately."

"So, I guess you'll be hanging around here tonight then."

"I can catch a nap later. Thanks for your help, Shondell." He entered his office and closed the door, dreading what might be ahead. His staying overnight at the hospital wouldn't make a difference to Mona. She couldn't get any madder than she already was.

After Mona dropped Trey and Julian off for their swimming lessons, she drove to the tea room nestled among the antique shops in the Chamblee antiques district. She loved the spot for its Asian décor and serene atmosphere, and serenity was exactly what she needed in order to share the decision she'd made with her friend. Daphine had not yet arrived, so Mona ordered her favorite green tea iced matcha latte and found a spot at one of the dark wooden tables away from the heat of the front window to wait. She smiled when her friend came through the front entrance looking cool and stylish in a sundress she'd picked up the last time the two of them had been shopping together.

"Hi! Have you been here long?"

"I just got here a few minutes ago. The dress looks great on you. Go order your tea then we can talk."

Daphine went to the counter and placed her order then rejoined Mona at the table. "You know what I want to hear about." She folded her hands beneath her chin and grinned. "Start talking, girl."

"I don't understand why everybody thinks there's something to tell."

"Everybody who?" Daphine asked with raised eyebrows.

"Vic for one. He all but gave me the third degree after he saw the pictures in Jezebel and Rolling Out."

Her friend licked her lips as though she couldn't wait to hear what Mona was about to say. "What did he ask you?"

"Believe it or not, he wanted to know if I was sleeping with that kid." She crossed her arms. "All because of a couple of pictures taken at a public benefit."

Daphine momentarily left the table when the counter girl called out her drink. "Mona, I have to be honest. The shot where it looked as if he was about to kiss your neck even made *me* wonder," she whispered after she returned.

"Wonder what? If I had a boyfriend on the side? Don't be ridiculous, Daph. He was nice, friendly and fine as hell. I came to the affair unescorted, so I appreciated the fact that he wanted to spend the evening with me. He also made a two thousand dollar donation."

"Really? Well, I guess that makes having to endure the gossip worthwhile."

"Who's gossiping?"

"Everyone who's seen the pictures, Ramona! I got a couple of phone calls from members of the committee asking what was going on between you two, and that it didn't look respectable."

"Unbelievable! Those bitches have the nerve to talk about what's respectable? They're forgetting I know a lot of their little secrets. I mean, Ray is handsome and rich, but he's probably only ten years older than Trey. If I did get somebody on the side, he'd at least have to be a grown man." She chuckled. "But that's not the reason I asked you to meet me today. I've decided to step down from the committee. In fact, I've decided to bow out of all my charity work."

Her friend's mouth dropped open. "Why on earth would you do that, Ramona? You are so good at it."

"And so are you, which is why I'm asking you to take my place as the chair of the juvenile cancer fund."

"Wait a minute. Back up and tell me the part about what brought this on."

"It's just time, Daph. I've worked on more committees and led more groups in the past ten years than I care to remember."

"I'm honored you'd consider me, really I am, but I have to know why you want to leave."

"I can't go into detail right now, but you'll know soon enough. There are some things I have to work out first."

"Is everything all right?"

Mona considered Daphine her best friend, because they socialized in the same circles and their husbands were good friends, but they didn't have the kind of relationship where they shared intimate secrets. She was a good friend, but they weren't so close that she felt comfortable revealing what was really going on between her and Vic.

Ramona didn't have that kind of friendship with any other woman except her mother-in-law. Her own mother tended to believe if you had enough money, any problem was bearable. She'd never had any money of her own, and she'd married a middle class worker bee who ended up divorcing her after ten years of marriage leaving her and Mona with nothing.

"Everything is fine. I'm making some changes, and just

won't have the time to do everything I was doing before. I'll be sending an e-mail to each of the committee members to explain, and I'd love to be able to tell them you've agreed to step in for me."

"UmI don't know what to say, and I don't know how the rest of the committee will feel about it. Maybe you should suggest they take it up for a vote."

"No. I started the group, so I have the right to choose my successor. You're the only one who will do things the right way."

Finally, Daphine smiled. "Thank you. I'll do my best to uphold your standards. When will you be leaving?"

"Immediately. If you have time to stop by my house in the next day or so, I can give you all of my files."

"I will, if you're sure about this. It seems so sudden."

"It's not. I've been thinking about it for a while. Thanks, girl. I knew I could count on you."

Mona checked her watch. Trey and Julian still had another forty-five minutes to go in their lesson, so she suggested they get refills. As soon as they settled back at their table, her phone rang. She gazed at the caller ID and bit her bottom lip. She considered letting the call go to voicemail and then thought again. What was there for her to be ashamed of?

"Excuse me, Daph. I need to answer this. Hello," she answered cheerfully.

"Hello, Ramona," the deep voice caressed her senses. "It's Rayvon. Can you talk?"

"I'm at lunch with a friend right now, but I have a few minutes." She smiled and gave Daphine a fleeting glance. "How are you?"

"I'm good. I'm calling to find out if you've seen the

photos from the ball? There are a couple in Rolling Out and some magazine called Jezebel."

"As a matter of fact I have, and so has everyone else it seems, including my husband."

"Hope it didn't cause a problem for you."

She detected an air of humor in his tone. "Nothing I can't handle."

"My reason for calling is I'd like for you to join me for dinner one night this week."

"Lunch would be better. My boys start school on Monday, so I'm free during the day."

"One of my teammates said The Capital Grille is good. Is that okay?"

"The food there is excellent. When?"

"Can you make it Monday at one?"

"I think so."

"I'll wait for you at the bar."

When she put her phone back into her purse and looked up, Daphine was staring at her with her lips forming a little O. "Well, it's obvious you were talking to a man, and I've never heard you speak to Vic that way."

"Mind your business, Daphine. It's not what you think."

"I sure hope you know what you're doing."

Mona smiled and stood. "I do. It's time for me to get the boys. Finish your tea. Let me know when you want to pick up the files." She left her friend wearing a curious frown as she walked out of the teahouse.

Maite met her in the foyer when she got home. "Ms. Ramona, Mr. Vic called and said there was an emergency at the hospital and he would be staying there tonight."

All she could do was laugh. "So what else is new? Thanks."

While Vic was gone, Mona spent the time getting the boys' closets organized to make their mornings go smoothly once they began school. They wore uniforms, which simplified life a bit, but both of them were notorious for losing socks or ending up with one shoe when it was time to walk out the door to the school bus. Hoping to avoid the early morning craziness this year, she'd made sure they each had five complete sets of uniforms and five pairs of school shoes. Maite made their mornings easier by having breakfast ready when they came downstairs. If they were running late, she had a stash of what appeared to be a year's worth of small disposable containers in the pantry. She would send them out with what she called *bus breakfast* and then go on with her chores for the day. Mona didn't know what she would do without her.

An hour later, after she had showered, applied her makeup and dressed, Mona left the house and headed to her appointment. The possibility she was making a huge mistake nagged her the entire time she drove on I-285. Not since she'd stepped into the foreign waters of charity fundraising, had she made such a major change in her life. She hadn't talked her decision over with anyone, because no one knew what she needed but her. Vic was right. She needed something to satisfy her apart from him. Something which belonged to her alone and had nothing to do with medicine, hospitals, or diseases. The pageants and the preparation for them which had monopolized her childhood and teens had been her mother's dream. In college she majored in business, because her mother insisted it was something she could always fall back on if necessary. Only one thing fascinated her, and today she intended to reclaim that passion.

When she turned off of Ponce de Leon onto Court Square and parked in the lot, a surge of adrenaline ramped up her senses. Once she was inside the building, though, a feeling of foolishness came over her. Students who were young enough to be her kids traversed the halls. After all, some of them were eighteen, and she was thirty-six.

She approached the young woman at the front desk with trepidation. "Can you tell me where the Admissions Office is, please?"

"Yes. Go down this hall to the second door on your right."

Mona headed down the corridor strangely energized by the verve that seemed to radiate throughout the building. Inside the Admissions office, a painfully thin young man who reminded her of that Napoleon Dynamite kid Trey seemed to think was so hilarious, offered his assistance. "May I help you?"

"My name is Ramona Stafford. I have an appointment for a tour with a Ms. Geller."

"You can have a seat, and I'll tell her you're here. Fabulous blouse," he added before he picked up the phone. "Dolce, right?"

"Yes. You have a good eye."

"Fashion is my major," he said proudly. "I just work here in the office part-time." He lifted the phone, pressed a button and said, "Ms. Stafford is here. Okay." He hung up and smiled. "She'll be right out. Please have a seat."

When the advisor appeared in the doorway and asked her to come in, Mona breathed a sigh of relief. This was the same woman she had spoken to on the phone, and she appeared to be in her late thirties or early forties. At least she wouldn't have to tell her story to a child.

"Ms. Stafford, it's a pleasure to meet you. When we

spoke the other day, I recall you saying you're interested in our Fashion Design program."

"Yes, I want to create my own line, and design the clothes myself, and I need to learn how to go about it the right way. But before we get into anything else, how long is the course and how much does it cost."

"That's admirable, Ms. Stafford. Our fashion design program is four years, which is a major commitment. The cost is approximately ninety thousand including books and supplies, which is a major investment. Are you prepared to go the long haul?"

"You mean *at my age*?" Mona asked with a chuckle. "Yes, I am. My boys are eight and twelve now, and I can attend classes during the day while they're in school."

"The reason I bring this up is because the program is designed to take forty-five months to complete. Fewer than ten students completed this program last year." She paused to allow this information to sink in.

She had the feeling the woman assumed she was probably a washed up fashion model trying to create a secondary career. "Ms. Geller, I graduated from UGA with a B.A. in business administration in 1998, got married, had two children, and now my time is basically my own. My finances are such that financial aid won't be necessary. Can we take the tour now?"

A shadow of surprise drifted across the woman's face. "Yes, we can." She rose from her chair, and Mona followed her out into the hallway bustling with students. As they walked, Ms. Geller described the fashion design program, which included patternmaking, technical drawing, fashion drawing, and sewing technique. She also briefly described other courses, such as event and fashion show production, Trends & concepts in apparel, gaining a great understanding of global trends, and the use of technology.

Mona got a chance to peek into the different classrooms. In the midst of describing the function of each room, the advisor stopped.

"I'm afraid I need to ask you this question, since I strongly believe you should think about it." She looked up at Mona with an expression of concern. "Have you considered how you might feel being in classes with people who are half your age?"

"I hadn't until I walked into the building, but actually I think it would be refreshing."

"They think differently and act differently and might not understand your situation."

"My situation? You mean having someone their mother's age who's decided to return to school?"

"Well…yes. I interact with these young people every day, and I realize they consider me a relic because I'm forty-two. It's not an issue for me, because my job is to counsel them, something they're used to older people doing. But to have an older person as a peer is a different story."

"Are you trying to dissuade me, Ms. Geller?" Mona asked, locking her gaze with the other woman's.

"No, but I wouldn't be a good advisor if I didn't make you aware of what you might be facing. You definitely aren't our average student, but we do have a handful of students over thirty, and we would be thrilled to have you. Since you missed our summer start in July, the next start date will be on October 5th."

They continued walking while she told Mona about learning while doing—hands on, taking what's in the mind as an idea and having it manifest as a piece of real clothing. Mona's blood rushed at the concept of turning an idea into reality. That was something she had never done. Trey and Julian were the only things she had ever created from nothing. And even then, Vic had something to do with it. She loved clothes, and before she'd met Vic she had been considering going to fashion school once she graduated from UGA. But when their relationship blossomed, she filed the idea away. Her life became all about Vic. On her mother's advice, she spent her free time finding out about *his* future career, and when he became Dr. Stafford, she concentrated on making him look good. At the time she loved the idea of becoming a doctor's wife, and even though preparing herself for the task overshadowed any plans she'd had, she hadn't cared. Now she regretted losing herself.

At the conclusion of the tour, they returned to her office, and Ms. Geller handed her a thick package of information. She then explained how Mona could complete her application online before the deadline date, shook her hand and wished her well and told her to call if she had any further questions.

Mona still had time before she was supposed to meet Ray, so she sat in the car and looked over the literature. What she read renewed her interest in her old passion, and at the same time, scared her silly. Under the fashion design section it read, *"Make a name for yourself. The fashion industry has its own creative energy. In our programs in the area of Fashion Design, that energy flows from the instructors, who'll guide and support you as you develop your individual style….Everything we do is focused on preparing you for such entry-level positions as assistant designer or patternmaker, production assistant, fashion stylist, fashion illustrator, or wardrobe assistant for employers including apparel manufacturers, boutiques, and department stores.[1]"*

As she studied the brochures and pamphlets, Vic's words repeated in her mind, *I know you have nothing to occupy your time, and that was your choice.* After all the years she'd spent catering to him, how would he take her decision? His family always joked about her being spoiled, but they didn't understand how spoiled Vic was. For almost two decades he'd had a woman at his beck and call who'd spent most of her waking hours thinking about what she could do to further his career.

As soon as the dashboard clock read twelve-thirty, she drove up to Paces Ferry Road to meet Ray. She thought The Capital Grille was a bit staid for someone Ray's age, but as she exited the car, she smiled knowing he'd chosen the location for its status. He obviously wanted to impress her. The host escorted her to what was called the Penthouse where Ray was already seated and said he would send a server to their table.

Ray glanced up when he saw her coming toward him and greeted her with his devastating smile. He stood and pulled out the other chair at the table. "Ramona, you look beautiful."

"Thank you."

"Care for a drink before we order?"

"No alcohol. I'd like a San Pelligrino, lemon or orange."

When the server arrived with their menus, Ray ordered two sparkling waters. They studied the menu for a few minutes and ordered lunch when he returned with their beverages.

"What did your husband have to say about the pictures?" he asked, pouring the bubbly drink into their glasses.

"Do we have to talk about that?"

He peered over the top of his raised glass. "You said it wasn't anything you couldn't handle, but to me that meant he was pissed."

"That's putting it mildly. He blew the whole thing out of proportion."

"But even so, you're meeting me for lunch today." Rayvon settled his gaze on her face.

She smiled. "I am a grown woman, and I can have lunch with whomever I please. What have you been up to since last week?"

"Practicing, working out and trying to find a house. I only have a month before training camp opens. The season doesn't officially start until October."

"Where do want to live?"

"I'm really not sure, since I'm from Ohio and I'm not too familiar with Atlanta's residential areas." Their server reappeared with their meals. "All I know is a little about the night clubs and health clubs in Atlanta from the couple of times I visited here." He enthusiastically dove into the Grille's Signature Cheeseburger.

"Do you want to be inside or outside the perimeter?"

Ray swallowed and laughed. "I don't have any idea what that means."

"Inside I-285 or outside? In the city or in the suburbs?" Mona started on the side salad she'd ordered to go with her Lobster and Crab Burger.

"I don't want to be too far from the Arena. The team will be practicing in the Atlanta Sport and Social Club inside Philips."

"So you want to stay in town. Do you have a real estate agent?"

"Yes, the team provided someone. We've been going out every day to look at properties."

"There are so many beautiful homes in Atlanta. What's the problem?"

"I guess I'm not sure of exactly what I want. That's one of the reasons I asked you to lunch today. You seem like a woman with great taste. Would you help me find a place?"

She frowned. "I'm not a Realtor."

"I know, but I'd love to hear your opinion on some of these houses and neighborhoods."

"That's what your agent is for."

"But her job is to make a sale. I trust you to give me your honest opinion."

"You don't really know me, Ray."

"True, but somehow I know you wouldn't steer me wrong." Her foolish heart skipped several beats at the way he smiled. "Just go out with me and her a time or two and give me your thoughts."

Mona thought about it for a moment. "Sure. Why not?"

Chapter Seven

Vic came home the next morning to grab a shower and a couple of hours of sleep. Mona's car wasn't in the driveway, so he let Maite know he was in the house and went directly upstairs. Before he'd left the hospital, Marv had stopped by his office and dropped a bomb on him. As though he needed any more bad news.

"Hey," he said poking his shiny, bald head in the partially-open office door. "I heard the CRE news. How're you holding up?"

"I'm okay. Spent the night here on the sofa."

"Daphine told me about Mona's decision. What brought that on?"

Vic squinted. "What decision?"

"Stepping down from all of her charity work."

He almost choked but fought to keep his expression blank. Mona hadn't said a word to him about this, but they hadn't communicated with each other since the other night in the guest room. And it wasn't exactly verbal communication. "Oh, that," he said, pretending he knew what Marv meant. "It's her decision, man. The begging will always go on without her." He gave a mirthless chuckle.

"So, is she finally going to Hollywood like I've been suggesting?"

"I wish you'd keep your crazy ideas to yourself. Knowing Mona, she might just listen to that nonsense."

Marv laughed. "Come on, Vic, with her looks and sense of drama, you might have a movie star on your hands."

"My hands are full enough already. Get the hell out of here, man. I need to check on these CRE patients and go home for a while."

"I'll talk to you later. Get some sleep."

What was Mona up to now? Why would she give up the one thing she excelled at? He needed to talk to her about it, but not until he got some rest. Without it, irritability and exhaustion would prevent him from being rational. After a long hot shower, he stretched out on the bed and pulled a throw over his body rather than disturb the bed Maite was always so diligent to make up each morning. In a matter of minutes, he was unconscious.

The sound of his sons charging up the stairs woke him. He glanced at the clock, surprised it was close to four o'clock, and they were coming in from school. When he heard Mona's voice chiding them for all the noise, he got up and opened the bedroom door.

"Hey, guys," he called out to the boys who had disappeared into their rooms.

Julian was the first to respond. "Daddy, you're home!" He crossed the hall and rushed to hug Vic around the waist.

"Hey, Dad," Trey said from the doorway of his room.

"How was the first day of school?"

"Okay," both boys mumbled in unison.

"Just okay?"

"We don't do anything on the first day," Trey explained.

"Did you see Megan?"

"Yuck!" Julian scrunched up his face and retreated into his room.

His oldest son grinned then looked away. "Yeah, she was there."

"Remember what I told you." Vic smiled back at his namesake, amazed at how quickly he was growing up.

"I will, Dad."

"Where's your mom?"

"I think she went downstairs."

"Okay. Do you have any homework?"

"A little."

"Julian?" he called out. "Do you have any homework?"

His youngest stuck his head out of the door to his room. "All I have to do is read."

"Both of you change out of your uniforms and get started."

Vic headed downstairs and found Mona in the kitchen talking to Maite. "Can I talk to you for a minute? I told the boys to change and do their homework."

"What's the matter?"

He opened the refrigerator and removed a bottle of water. "Let's go in the den."

She gave him a suspicious frown and followed him into the other room. They both sat on the sofa.

"Marv Weber stopped in to see me this morning." She gazed at him with an almost imperceptible lift of her brows as though she knew what he was about to say. "He told me something you should've told me yourself."

"I planned to tell you…whenever you decided to come home."

"But I thought you enjoyed fundraising, and you're so good at it. What's going on with you?"

"I've decided to do something else, and I won't have the time for both."

Vic frowned. "Do something else? You mean for the hospital?"

One corner of her mouth rose into a half smile. "For me, Vic. I'm finally going to do something for myself. I think I'll call it Project Ramona."

"Is Rayvon Patterson part of that project?"

"Why can't you just drop it? I told you there's nothing going on between us. If you don't believe me, it's your problem."

"Maybe it is," he answered, holding her gaze. "We'll see. What is this project all about?"

"I don't want to talk about it now. You'll find out when I have everything worked out. I'm going to take a shower. I'm still hot from being outside."

Vic watched her leave the room then waited a few minutes before going upstairs to their bedroom. Just as he'd hoped, she'd left her purse in the chair in the corner when she'd come upstairs. He sat on the bed and waited until he heard her turn on the shower. After a few more moments, he went to the chair and took her phone from her purse. Contrary to his suggestion, Mona had never added a password lock, so he went directly into her recent calls. His jaw clenched when Ray Patterson showed up in the list. What the hell? He studied the display with shaking hands. The last call was from earlier this afternoon. Now he didn't feel the least bit guilty about having McClendon follow her. In order to keep the number, he pulled out his phone, entered and saved it.

The sound of the water running continued, so he figured he might as well scan through her photos while he had the opportunity. Nothing incriminating there. All she had were pictures of the boys during their recent visit to one of those local game spots and a couple of shots of shoes she'd taken in the store. The one photo of a new Fiat parked on the street confused him though. Economy cars were definitely not her style. What reason would she have for photographing a twenty-thousand dollar vehicle? When the water stopped running in the bathroom, he placed the phone back in her purse, but not before he searched through the bag to see what else she might be hiding. Lipstick, compact, breath mints, tissues, car keys—nothing out of the ordinary.

Mona stepped out of the bathroom wrapped in towel. His gaze followed her long, beautiful legs as she crossed the room and disappeared into her cavernous closet. Her routine after she got out of the shower was to sit on the ottoman in the center of the bathroom and faithfully apply her creams and lotions. Their master bath was the size of a living room in an average house. In times past he'd sit in one of the chairs and watch the sexy display as she prepared to get dressed. Every now and then he would dip his fingers into the luxurious cream, stand in front of her and lift her foot up to his crotch. Rubbing the fragrant cream up and down those incredible legs used to be one of his favorite pastimes, and nine times out of ten this scene ended with her bent over the ottoman with him on his knees behind her. Their bathroom sex was the best sex they had, maybe because it seemed so illicit, even better than in the pool. That hadn't happened in a *very* long time. At the moment, he didn't want to think about those times. All he wanted to do was put some distance between them.

Before Mona emerged from her closet, he was on his way back to the hospital carrying a duffel bag packed with three changes of clothes. Before he left, he'd said goodbye to the boys and explained why he needed to return to work, then promised to call them the next evening. Julian hugged him, and Trey mumbled something. Considering the choice, he'd rather share space with a bacteria-resistant virus than with a lying, adulterous wife.

The situation on his surgical service hadn't improved in the hours he'd been at home, but they quickly deteriorated by morning when Chauncey Higgins, the first patient to contract the CRE virus, expired. After he alerted Dr. Sternhagen of the death, the chief said he would contact the CDC to update them. Vic had the sinking feeling the bacteria wasn't done. They had isolated the affected patients, which was all that could be done. There was little chance an effective drug to kill CRE would be invented in the coming years. According to the feds and industry experts, the pharmaceutical companies had no new antibiotics in development that showed promise, and there was little monetary incentive because the bacteria adapted quickly to resist new drugs.

By Thursday afternoon, Vic had had his fill of meetings and revisiting the possible causes of the infection. The story was leaked to the local news, and Dr. Sternhagen was forced to make public statements to the press reassuring the public they were in no danger. Sleeping on the sofa in his office did nothing for Vic's sour disposition. He had to remind himself not to take it out on his staff. They were doing the best they could given the situation, and they certainly weren't responsible for his crumbling home life.

After Shondell left for the night, he downed his fourth cup of coffee of the day. As he contemplated whether or not to go home, he scrolled through his calendar. Seeing an event he'd forgotten about, he called Nick, his baby brother. "Hey, it's Vic. Are you at work?"

"Yeah, but I can talk. What's up?"

"I was just checking my calendar, and I totally forgot about this men's health seminar the 100 Black Men of Atlanta are co-sponsoring with the Cancer Society on Saturday. Since you're considering men's medicine, I thought you might want to go."

"Saturday looks clear unless they change my schedule. Thanks."

"Hopefully, no hospital emergency will keep me from going." Vic gave his brother the details and location, straightened up his desk and sat for a few minutes contemplating whether or not to go directly home. He locked up and stopped by Marv's office. "I'm heading out. Do you want to get a brew?"

Marv looked at the clock. "Okay. Where should I meet you?"

"How about the Midtown Tavern?"

"I'll be there in about thirty minutes."

Vic picked up his pace leaving the hospital, hoping he could get out of the building before someone stopped him with a question or an issue they believed no other human on the planet could handle. Once he made it to his car without being accosted, Vic blew out a relieved breath and started the engine.

The Midtown Tavern wasn't a doctor's hangout, and that's why he liked it. There he wouldn't be pulled into conversations about patients, diagnoses or hospital business. With its laid-back, friendly atmosphere reminiscent of *Cheers*, he could just sit and watch people play darts, pool or compete in trivia games. Or he could participate in a game, if he desired. Normally, he didn't. Typically, the crowd was younger than him, and all he wanted after a long day at work was to relax with a cold beer.

He ordered a Heineken and waited for Marv to arrive. While he observed the after-work patrons trickling in, he made up his mind not to mention what was going on with Mona. Nobody else needed to know what kind of turmoil his marriage was in until it could no longer be hidden.

Marv was a pediatric surgeon who spent a good deal of time on Vic's floor seeing to children who were in need of surgical intervention. His personality suited his specialty perfectly. Vic had known him for several years, and he'd never seen Marv be surly or short-tempered with patients, their parents or his colleagues, no matter how tired he was. Spending a little time with him always improved Vic's mood. He came in about fifteen minutes later looking no worse for wear.

"Are we eating, 'cause I'm starving," were the first words out of his mouth.

Vic had to laugh. His friend probably hadn't missed a meal in years. Marv consistently hovered at around forty pounds overweight, but his jovial personality and hearty laugh matched his appearance, kind of like a jolly black Santa Claus minus the beard and red suit, the reason his mini-patients loved him.

"Sure." Vic waved to the server, and since he and Marv knew the menu by heart, it only took a minute to place their orders.

The CRE problem at the hospital and Mr. Higgins' death dominated their initial conversation, but the matter had turned into a waiting game. Vic had nothing new to report, and the conversation gradually petered out. Marv popped the top on his beer, took a long drag and said, "Daphine was shocked at Mona's news, but she was honored Mona asked her to step in."

"It just makes sense," Vic played along. "The two of them have worked together for a while."

"I think her feelings were hurt because Mona didn't seem to want to share what her next step is going to be." Marv smiled at the server as she placed their plates on the table.

"Tell her not to worry about it. I don't even know what Mona is up to, and I live with the woman," Vic finally confessed. Marv's eyes rounded. "She's going through some kind of crisis, and she won't talk about it."

"Damn. Sorry to hear it, man. I'd say she could be going through menopause, but Mona has a good twenty years before that happens. Do you think she's bored?" Marv stuffed a bunch of fries into his mouth and hummed his approval.

"Could be. I guess the fundraising and charity stuff isn't enough for her anymore." Vic savored the flavor of his grilled chicken, zucchini, and peppers. He wanted to tell his friend more, but thought it best to keep quiet. "I need to ask you a favor, though."

"Anything." He opened his mouth wide to accommodate the huge and appropriately-named Fat Frenchmen Burger. "What do you need?"

"Let me know if Daphine tells you anything out of the ordinary. Don't let her know I asked. Let's keep this between the two of us, okay?"

"Anything out of the ordinary like what?"

"Come on, Marv. Anything that sounds strange or out of character for Mona."

"Will do, man."

Vic felt conscience-stricken for a moment then reminded himself that he had to do whatever was necessary to learn what his wife was up to. "Thanks."

♥♥♥♥

Ray called Mona on Thursday morning. "I'm sorry to call you so early, but my Realtor said she has another group of houses to show me today at ten-thirty. Will you be able to come with me? I can pick you up."

She mulled it over for a moment. "I don't have anything planned this morning. Give me your address, and

I'll meet you there."

He agreed, and she typed the street address, gate code and apartment number into her phone. Two hours later, she drove up to the entry gate of The Heights, a luxurious apartment home community in West Midtown. She punched the numbers he'd given her into the keypad, and his voice came through the speaker.

"I'm here."

"Hang on, I'll buzz you in. Come in the front entrance and take the elevator to four. I'll wait for you there."

The brightness of his smile met her when the elevator doors opened. He was leaning against the wall with his arms folded. "Hi." She stepped out, and he reached for her hand. "My apartment is down the hall. Carrie should be here in a few."

"This is a lovely community, especially for a single man. I don't understand why you want to move."

"It's one of the places the team recommended. You're right. It has everything you could want, but I'm used to living in a house. Even with the cyber lounge, the library, and the free breakfast, having people across the hall from me is still not appealing. I make almost four million a year, and I want to buy a house–my own house."

"Well, all right then," was the only response she could come up with. *Four million dollars a year. At his age.* She couldn't even imagine it.

"I forgot my manners. Can I get you something to drink?"

Mona sat on the sofa and her eyes took in the apartment. "Do you have any bottled water? I want to take it with me when we leave. It's disgustingly hot out there."

Ray went into the kitchen and returned with two bottles

of water. As soon as he handed one to her, the intercom buzzed and his Realtor announced her arrival.

"You don't have to get out of the car, Carrie. We'll be down in a minute. Just pull up to the front entrance. We'll follow you."

After he introduced Ramona and Carrie, they followed her up to Buckhead where they looked at five homes, all so huge it took them nearly an hour to tour each one. They all contained every bell and whistle imaginable.

And I thought my house was big. I could put mine inside these three times.

Although Ray said Carrie was experienced at showing high-end properties, she seemed visibly annoyed when he insisted on asking Mona her opinion on everything. Mona told him what she thought. "But Carrie knows more about these things than I do," she added in an effort to smooth the agent's ruffled feathers.

By the middle of the day, Ray decided to make an offer on a house in Tyler Perry's neighborhood. It was much more traditional than she expected, but it was the perfect house for entertaining with several spacious open areas and a pool area that looked like it belonged at a Las Vegas hotel.

She didn't know what had given her the impression he wanted a *normal* house, and she finally had to ask, "Why do you want something so huge when it's only you?"

"It's not just me. Once I find something, I'll be bringing my family here."

His *family*? Her body stiffened. She had no right to be affronted by the revelation in view of her own situation. But at least she'd had the decency to tell him she was married right out of the gate. Her stunned gaze caught the agent's for a fraction of a second then Carrie looked away. "Your family is coming to Atlanta?"

"Yeah, I promised them if I ever got signed to the NBA, I was going to buy a house with enough space for everybody."

She studied the gleam in his eye and tried her best not to sound irritated. "And how many would that be?"

Carrie turned her back to them and walked over to the windows leaving them standing in the middle of the room.

"Five altogether."

"Five? Amazing." Mona had heard about the sexual escapades of professional athletes, and she knew she had no reason to be irked, considering she had two boys at home. But wasn't he awfully young to have four kids and a baby mama already? She kept her composure. "Why didn't you tell me about them? How old are they?"

"Leshan and Leshanique are thirteen. Ja'Vante is fifteen. And Tyrez is seventeen.

Completely baffled at this point, she asked, "I thought you said you were twenty-three?"

Rayvon's confused expression reflected hers. "I am. What are you…" Suddenly, he broke into a fit of laughter. "Did you think I meant my family like my *wife and kids*? I'm talking about my mother and my brothers and sisters."

Now she felt like a complete idiot, but when he put his arm around her shoulders and pulled her into his side, she felt something completely different. She shivered when his bicep rippled against her back and wanted to close her eyes and inhale the fragrance of his cologne. The second she pulled out of his embrace, he smiled as though he sensed her attraction then said, "Let's get these papers signed so Carrie can be on her way."

Less than thirty minutes later, he'd made a fourteen million dollar offer on the nine-bedroom, eleven-bath, twenty-four thousand square foot, fifteen-million-dollar house. Some papers were signed, and as soon as Carrie left the premises, she and Rayvon stood outside of the enormous European-style mansion known as LaVictoria, which was said to be the twelfth largest in the country.

"Ray, maybe…" she began hesitantly. "Maybe I have no business saying this, but I have to. This house is incredible, if you like that style, but the price of this house is more than your entire contract."

He tilted his head with a smirk. "I don't plan to play for only three years, Mona. I got this covered, and what do you mean by, if you like that style?"

"It's not my taste, but I can see why you love it."

"I've wanted this house since I saw it in the movie, *Zombieland*. You know it's owned by Big Papa, Kim's former man on the Real Housewives."

"No, I didn't know," she answered, totally disinterested in the property's history. "Just hear me out, Ray," she continued. "I understand you're excited about signing such an incredible contract, but have you considered what might happen if you get injured? You read about it all the time."

His eyebrows rose. "Not going to happen."

"How do you know? It's a scary thought, but it *is* a possibility."

"Why did you come today if you felt that way?"

"I had no idea we were coming to look at fifteen-million-dollar houses."

"Mona, I only asked you because I thought you'd appreciate a house like this."

"It's a little too ornate for me. You're not listening, Ray. I'd hate to see you get in over your head."

To her surprise, he cupped his hand under her chin. "No need to worry."

She should've backed away, but when she didn't, he bent down and touched his lips to hers in a soft, gentle kiss. When their lips parted, she took a shaky breath. "Ray, I think I need to make it clear that we're just friends. There can never be anything deeper or sexual between us."

He grinned and her knees threatened to give out. "It was only a kiss."

"Our first and our last."

"If you say so." His reply seemed a bit too confident. "How about some lunch?"

"Okay, but I have to be home by three."

Once they were seated and had looked over the menu, she asked, "Do you always eat twenty-dollar burgers with ten-dollar sides for lunch, or are you trying to impress me?"

Rayvon chuckled. "I guess I'm trying to impress you a little."

"That's not necessary. I'd be fine going to a regular burger restaurant."

He gave her an exaggerated head-to-toe scan then laughed. "No you wouldn't. Let's order."

The server took their orders, and the moment she left, Mona blurted out, "I've decided to go back to school. Do you think that's crazy?" She needed to tell someone, and he was her first choice.

"That's great. Why would I think it's crazy?"

"I'm almost forty years old, Ray. Most of the students are in their late teens and early twenties."

"So. What does that have to do with you?"

She thought about it for a second. "I don't know if I can compete."

"You wouldn't be there to compete. What school?"

"The Art Institute. I love fashion, and I want to create my own fashion line, but I know nothing about where to start."

He sat back in his chair and studied her with an intense expression. "I can see you doing that. You have a great sense of style, and everything you wear looks beautiful on you."

She lowered her gaze, afraid of what she might see in his eyes. "That's sweet of you."

"Just speaking the truth. So when do you start?"

Their lunch arrived, and she waited until the server disappeared. "The first week in October, but my tuition has to be paid before then."

He rested his burger on his plate. "Do you need my help with that?"

"I wasn't telling you to ask for help. You have to stop being so willing to give away your money. It's not going to last forever."

"I plan on making more every year, you know. There's no way I could spend it all on myself. I'd be glad to help you, Mona."

"I appreciate the offer, but I'm going to pay for the entire course at once. And I think I've come up with a way to do it."

Ray squinted. "Why do you need to come up with a way?"

"I don't want my husband to know just yet." She sighed and toyed with her Chinese Chicken Salad.

"How are you going to keep something like that from him, and why would you want to?"

"It's a long story. I don't want to bore you with the details."

He stroked his chin and kept his gaze fastened on hers. "How much is it going to cost, if you don't mind me asking?"

"Tuition for the full forty-five months is ninety thousand. Books are another twenty-five hundred."

His high-pitched whistle filled the air. "You can get your hands on almost a hundred grand without your man knowing it?"

"I'm going to sell my car. I should be able to get one-seventy-five for it, since it's only a year old."

"Then how do you intend to get around?" Ray continued his inquiry.

"I'm going to buy something small and good on gas, because I'll be driving back and forth every day."

"Mona, I'll give you the money, if you need it. You don't have to sell your car. I know how much you love it."

"I do, but I didn't buy it to begin with. It was a birthday gift."

He sat silently for a long moment. "From your husband."

"Yes."

"You're going to sell the car he gave you?"

"If it was a gift, that means it's mine to do with as I please. I don't want to ask him for the money, because I don't want him to know I'm going to school until I'm ready to tell him."

"Don't you think he'll be pissed when he finds out what you've done?"

Mona shrugged. "I guess I'll just have to cross that bridge when I get to it." She shook off the momentary feeling of shame at Ray's questioning gaze. He didn't know what was going on between Vic and her, and she wasn't about to explain it. Instead, she changed the subject. "What's your plan for decorating that palace, if the sellers accept your offer?"

"What do you mean *if*? If they don't, then I'll make a counter-offer."

"You obviously want that place, so I'll just keep my opinions to myself from now on."

His voice softened. "Mona, you never need to be afraid to speak your mind around me. I like to know your opinion on things."

That sure was refreshing to hear. These days, no matter what she and Vic discussed, it ended up in an argument. Whatever she said was always the wrong thing. "Do you know anything about cars?"

The way his head jerked up, she assumed he'd expected her to say something else. "A little. What do you want to know?"

"I need someone to go with me when I buy the new one. It's always better if a woman has a man with her when dealing with car salesmen."

"Yeah, I guess you can't very well ask Mr. Mona to help you after you ditch his gift." He snickered. "You came house hunting with me. Sure, I'll go with you."

"Thanks, Ray, and thank you for not asking about my home situation."

"No problem. It's plain to see that you love him, no matter what's going on. I can respect that."

"I do love him, but I need a friend right now–someone I can trust."

Chapter Eight

Vic and Marv played a game of pool, had one final beer, then said goodnight and headed home. Every night that he stayed at the hospital, he called Trey and Julian to say goodnight, but he hadn't spoken to Mona. By the time he pulled into the garage, it was after eight o'clock. Maite had already left for the night, and the first floor was dark. He trudged up the staircase expecting the discussion with his wife to continue where they'd left off. To his surprise, she wasn't in their bedroom but was standing in the door of one of the guest rooms with her arms crossed.

She didn't acknowledge his three-day absence and instead said, "I'm going to redecorate this room," as though they had been in the middle of a conversation.

"What's wrong with it?"

"Nothing. It's just not what I need anymore."

"Hmph." He turned his back, went to Julian's room and knocked. "J-Man, it's Dad."

Vic smiled at the sound of his son footsteps racing toward the door. He opened the door with a big smile. "Hey, Dad! I didn't know you were home."

"I just got here." Vic entered the room and sat on the bed. "How's school going?"

"It's okay. I have to get a book for a stupid book report."

"What book?"

"It's about some girl named Helen Keller. It's a *girl's* story," he whined.

Vic laughed and rubbed his son's head. "It's not a girl's story. I read it when I was in school."

"You did?"

"Yeah. It's a book that makes you think."

"About what?"

"What you would do if you were deaf and blind."

"That's what it's about?"

Vic rose. "Uh huh. I want to hear what you think about it when you're done. Let me go see Trey then I need to get some sleep. Have a good night." He put an arm around Julian and pulled him against his chest.

"Do you have to go back to the hospital?"

"As long as we're dealing with this infection, I have to go in every day just to see what's going on. Sorry, J."

"It's okay, Dad." His sad tone might as well have been a punch to Vic's gut.

Perched Indian-style in the middle of his bed with his earbuds in, Trey didn't hear him knock. He glanced up when he saw his father step into the room. "Oh, hi, Dad. I didn't know you were here."

"I just got here a few minutes ago. How're you doing?"

Trey shrugged.

The older Trey got, the harder it was to engage him in conversation. "Do you like your teachers so far?"

"They're all right." Strike two.

"Have you talked to Megan?"

That brought a shadow of a smile to his son's face.

Bingo. "Yeah, we sat at the same table at lunch today. She told me that a bunch of kids are going to the mall on Saturday. I guess she wants me to go too."

"That's what it sounds like to me. Let Mom or me know the details and if you need a ride, okay?"

Trey's lips spread into a wide-open smile. "Okay, thanks."

"I'm going to bed. See you in the morning before you catch the bus."

Mona still hadn't come into the bedroom, so Vic hurried to take a shower and get into bed. When he awoke during the night she was sleeping on the far edge of the king-size bed, hugging her pillow. He rolled over and went back to sleep. In the morning, when his alarm went off, her side of the bed was vacant. After he washed up and dressed, he went directly to the kitchen where Maite was preparing freshly-cut fruit, muffins and coffee.

"Good morning." He sat and reached for one of the mugs she had waiting on the island. "Have you seen Mona?"

"Good morning. Yes, she said she was going to take a dip in the pool before the boys got up for school."

He scratched his head. "Are you sure that's what she said?"

"Yes. Come see." The housekeeper pointed out the window overlooking the pool.

Vic rose and joined her at the sink and stared through the glass in disbelief. "She hasn't done that since we first moved in."

"Miss Mona said she's not going to the gym anymore, and she's going to swim instead. She looks amazing."

His wife did look amazing, and she could give any twenty-five year old a run for their money. That never bothered him until now. Her new association with Rayvon Patterson had him wondering if she'd suddenly started believing *she* was twenty-five. He pondered the question and watched her graceful limbs traverse the water, until his phone rang.

"Vic, Doug McClendon. My first weekly report is ready. I wanted to call you early to see how you want me to handle it. Do you have a private e-mail or do you want to pick up a hard copy at the office?"

"Could you have it hand-delivered by courier to the hospital?"

"Certainly. For your signature only, correct?"

"Right. I'll be there in the next thirty minutes. The courier might have to wait a few minutes while my assistant locates me in the building. Anything concrete?"

"It appears so."

Vic swallowed the lump in his throat. "Thanks, Doug." He grabbed a muffin, wrapped it in a paper towel and asked Maite to put his coffee in a travel mug then went back upstairs to say goodbye to his sons before he drove to the hospital. His heart pounded at the prospect of what McClendon's report might include. Once he'd said the report contained something definite, Vic's appetite disappeared, but he knew he needed some sustenance before the day got underway. By the time he drove into his reserved spot in the hospital garage, his cup was empty and only crumbs remained in the napkin.

Not more than an hour after he arrived, Shondell buzzed him. "Doctor, there's a courier here. He needs your signature for an envelope."

"I'll be right out." Vic held his breath, slowly rose from his desk and went to the outer office. He signed, and the courier handed him the manila envelope. "I need to go over this information, so hold my calls for the next half hour, please, Shondell."

Rarely did he lock his office door, but he wanted to make sure no one interrupted him. He opened the envelope as though the contents might jump out and grab him around his neck. McClendon had provided a typed report, but Vic went right to the photos which were photocopies of the originals. His hands clenched at what he saw. The first picture was of Mona and Patterson sitting at a table in a restaurant that looked familiar. The next one was also in an eatery he didn't recognize. The last couple of photos were the most damning. They showed his wife and her young companion along with a third person standing outside of an enormous Euro-style mansion. The final shot had captured her and Patterson sharing a kiss outside the gate of the house. The sick feeling in his gut intensified. His breath came raggedly and burned in his throat. He had to swallow repeatedly to push down the bile rising in his chest, and drove his fist into his hand. Finally, he picked up the report and read the details. The other person was a Realtor from a local agency.

They're looking at houses together? She doesn't even know him. This is how she plans to repay me for giving her the kind of life she said she'd always wanted?

Vic rarely obsessed over looks. He and his brothers had never lacked female companionship. But Patterson's physically perfect body and dark skin were what many women drooled over. And it appeared that Mona was drooling. He couldn't imagine her with someone so much younger, but youth always seemed to have the advantage. The hoops star also had a serious financial advantage over him. A bitter jealousy stirred inside him, and his throat ached with defeat.

He probably makes ten times what I do, and he can offer her much more. I always knew she liked nice things, but I actually thought she loved me. Has she been biding her time all these years, waiting for something better to come along? How the hell am I going to explain to Trey and Julian that their mother has decided to go with the highest bidder?

Naturally, in nearly thirteen years of marriage, there had been times Mona had made him so angry he wanted to punch something, but never had he wanted it to be heruntil this moment. Thank God, she wasn't standing in front of him. Patterson was another story. Vic blinked furiously at the fleeting vision of slicing him from ear to ear with a scalpel and watching him bleed out. He couldn't begin the work day with his head swimming with these thoughts. Had they been visible, they could have sent him straight to jail or to the mental hospital.

Fighting the urge to vomit, he stuffed the photos and the report back into the envelope and stashed it in the bottom desk drawer beneath his gym clothes, sneakers, and iPodthings he rarely had time to use anymore. Right now he needed something stronger than coffee, but it would have to do for now. He steeled himself for a moment then unlocked the door.

"I'm going to get some coffee," he said, as he passed Shondell's desk.

"Are you all right?"

He came to an abrupt stop. "Yes, why?"

"You look like you just saw a ghost."

Her intuitive nature was one of the reasons he valued her as his right hand in the office. He knew she'd already made the connection between the courier delivery and his appearance. "I'm fine. Just have things on my mind."

"Obviously," she replied with a deep frown. "Don't forget you're meeting with Dr. Jhaveri, Dr. Schmidt and the people from Infectious Disease at ten forty-five."

He gazed at the clock on the wall across from her desk. "I'll be right back." If he didn't clear his head before the meeting began, he would never be able to focus on the matter at hand. Nothing so huge had ever infiltrated his personal life and hijacked his concentration. How could he focus on hospital business when his wife was making plans to abandon him?

Vic managed to acknowledge the people who spoke to him while he walked to and from the cafeteria. The pressure in his chest gradually subsided and his breathing returned to normal by the time he got back to his desk. Before he grabbed his iPad and relocated to the conference room, he pulled open the bottom drawer and checked to make sure the envelope containing McClendon's report and the pictures were well hidden.

At least the doctors had something positive to report on the source of the CRE infection. It appeared that the infected patients had been contaminated by medical scopes during endoscopic procedures. The scopes had been sterilized according to manufacturer standards. This meant that the infection had been pinpointed to a specific cause and wasn't running rampant through the entire hospital. From this point forward, they would need to use a decontamination process that exceeded the manufacturer and national standards.

Vic breathed a relieved sigh. The new decontamination process might cost more, but it was a relatively simple procedure that hopefully would put an end to the problem. The Infectious Disease guys remained after the other doctors left to educate him on the replacement equipment that would need to come out of his budget. Their discussion took another hour, and when they finally wrapped up, Vic removed the envelope from his desk and had to restrain himself from running out of the building. He needed to speak to McClendon as soon as possible. Instead of taking his car from the garage, He walked to a sandwich shop not far from the hospital, and then took his lunch to the park where he could talk without being overheard.

"Vic, I take it you got a chance to go through the package?" the investigator said when he got on the line.

"I did, and I need to ask if you saw Ramona sign anything when they met the Realtor?"

"No. The agent gave the papers to Patterson to sign."

"Are you sure?"

"Completely. Have you confronted her about this yet, because if you have, she'll probably start being more careful."

"Not yet, and I want you to continue to follow her for the next week or two. By then I'll know what I want to do."

Ray's offer to pay Mona's tuition left her astounded. His sweet, generous nature worried her, though. Like so many young professional athletes who were overwhelmed by their new salaries, his giving nature could send him to bankruptcy court before the end of his first contract with the league. She would hate to see that happen to him, and it occurred to her that perhaps she was the only person in his life who was concerned about him making wise financial decisions. Possibly his family and close friends were more focused on how his success might benefit them. She wasn't a big sports or music fan anymore, but she'd heard the stories of young performers and athletes who had lost everything because they ended up feeding, clothing and entertaining their entourage and other assorted freeloaders. Before she'd left him earlier yesterday, he agreed to go car shopping with her. She would use the opportunity to talk to him about his finances.

Today, Vic was attending some kind of men's health event. As he exited the kitchen and entered the garage, he mumbled something about going to pick up his brother, Nick, and that they would be gone most of the day. She wondered why he even bothered to tell her that much. They hadn't spoken to each other since he'd questioned her about her decision to step down from her charity work. She had asked Trey and Julian what they wanted to do for the day, and they surprisingly both agreed that they'd rather stay home, watch On Demand and play video games. Now that school was back in session, they weren't as gung-ho about going out on Saturdays.

Maite wasn't scheduled to work and said she had no plans for the day, so Mona asked if she would come into the main house and relax in the den. She showed up a few minutes later carrying the handmade blanket her mother made her for Christmas, an armful of magazines, a couple of cans of Coco Rico, her favorite soft drink and a Tupperware container of arroz con pollo and fried plantains. Maite never turned down a chance to pick up a few overtime hours when she had no other plans.

"I'll be gone until late afternoon," she told the housekeeper. "The boys can make their own sandwiches for lunch. There's turkey, peanut butter and jelly and fruit. My phone will be on if you need me."

An hour later, she picked Rayvon up at his apartment and drove to the Bentley dealership in Alpharetta. When they got out of the car, the proverbial huddle of hungry salesmen outside the entrance to the showroom was conspicuously missing. But once they entered the building, she immediately noticed the craning necks and hushed whispers. *Basketball fans. They must recognize him.*

"Do you know who I need to speak to?"

"Uh huh." They exited the car, and he took her elbow as they crossed the parking lot to the front entrance of the showroom. "The manager of the pre-owned department. Somebody will take us around to see him."

Just as Ray said, one of the salesmen rushed over and offered to escort them. He introduced Ray to the manager whose eyes lit up when the salesman introduced him as the new Hawks point guard. Ray introduced Mona then launched right into why they were there.

"This is my friend, Ramona Stafford. Right now she's driving a Continental coupe that's a little less than two years old. She wants to sell it and get a more economical family vehicle. Do you think you can give her a good price?" The sparkle in the manager's eyes dimmed considerably, yet he remained cordial.

"May I ask why you want to sell? Did the vehicle not meet your expectations?"

"It's an exquisite car," Mona explained. "But I honestly didn't have any expectations. It was a gift."

The manager's gaze jumped to Rayvon's face, obviously assuming he'd been the gift-giver. "I understand. Let's go out so I can take a look, Ms. Stafford, then I can give you a better idea of what kind of resale we're talking about."

She and Ray followed him out through the showroom to the front parking lot. "Very well-kept," he said, circling the exterior with a critical eye. She handed him the keys so he could examine the interior. "I assume you don't have any children."

Mona chuckled. "I have two boys, but they know better than to mess up my car. There's no eating, drinking or coloring with markers allowed. Now it's time for me to get a car we can all feel more comfortable in." Of course, that wasn't the reason, but she figured she'd go with it.

"Ms. Stafford, I need to have one of my men check the engine and put the car up on a lift. Please make yourself comfortable in the customer lounge." He pointed to the sign above a door at the end of the hall. "I'll come to get you when he's done."

"Thank you." She preceded Ray into the lounge, which looked more like an upscale doctor's waiting room. The upholstered dark maple furniture was a surprise. Two of the walls were lined with a counter and stools where customers could plug in their laptops or charge their tablets. A large flat screen television anchored one corner near the ceiling. Bakery-quality pastries, finger sandwiches, fruit, and assorted beverages covered a table in the opposite corner. She and Ray fixed themselves a dessert-size plate and sat across the room from the others waiting for their vehicles.

"I need to ask you something," Ray said in a whisper. "Do you think it's a good move to sell your car?"

She squinted. "What do you mean?"

He cleared his throat. "If I'd given you that car, and you decided to sell it, I'd be hurt." He stared at her until she looked away.

The consequences of doing this had plagued her since she'd come up with the idea. "I know what you're saying, but I don't have any other option. There's no other way for me to come up with ninety thousand dollars. Vic will just have to understand."

"What if he doesn't?" He asked, pinning her with his dark gaze.

Her gaze dropped to the floor. It was all she could do to keep from telling him how Vic had called her clingy and had implied that she was lazy. He'd never said anything so hurtful before, and she intended to prove him wrong.

"Have you considered doing it the way the stars do?

Carmelo Anthony's wife, LaLa, started her own line with her stylist. From what I hear it's doing pretty well."

"I could venture right into the business rather than spend four years in school, but either way I'd still need a lot of cash. Do you know her?"

"La? Not well. I know Carmelo, though. If I can get in touch with him, maybe we could hook you two up for a conference call or something."

Mona sat forward in rapt attention. "Do you really think she might talk to me?"

"All she can do is say no. Nothing ventured, nothing gained, right?"

The manager returned carrying a paper. "Ms. Stafford, my crew has checked out your car. It's in excellent condition. This is what we're prepared to offer you today." He handed her the paper.

Mona glanced at the bottom line and smiled. "That's more than I expected."

"That number is good for the next seven days. If you're not ready to sell it by then, we'd have to recalculate."

She folded the offer and placed it in her purse. "I understand. I'll be sure to get back to you before then. Thank you so much for your time."

He gave Mona and Ray each a business card. "It's a pleasure meeting you, and I hope to see you again."

She and Ray left the building and crossed the parking lot. "Do you have time to go to the Fiat dealer with me?"

He placed his hand on her back and steered her toward the car. "You have me until training camp starts."

The sensual edge in his tone made her stomach quiver. Again, he hadn't said or done anything out of line, but she internally questioned his motives. "Okay, it's down on

Peachtree Industrial Boulevard."

"Do you mind if I drive? This might be my only chance to pilot a Bentley."

"Help yourself before it disappears." They both laughed, and she dropped the keys into his open palm.

The mall, European-looking vehicles at the Fiat dealership spoke to a different part of Mona's consciousness than her Bentley had. She loved the trendiness of the brand, and the idea that she'd chosen it for herself. After an hour of checking out different models, she had tentatively decided on the 500X crossover, because it had enough room to carry the boys. She explained to the salesman that she needed to sell her car first, and promised to return.

"I can't picture you driving that," Ray said with a curious frown on their way out.

"Why?"

"It just doesn't look like you, and you might need something bigger if you have to haul stuff for your business."

She rolled her eyes. "I'm not starting a construction business."

"No, but what kind of things would you have to carry?"

"Fabric, garment racks, samples…." She stopped walking, folded her arms and gave him a thoughtful smile. "You see. That's why I needed you to come with me. Do you have time to make one more stop?"

Ray stretched his long arms out to each side and grinned. "I'm wide open, as we say in *my* business."

"There's one other car I like, and it's larger than the Fiat."

He held the keys out to her. She waved them away, stood beside the passenger door and waited for him to open it, then she looked up their next destination on her phone and put it into her GPS.

After they rode for several minutes, Ray surprised her by asking, "Where is your husband today?"

"He and his brother had some kind of men's health event they had to attend. Nick recently graduated from medical school and plans to specialize in men's health."

"Hmm. A couple of doctors in the family, huh?"

"Yeah," she answered unenthusiastically. "More than a couple."

His gaze left the road and rested on hers momentarily, but he didn't respond.

The afternoon finally came to an end after she had changed her selection to an Audi Q7. After seeing it in person, she was convinced it would give her some of the luxury she was used to and twice the interior space. Now that she'd made up her mind, she suggested they go to lunch, after which she took him back to his apartment.

"Thank you so much for your help, Ray. I'm going to take the Bentley dealer up on their offer before the price expires. I need to get home now, so I can drop my son off at the mall."

"No problem. Before you go, I just wanted you to know that I had to make a counter-offer on the house, and the seller accepted it."

Ramona didn't know whether to smile or groan. "I'm glad it worked out for you. When are you supposed to close?"

"Since the house is unoccupied and the furniture is included, I might be able to close in a month. My family could be here by the fall."

"I know you're excited about this, and I'm happy for

you. If you're interested, I can give you the name of a good financial adviser to help you with your expenses and investment strategy."

She had to look away from his knee-weakening smile when he said, "You're worried about me, aren't you?"

"I'm not worried. I just care what happens to you. It probably feels like your money will never run out, but it could, and I'd hate to see you end up broke."

His smile widened. "You're worried about me."

Chapter Nine

The men's health event marked the first time Vic attended a medical event with his baby brother. Until a year or so ago, he still thought of Nick as a kid. Now that he was an intern at one of the other Atlanta hospitals, Vic had to let go of that image. The last of the Stafford brothers was about to make his mark on the medical world, and Vic was determined to help him in any way he could. Being a member of Atlanta's 100 Black Men offered Vic the opportunity to rub elbows with doctors, lawyers, entrepreneurs, educators and religious leaders. The organization had a stellar reputation for its programs that supported Atlanta's challenged communities. Its members were actively involved in educational issues affecting youth, public policy, as well as economic, social and health issues impacting the communities it served. Today they were talking to men about prostate cancer and prostate health.

"Morning. Thanks for picking me up," Nick said, as he opened the passenger door of Vic's car.

"No problem. So, what's up with you, man?" They hadn't seen each other since the discussion about their mother's birthday party.

Nick shrugged. "Just work. By the time I give the hospital my eighty hours, all I'm good for is grabbing something to eat and falling into bed."

"By yourself?"

"Yeah, most of the time. Since Cher and I split, I

haven't had the time or interest in getting out there to meet anyone.

"I remember those days," Vic said with a cynical snort. "It's funny how I thought I was tired back then."

"But at least they're paying you the big money to be exhausted now."

"Yeah, I had the idea that the salary would compensate for feeling like I've been run over by a steamroller, but it doesn't. This job has cost me more than I imagined."

Nick tugged on his earlobe. "Are you talking about Mona?"

"Yeah."

"We all figured something wasn't right when she dragged me out onto the dance floor at the barbeque. Rhani assumed Mona was trying to get your attention."

"What was everybody doing, standing around discussing what they thought was wrong with my marriage?"

"Well…yeah. You didn't handle that too well, you know."

"I know, but Rhani wasn't in any position to give her *professional* opinion on anything. She was screwing a client."

"Hey, don't be pissed with Rhani. She only speculated because somebody asked her what she thought."

Vic recalled the pure humiliation of that day. "I couldn't believe what I was seeing. In the fifteen years we've been together, Mona's never acted like that, even when we were drunk. It pissed me off that she decided to act a fool in front of the whole family and Mama and Daddy's friends. I wanted to crawl in a hole, man."

His brother hooted. "We were shocked, but it wasn't the end of the world."

"I'm not so sure about that. Look, let's talk about something else. I want to mention this before we get busy today and forget. The 100 Black Men are having our black tie event on the twelfth of next month. It's an annual affair and we have to raise money for mentoring programs and scholarships. I'm expected to buy at least two tickets. Since Mona and I aren't exactly on speaking terms, do you want to be my date?"

"For real?" Nick asked with a frown. "This business with Mona must be worse than you're willing to admit. Sure, I'll go if you need me to."

"Appreciate it, man. Do you own a tux?"

"What would I do with a tux, wear it to work the late shift in the ER?"

The brothers laughed at the mental vision. "Maybe we can skip out early today, stop by Savvi and reserve yours–on me, okay?"

"Thanks. You can add it to my tab. What I owe you since freshman year in college must be up in the thousands by now."

"Our family doesn't keep track of dollars and cents when it comes to helping each other out. If that was the case, I'd be paying Daddy and Mama until the day I die."

The afternoon proved to be informative to the attendees, and beneficial to Nick. Vic made sure he introduced him to all of the other medical men who had come out to volunteer their time. Before he dropped Nick back at his apartment, Vic made sure he'd reserved a decent tuxedo for him to wear to the Black Tie Affair.

On the way home, what Rhani had told the family about Mona's behavior on the Fourth repeated in his mind. Had he really neglected her so much that she felt compelled to act out in order to get his attention? If that was true, what did it say about him as a man, as a husband? On the other hand, was devoting her free time to another man the right way to handle their problems? If he were honest with himself, though, he'd have to admit that she'd come to him many times and tried to tell him how she felt. He hadn't listened.

He and Mona avoided each other for the next two days, and on the third day he got a call from Doug McClendon saying his weekly report was ready. Vic made the same arrangements as he had the previous week and told him to have the report hand-delivered to him by courier at the hospital. After he asked Shondell to hold his calls, he locked the door, opened the envelope and went to the pictures first. His lip curled at the sight of his wife and Patterson entering the Bentley dealership. The next two shots were of them walking around at another car dealership. The others showed them having lunch at a restaurant. His throat tightened seeing the last one of Patterson behind the wheel of the Bentleythe one he'd bought her. He pressed a fist against his mouth, puffed out his cheeks and blew out a long tense breath. At least this time there were no kissing shots. He grimaced and uttered a curse. What was she up to? He'd be a fool to wait around for her to announce that she was leaving him and moving into that Buckhead mansion. He needed to act now.

A sickening jumble of emotions–anger, disappointment, and dread–rendered him immobile. He stared down at the photos spread out over his desk, mocking him. Everything within him screamed, "Leave her!" Being the logical man he was, he did what he had always done with his work. He set out to get an expert consult first. He picked up the phone with a groan and dialed.

"Daddy, it's Vic. Can you talk now?" At this time of day, his father was usually in his office seeing patients.

"Hey, son. I'm in between patients, so I have a few minutes."

"I haven't talked to Mona about venues for Mama's party. We're not speaking right now."

"Hmm. How serious is it?"

Vic hesitated for a few beats. "Divorce court serious."

"Do you want to come by and talk about it?"

"Yeah, I would, but please don't mention this to Mama. *Please.*"

"I won't. When are you free, and where do you want to meet?"

"*Gladys and Ron's.* I can leave here about six. If there's any hold-up, I'll call."

"I'll order a drink and wait for you. See you this evening, son." His father ended the call.

The day couldn't have gone by fast enough for Vic. Once Shondell left to go home, he took both envelopes from beneath his workout clothes in the bottom drawer and stuffed them into his briefcase.

His father was sitting in a booth at the popular restaurant with glass in hand when he arrived. Vic slid in on the other side of the table and glanced around for a server. He needed a drink before he opened this can of worms. "Thanks for coming, Daddy." He signaled the server and ordered a Johnny Walker Black on the rocks. "I need your advice."

"When we talked July Fourth weekend, you didn't seem to know what was going on with Mona. Has that changed?"

Rather than explain, Vic opened his briefcase, took out the envelopes and placed the photos in front of his father. The older man took his glasses from his breast pocket and silently studied what was before him. After he groaned once or twice, he finally asked, "Who is he?"

"Rayvon Patterson, the new point guard for the Hawks," he said, avoiding looking his father in the eye. "They met at the masquerade ball she put together a few weeks ago."

A melancholy frown flitted across the older man's features. "How did you get these?"

"I hired Doug McClendon, the investigator Jesse used when you had that theft problem at your office last year."

"Jesse knows about this?"

"He's the one who suggested I hire McClendon to be sure of what Mona was up to before I confronted her. I've questioned her about where she's been lately, but I haven't shown her the photos. That's why I wanted to talk to you."

His father's azure gaze rested on his face. "It's hard for me to believe Mona's cheating. That girl has always adored you. What's happened between you two?"

"She says I've neglected her since I was promoted to Chief."

"Have you?"

His gaze jumped to meet his father's. "I've tried over and over again to make her see what kind of pressure and scrutiny I'm under. We're living in Atlanta, but there are lots of folks here, black, white and others, who would be thrilled to see me fail. She doesn't seem to understand that."

"You didn't answer my question. Have you neglected her? You and Mona always seemed to have a deep connection. Anyone could see that from a mile away. Is it still the same?"

Vic hung his head. "How could it possibly be the same? I'm working like a slave, and I'm exhausted most of the time."

"I understand that, you know I do, but for the sake of argument, let me plead her case here. Have you given her reason to look for time and attention from another man?"

"Everything I'm doing, I'm doing for her and the boys."

"That might be true, but that excuse doesn't fly with a woman. Have you ever heard the saying, "If you're getting more of his money than his time, then what you're getting isn't really worth anything.?""

The direction of the conversation had started to grate on Vic's nerves. "I thought *you* would understand."

"Believe me, son, I do. Your mother and I nearly separated for the same reasons back when I first started my practice. I was so driven and so obsessed with being successful, I almost lost the best woman in this world."

"But Mama never started creeping with some other man, though."

"No, but I guess I couldn't have blamed her if she had. Your mother was and is an amazing woman. While I was busy making a name for myself, she took care of the house and raised you boys basically by herself. Looking back, I don't know how she did it. And you and your brothers wonder why I go overboard for her now. I thank God she didn't leave me."

Vic squinted at the man he most admired in the world. "I thought I'd get some support from you."

"You have my support, but I'm trying to get you to look at things the way Mona probably is. If she isn't already at the point of no return, make her sit down and talk to you. When a marriage runs into trouble, it's almost never the fault of one partner alone. Yes, Mona's making a mistake, but you've made a few yourself. Do you still love her in spite of what she's doing?"

"I don't know." Vic swallowed the lump in his throat. "She's having a public relationship with a kid! I can imagine what my colleagues think. It's humiliating. At the same time she's house hunting with him, she's talking about redecorating one of our guestrooms. What the hell is that all about?"

"And making her live like a single woman for years isn't humiliating?"

He slammed his glass down on the table. "All right! Since I'm such an awful husband, how do you suggest I fix this mess?"

"Keep your voice down." His father gave a self-conscious glance around at the other patrons sitting near them and whispered. "Nobody said you're an awful husband. You just have to decide what your priorities are at this point in your career, and you need to ask Mona that question then *listen* to what she says. The only people with the answers are you and her. It might be a good idea to go somewhere away from home where you won't be distracted, even if it's just a hotel room in town."

Dumbfounded by this unexpected advice, Vic sat back in the booth and smiled. "The older you get, the more you surprise me."

His father smiled, and lines crinkled around his eyes. "There's no point in getting older if you're not getting wiser."

Vic chuckled as he stuffed the photos back into the envelope then stood and put a couple of bills on the table. "Guess I'd better go home and face the music." He patted his father's shoulder. "Thanks, Daddy."

"I hope it goes well, son."

Mona wanted to laugh when she saw Trey pacing around the foyer like an expectant father outside a maternity delivery room.

"Mom, what took you so long?" His voice rose into the squeaky, high-pitched realm it had started visiting lately. "I'm supposed to be at the mall at five o'clock!"

"Calm down, Trey. It's only four-thirty. We have plenty of time. Sit down and take a deep breath while I use the bathroom. Where's your brother?"

"In his room."

"I'll be right out. Ask him if he wants to ride with us." She went into the master bathroom wearing a smile. *Look at my baby, all excited about meeting a girl. I blinked and he grew up. Gotta stop blinking.*

Several minutes later, she and her sons were in the car heading for the mall. As usual, the first thing Trey did was change the radio station. She immediately turned the volume down. "I know your Dad already talked to you about how to behave, but I want to remind you to be a gentleman and not do anything that might get you into trouble at the mall. The security people will have an eye on you. They might even follow you around in the stores."

"Why?" His eyes widened in an innocent stare.

"Because you're a black boy, and they expect you to steal."

"Why would I steal?"

"It doesn't matter. Don't pick up anything unless you plan to buy it, and don't leave the mall for *any* reason. By the way, how much money do you need?"

"I don't know. I guess we're going to eat, and I might

want to buy a shirt or something."

"Okay. Is forty dollars enough?" She reached into her purse and handed him two twenty-dollar bills.

He grinned. "Thanks, Mom."

"Can I have forty dollars too?" Julian asked from the back seat.

"Not until you're twelve, and you're going to the mall with your friends."

Trey laughed.

"Shut up, Trey," Julian snapped with his lips poked out and his arms crossed.

"Where are you meeting your friends?"

"In front of the ice cream store in the food court."

"Okay. I'm coming in to make sure they showed up. Don't worry, I'll observe from a distance. What time should I come back?"

"Megan said eight o'clock."

"Fine." She set the alarm on her phone. "I'll meet you outside the same door we go in at eight o'clock *on the dot*."

"Okaaaay, Mom."

Mona parked the car, let Trey go in first, and then did her covert surveillance from a table in the food court. Once satisfied that her soon-to-be teenager was in fact meeting a group of friends and not just this Megan child, she and Julian got takeout for dinner then headed back home.

Before they finished eating, Vic came through the kitchen door from the garage. Three lines separated his thick brows and his eyes were narrowed into a squint, but that wasn't anything out of the ordinary. From the time they had started dating, she constantly told him he needed to smile more–that it was good for him. He was a thinker and his mind was always contemplating some serious matter. Back then Jesse and Greg credited her with being the only person who could make their brother laugh. And she used to have ways of making Vic smile that nobody knew.

"Hey." He rested his briefcase on the floor with one hand and ruffled his son's curls with the other. "How're you doing, man?"

"I'm bored," Julian answered with a pout. "Trey went to the mall with his friends, and I'm stuck here all by myself."

"Well, thanks a lot!" Mona said, faking offense.

"You know what I mean, Mom."

"I need to talk to Mom for a minute, buddy. Can you go up to your room until we're done?" Her wary gaze followed him as he patted Julian on the back and walked him over to the door.

Vic made sure Julian had gone up the stairs then turned to face her with his hands in his pants pockets. "I reserved a room at the Ritz-Carlton downtown for tomorrow night, because I need to talk to you without any interruptions. Make arrangements for the boys. See if they can spend the night with friends instead of Mama or Maite. We'll be back early Monday morning."

"Why do we need to go to a hotel?"

"There are some things we need to talk about, and I don't want to do it here. We can leave after church tomorrow. Pack an overnight bag."

"I hadn't planned on going to church tomorrow."

His voice hardened. "Don't make this difficult. Is it that hard for you to pretend everything is okay between us for ninety minutes?"

The thought of putting on a smile for his parents and

other church members turned her stomach. "Fine. Whatever."

He exhaled a long breath. "All right then."

"There's a plate in the microwave, if you want it."

"Okay, I'll eat it later."

She watched his back retreat into the hallway and up the stairs. What was he up to, and why was it necessary to get a hotel room overnight? His ominous tone told her this wasn't going to be an apology dinner and a hot night between the sheets. The alarm went off on her phone and drew her out of her thoughts. Time to go get Trey. She yelled up the stairs, "I'm going to the mall to pick Trey up." When she didn't get a response, she picked up her keys and left the house.

He was waiting with two girls and another boy, outside the door where she'd told him to be when she arrived. Something in her chest clinched when she saw him laughing with his friends. *That must be Megan.* The strange feeling that her first-born son was developing his own life with friends she didn't know saddened her. Of course she wanted him to have a social life, but at the moment it felt as though he was somehow leaving her. Not a good feeling. She already felt as though Vic had deserted her.

Trey glanced up and saw her pull up to the curb but continued to talk to the brunette for a few minutes. Eventually, he walked toward the car. Mona didn't blow the horn or do anything that might embarrass him.

"Did you have a good time?" she asked once he climbed into the passenger seat and waved to his friends.

"Yeah, it was fun. I got a shirt." He raised a bag from one of his favorite stores.

"Was that Megan, the one with the long brown hair?"

"Uh huh," he said with a hint of a smile.

"She's cute. I can see why you like her."

His smile widened to a grin. "She's funny too. Next time I'll introduce you."

"Oh, there's going to be a next time?"

They both laughed, and after he changed the radio station, they rode in companionable silence. He seemed so content. That clinch in her chest came again as she wished he could always be this happy. Only she knew that was impossible. His heart would get broken many times, and hers would break for him. "When we get home, will you call Darien and see if you can spend the night? Daddy and I are going out tomorrow afternoon after church, and we'll be staying overnight at one of the hotels downtown. I'm going to see if Julian can stay with Anthony. That way I don't have to ask Maite or Grandma."

The next morning the family attended church together. The boys went next door to the children's ministry, and she and Vic sat side-by-side in silence. When the pastor told everyone to hug the person next to them, she busied herself with searching inside her purse for something so Vic wouldn't give her a phony church hug for everyone else's benefit. Mona didn't miss her mother-in-law's curious glance. When the service ended, they dropped Trey and Julian off at their friends' houses and headed directly to the hotel.

Vic made quick work of checking in at the desk then picked up their overnight bags and inclined his head toward the elevator. He had requested an upper floor, so the wordless ride proved to be more unnerving than she'd expected. The elevator reached their floor, and Vic stepped out. She exited behind him feeling as though she were on a walk to the gallows. When they used to travel, they would examine the room before he even put their bags down. If it met with her approval, he would close the door and rest their luggage on the floor. This time he didn't bother to ask what she thought of the suite, and merely shut the door.

She sat on the loveseat, and her gaze fell to his briefcase on the cocktail table in front of her. *I know he didn't bring me here to watch him work.*

He turned on a lamp, and called room service for a bottle of wine and sandwiches for their late lunch. Her nerves couldn't take the silence any longer. "What are we doing here, Vic?"

"I have something to show you," he said in a matter-of-fact tone while he removed his tie and threw it over the back of the chair opposite the loveseat. "But I want to wait until room service gets here. You might as well make yourself comfortable."

He had to be kidding. Everything he did made her uncomfortable today. It wasn't often that Vic appeared secretive, but the way he avoided any explanation, rankled her. The stilettos she had worn to church had been pinching her toes for hours now, so she unbuckled the ankle straps and set them aside while he turned on the television and found a jazz music station. Vic went into the bathroom and returned a few minutes later. She did the same, and by the time she re-entered the sitting room, the girl from room service was knocking on the door. She set up their food and beverages on the table in front of the windows overlooking the city. Vic thanked her; she collected her tip and left.

He picked up the briefcase, brought it to the table then opened the wine and poured a generous amount into a glass for each of them. "Here." He held up a glass to her and took a bite of one of the sandwiches.

Mona approached him cautiously and took the glass from his hand.

"Sit down, Mona."

Her gaze tracked the skillful hands that had given him the status he enjoyed. He opened the briefcase and removed a large manila envelope. "What's that?"

"You tell me." Not one to be threatened by conflict, he reached across the table and spread the contents of the envelope in front of her with a flourish she considered unnecessary.

She uttered a small gasp when her gaze fell on the eight-by-ten pictures. Her manicured hands trembled, as she picked up the images one at a time. "You had me followed?"

"Did you give me any other choice? I asked what was going on between you and Patterson." He took a long swallow from his glass and immediately refilled it without taking his laser-like gaze from her face. "You wouldn't give me a straight answer, so I had to find out for myself."

"It's not what it looks like, Vic."

"Really? Because it looks like you're house-hunting and car shopping with him. It looks like you're kissing him out on a public street. He's not driving the car I bought you? What kind of a fool do you think I am?" His voice rose with each question until the last few words came out on a scream. Hurt underscored the anger in his voice.

Vic had never yelled at her like that, and she gulped from her glass taking those few seconds to come up with an answer that didn't sound insane. "Please calm down. I can explain." Her mind scrambled for a logical explanation, only she knew nothing she might say would come across as sensible or truthful. "I wasn't house-hunting with him. He's looking for a house, and he asked for my opinion."

Vic scrubbed his chin. "I don't believe you, and why the hell did you think it was your responsibility to help him?

"It wasn't my *responsibility*. I was just doing it to help

him out."

"Why?" Vic asked, his face twisted in confusion.

"Because he's new in town, and he asked me to."

Her husband glared at her with fire in his green gaze. "What else has he asked you to do? If you're so willing to kiss him, what else has he convinced you to do for him?"

"I'm not sleeping with him!" Her voice trembled. "And I didn't kiss him; he kissed me. I told him right away it was the first and last time."

"You don't see a problem with that, Mona? You're another man's wife. What the hell is wrong with you? All these years I believed you had some standards, that there was a line you wouldn't cross, but I guess I was wrong. You've just been playing me until something better came along. You had a reason for getting involved with Patterson. I suppose it's that big contract he just signed, and you know I can't give you that."

Fear crept into her heart hearing his disgust. She pressed her hands to her stomach and blinked back tears. "Vic, I'm the one looking for a car," she pleaded. "I knew you'd be mad if I told you I wanted to sell the Bentley, so I asked him to go with me just to have a man to help me negotiate."

"What reason do you have to sell your car?"

"I need the money to…I want to…to start my own business, and I need the money either for the initial investment or to pay for classes. I didn't want to ask you for the tuition," she blurted out.

His loud, mocking bark of laughter filled the room and might as well have been an ice pick to her heart. The tears pushed past her lashes and ran down her cheeks.

"Oh, come on. You can come up with something better

than that! What do you really want the cash for?"

"I want to create my own fashion line." She sniffed and wiped a hand across her eyes. "That's the truth, Vic."

He stared at her for a long moment. "Maybe that's the truth about the car, but you're a really bad liar. There's more than just a buddy-type friendship between you and him, and the sooner you own up to it, the sooner we can decide where we go from here."

Her stomach lurched. "What do mean by that?"

Vic's expression turned even more grim. "You disrespected me in the worst way, and if I find out you're sleeping with him, we're done. Don't ever let him get behind the wheel of your car again. And if find out you've had him in *my* house, I'll burn it to the ground with both of you in it. I'm only giving you one choice. Stop seeing him right now."

Seeing this side of her husband frightened her, and she stopped breathing for a moment. "It...it was just...so nice to...," she blubbered through tears that now flowed freely. "To have someone who wanted to spend his time with me. I swear, there's nothing going on between me and Ray."

"Prove it." He emptied his glass in one long swallow and rose from the table. "You can stay the night here. I'm going back to the house. Call an Uber car in the morning."

Mona found herself sitting in the suite alone staring in shock at the door he'd just slammed. She'd been so desperate to get his attention, and her whole stupid plan to make him jealous had blown up in her face. Now she had to clean up the disaster she'd created before she lost the only man she'd ever loved.

Vic's hasty departure from the hotel room left Mona sitting shocked and shoeless staring out the window at the city skyline. What a royal mess she'd made of this whole plan to get his attention. Now she felt like a complete fool. She should have known her husband was too smart to fall for her simple little scheme. He'd been one step ahead of her the whole time. The only thing on her mind now was if the worst happened and Vic decided to file for divorce.

When she finally glanced at the digital clock next to the bed, it read seven o'clock. She reached in her purse for her phone and dialed Ray.

"Hello," he said in that deep, smoky voice.

"I was hoping you would answer. Are you in the middle of anything right now?"

"Nothing I can't do later. What do you have in mind?"

"We need to talk. Can you meet me somewhere?"

"Name it. I'll be there as soon as I change clothes."

"I'm downtown at the Ritz Carlton. Can you come here?"

"Give me a half hour. Are you all right, Mona?"

"Yes and no. I'll wait for you at the bar and explain when you get here."

She reluctantly stuffed her still-throbbing toes back into her shoes, hobbled into the bathroom to check her hair and makeup then took the elevator back to the ground floor. Once she positioned herself onto one of the burgundy leather bar stools, she casually glanced around. Now that she knew she was being followed, everyone she saw was suspect. Since everyone could capture their surroundings on their phones, the guilty party didn't have to be a man holding a professional-grade camera with a foot-long telephoto lens. Knowing it could be anyone in the room, she nervously smoothed her skirt and tried her best to appear as though she wasn't self-conscious.

Rayvon came in the door looking wonderful as usual in a crisp open-neck white shirt and khaki pants. The minimal gold jewelry he wore sparkled against the darkness of his skin. He approached her with a tentative smile and bent down to kiss her cheek. "Hi." She backed away with a frown.

"Sorry. It sounded urgent on the phone, so I got here as fast as I could. What's up?"

"Get yourself a drink first."

"That bad, huh?"

Her head bobbed up and down in agreement, and her hair fell down to cover one eye. She brushed it back with one hand. "Yes."

Ray signaled the bartender and ordered a drink. "Tell me what's wrong."

"My husband hired an investigator and had me followed," she whispered even though no one was sitting near them. "He had pictures of us everywhere we've gone, including ones of you kissing me and driving my car. He was livid."

His eyes stretched wide. "What did he say?"

"A lot, but of the things I *can* repeat he said, if I ever see you again, our marriage is finished."

"Didn't you tell him we don't have an intimate relationship?"

"Of course I did, but he doesn't care. I love my husband, and even though I value your friendship, I'm not willing to risk my marriage. I'm sorry, Ray."

"I'm sorry too." A pained expression marred his handsome face. "You're a special woman, and he's a very lucky man. It's too bad, because I wanted you to meet my family, and I was hoping you could give me some pointers on what to do with the house." His currant-black eyes seemed to plead for friendship.

"I can recommend you to an interior designer I know.

She'll do a great job for you. You don't need my help."

"I know I don't *need* your help. I enjoy being with you."

"Me too." She stared down at her hands and tried to comprehend the heaviness in her chest. "I hope everything works out for you and your family. You know I'll be rooting for you once the season starts."

"You don't watch basketball." His normal youthful happiness faded.

"True, but I can still root for you in my head." When she glanced up, he was looking at her as though she had just given him a precious gift. "I think I'd better leave now." Mona rose from her seat and let her gaze linger on his face as though trying to memorize his features. "Goodbye, Ray." She left the bar, willing herself not to turn around and went back upstairs to the room telling herself he would get over it. She didn't believe it was true, because Ray had come to rely on her for advice and support. He'd just have to find someone else.

Chapter Ten

*T*hat wasn't exactly the way Vic intended for it to go. He had hoped Mona would fall into his arms and beg for his forgiveness, but she didn't. The look of shock and panic when she'd seen the pictures had given him a twisted sense of pleasure. He'd wanted to stun her and make her feel the way he'd felt when Marv blindsided him with the magazine photos. Hitting her with the photographic evidence right out of the blue also hadn't given her time to concoct an elaborate story.

It was quite possible she was telling the truth about the kiss. Hadn't what happened to him in Chicago been the same thing? He hadn't kissed that woman. She'd kissed him. He hadn't confessed his transgressions either. Nor had he asked for her forgiveness. The difference was Mona had an on-going relationship with this guy whether it was just friendship or something more. In all their years together, not once had Mona ever cried like that. In his heart he wanted to believe there was no intimate relationship between her and the round ball wunderkind, but he wasn't going to be a fool. She would have to prove it to him in no uncertain terms.

Vic stared up at the house when he pulled into the driveway. It looked so different now. Beautiful, yet empty of the things that made a house a home. The joy was gone from his marriage, and it had been replaced by suspicion, fear and anger. What would happen if he and Mona couldn't work out their problems? No one on the Stafford side of the family, including his uncles, had been divorced. Both of his father's brothers had been married for thirty-plus years.

God, he didn't want to be the first to have that dubious honor. His father's mantra kept repeating in his mind, "Stafford men take care of their women." Vic couldn't deny that he'd done a stellar job materially, but he had deceived himself into believing that he'd taken care of his wife's emotional and physical needs in the two years since his job had taken over their lives. It put a sharp pain in his chest to admit that he was actually responsible for this mess. He wanted more than anything to blame Mona, but in spite of his anger, his conscience kept reminding him of all the times she had begged him for his companionship, and he'd refused for one reason or another. Because he believed his work was more important than being an escort to social functions, he'd allowed her to attend them alone. All she wanted was to be with him, and he'd been too preoccupied to listen.

He hit the button on the visor for the garage door to open, but before he exited the car, he sat contemplating whether or not to go inside. Normally, he would've looked forward to the peace and quiet, only tonight all that silence would only remind him how empty his life had become. Eventually he entered the kitchen, disabled the security system and went directly to the bar in his man cave. He filled a lowball glass with his favorite Scotch, took it upstairs to the bedroom and set it on the dresser while he peeled off his clothes. Even though it wasn't dark yet, he crossed the white carpet, threw back the white comforter and slid beneath the white sheets taking the glass with him. The room, which at one time he'd considered clean and stylish, now seemed nothing more than sterile and cold. Just like his marriage, it needed some warmth and softness. Once he laid back, Ramona's scent wafted into his nostrils from her pillow. For years she had worn Oscar de la Renta's Ruffles, her signature fragrance, which he loved. Even while he made the rest of his drink disappear, the realization that he was drinking too much lately settled on him like a blanket of shame. He closed his eyes and prayed a silent prayer that his wife would do the right thing.

When he opened his eyes on Monday morning, he couldn't believe he'd slept ten hours straight. And it was a good thing, because before he finished his first cup of coffee, he got a call from the hospital and had to go back. In a way it didn't matter, because he knew it would be after eleven before Mona showered, did her hair and makeup and returned home. If there was one thing he appreciated about her, it was that she never went out in public looking unkempt. She always said, "Everywhere I go, I represent you," and she had done a superb job in that arena. Mona was fine as hell, and he understood why a man so much younger would be interested in her. He'd married her with the unrealistic expectation that no other man would be attracted to her. How stupid was that?

The moment he drove into the hospital garage, he forced thoughts of his messed up personal life from his head, changed into a set of scrubs and sought out the doctors who had requested his assistance. Like most surgeons, he felt the best remedy for his unsettled mind was to do what he did best–operate. He couldn't explain it, but even though it was often stressful, performing surgery soothed him. It was a different kind of stress, though–good stress, if such a thing really existed.

After he located his colleagues and listened to their predicament, he scrubbed in for the procedure. During the operation, the complicated details of the task pushed down thoughts of the complicated details of his deteriorating marriage.

Four hours later, after the surgery ended successfully, he returned to his office and checked the voicemail on his cell. Not that he was expecting Mona to call. She didn't like handling important matters on the phone. Part of him hoped their marriage was still important to her while another part tried to prepare himself for the worst. If she had reached the point of no return, as his father had said, Vic needed to be ready. With all of her denials, he still questioned whether or not they were sincere, and he wondered what it would take for him to believe her.

She came in while he was sitting at the kitchen island nursing his fifth cup of coffee of the day.

"Good morning." She went directly to the coffeemaker and reached for her favorite mug.

"Is it?"

"Do you have a few minutes to come outside to the patio?" she said, ignoring his question then turned to the housekeeper. "Maite, thank you for getting the boys off this morning."

The housekeeper smiled and waited for them to leave the room before she went on with her tasks.

Vic studied Mona's face for a moment, before he picked up his cup and headed out the door to the patio without a word.

Maite had her head lowered, but Vic knew she was watching them closely as they exited the kitchen. Their housekeeper knew more about what went on in their household than anyone else, but she never mentioned what she saw or heard to either of them unless they asked for her opinion.

He lowered himself into a chair at one of the umbrella tables beside the pool and waited for Mona to speak. When she did, her demeanor was different—more forceful and determined.

"Please let me get this out before you say anything, okay? All these years I believed you appreciated what I'd done to help your career image. It hurts so bad to know you see me as a leech." He opened his mouth to disagree, but she raised her palm and continued. "I can't go on being dependent on you, so that's why I'm selling the car. It's important for me to create a life for myself separate and distinct from being Mrs. Doctor Stafford." She paused, exhaled and looked at him eye-to-eye. "As far as the school idea goes, maybe you're right about me going back. There's another route I can take, but I'll still need a good deal of cash. I loved the car, Vic. It was a beautiful gift, but it's more important for me to have the cash right now."

He waited to be sure she was finished before he spoke. "I never said I thought you were a leech, and I didn't mean to hurt your feelings. When we got married, I vowed to provide for you, and I meant it. As the years went on, it seemed like you became more reliant on me rather than creating a life for yourself."

She answered with a staid calmness, keeping her features deceptively composed. "That's probably true, but I don't believe for one minute your reasons for wanting me to come up with a way to occupy my time are for *my* benefit, Vic. You just want me to be busy so I won't need you to spend time with me. My mother had me convinced that as a doctor's wife, my life should be all about making *you* look good and doing the things to help *your* career. So that's what I did, and you ate it up, Vic. Not once did I hear you complain. You were quite pleased with my life being all about you."

Was she right? Could it be he was just looking for an easy out? Most of the time he didn't want to attend any of those charity functions where everyone pasted on a phony smile and kissed as many butts as were necessary to reach a financial goal, but she probably hadn't wanted to attend the ones he insisted she attend with him either. He'd never asked her. "I don't deny that I liked the way our life was, but I see what it led to. You need friends and things to do of your own, Mona."

She pinned him with a piercing gaze in her perfectly made-up eyes. "As long as none of those friends are male, right? Well, don't worry. My hospital and charity fundraising

170

days are over. Oh, and by the way, you can call off your spy now. I met with Ray in person last night and told him we can no longer be friends." He squinted and shifted in his seat. "I thought it wouldn't be right to do it over the phone, since he's been nothing but kind to me. He understands, because there was never anything between us to begin with. As far as I'm concerned, ending our friendship is unnecessary, because there was nothing romantic or sexual between him and me. But you're my husband, and if that's what you want me to do, I'll do it. You mean more to me than any friendship."

He took hold of her hand. "I hope you're telling me the truth."

An expectant light suddenly flickered in her eyes at his touch and disappeared just as fast. He released her hand. "From now on, you have to take me seriously, Vic, I've done what you asked, and in return I expect you to do the same. No excuses."

"Name it."

"If you need to hear it again, fine. You have to make the boys and me a priority sometimes, if keeping our family together is what you want. I'm not going to tell you how, because you're smart enough to figure it out for yourself."

Even though anger still simmered between them, Vic studied her as she spoke. She still had an emotional hold on him that surpassed any conflict they might have. He wanted to grab her and pull her into his chest, but he still wasn't convinced she meant what she'd said. Time would tell.

He hadn't told McClendon to end his surveillance, and he wondered if the investigator had gotten photos of her farewell meeting with Patterson. His gut twisted at the mental image of her kissing him goodbye. His head told him giving her the chance to end her association with her young friend was the right thing to do, but his heart ached because some part of her had a need for another man. No matter how he tried, he couldn't deny his responsibility in this. A happy, fulfilled married woman didn't have to seek companionship elsewhere. Being honest with himself was painful, but he never shirked responsibility. What his father said was true. Since he'd taken the new job, he had given Mona everything but what she really needed–his time, attention and affection.

Vic and his brothers had the best example of a strong marriage. Their parents readily admitted to the trials they had faced during their forty-seven-year marriage, and Vic was certain they were more committed to each other now than ever. He gazed into the blue ripples ruffling the pool's surface and asked himself what his father would do. He recalled times when their Aunt Velma or Aunt Betty showed up unexpectedly and announced that they were staying at the house while their parents went out of town for the weekend. With six boys, it was impossible to find places for them to go for two days and three nights, so bringing in reinforcements must have been the only solution. As teens, they never speculated on why their mother and father just disappeared at regular intervals, but in hindsight, Vic understood. And he vaguely remembered his father wearing a sly smile when they returned.

Once he was convinced that Mona actually cut it off with Patterson, he had to figure out how to fix the disaster he'd created.

He still doesn't believe me. Mona threw the ball back in his court and waited for him to respond to her demand. "I've done what you asked; now I expect you to give me what I need. No excuses."

Now they seemed to be at an impasse. Vic remained

quiet, the reflection of the water flickering on his sculpted face, She finally broke the uneasy silence. "Can I count on your support with my business? Your emotional support, not financial."

"I know what you mean, and if this is what you really want to do, I'm behind you one hundred percent. My main concern is for you to get the right advice from people who are experts in the industry. You can't just jump into this blindly."

"You're right. Ray said the same thing." The second the words crossed her lips, she cringed when he glared at her. "You know Carmelo Anthony, right?"

"Of course." His brows drew together.

"His wife, LaLa, started a clothing line, and I understand she's doing very well even though she's not a designer with a degree in fashion. I might be able to get some pointers from her."

His gaze dropped to the floor, and he bit his bottom lip. "I suppose Patterson is setting this up for you."

"Well…" She sucked in her bottom lip and bit it. "He made the suggestion and said he'd try to get in touch with Carmelo. If it happens, the meeting would just be between LaLa and myself. Ray wouldn't be involved."

"Connections are important in any business." He poked his lips out. "Go for it. Just be sure Patterson doesn't use it as an excuse to stay in touch with you."

Mona gritted her teeth, forcing herself to remember she *had* given him cause for his jealousy.

"Tell me about your business idea." He angled his chair beneath the umbrella so the sun wasn't in his eyes then took a sip of his coffee as though he had all the time in the world.

His interest pleased her, yet she wasn't quite sure of

how to answer him. She didn't want to sound like an idiot. "You know how much I love clothes, and fashion is the only thing I've ever been interested in. My mother sent me to college to get a husband, but at least I got a B.A. in business administration out of it. Maybe some of what I learned is still up in there somewhere." She tapped her temple and laughed.

"I'm surprised you want to do this, but I think it's a great idea. When we got married, I think we both had unrealistic expectations. I thought my career should be just like my father's and our marriage should be just like my parents'. You made it your goal to be what your mother told you a doctor's wife should be."

"True, but you didn't disagree with it, Vic."

"You're right. I loved that your life revolved around me. Having you do everything to further my career made me proud, but it was selfish. It was all about me, and I didn't give a second thought to how it would affect you. You lost your identity."

She hung her head. "I don't think I ever had my own identity. When I was younger, it was all about what my mother wanted. I spent my free time preparing for pageants, which meant being made up to look like someone else. Then, once I met you, she convinced me to make my life all about you. I'm not really sure who I am."

His deep-set eyes settled on her face, and she saw something she hadn't seen unless he was talking about a patient.

"Well, now is your chance to find out. Whatever you need, baby, I'm there for you."

Rarely did he call her that anymore, and hearing the endearment warmed her heart. "Thanks, but I need to do this on my own. Right now all I need is office space, and I'm going to use the beige guest room until I'm forced to get something larger."

Vic chuckled. "Did you hear what you just said? You're already speaking growth. I like that."

His logical mind was always thinking one step ahead. "How do you plan to create your designs?"

"I'm going to talk to Jamila about that. She's been my stylist for three years now, and she might be interested in going in with me. If she isn't, I'm sure she'll have some ideas. In fact, I'm meeting with her later today to get her thoughts."

"Do you plan to ask for a cash buy-in from whoever partners with you, or will you be the financier?"

Already he was asking questions to which she didn't have answers. "I guess I need to call Cam for a referral," she said, speaking of Cam Southwell, their attorney, who was also a member of their church.

"He can handle the incorporation and general set-up for you."

"I know, but I want to use someone who specializes in representing small businesses."

Vic's eyes narrowed. "Plus, you don't want him knowing everything going on with you."

"Exactly." She gave him a small smile. "I'm supposed to be at Jamila's studio in an hour, and I have a stop to make first."

"Okay. I guess I'll see you later."

"You're not going in to the hospital today?"

"I already scrubbed in on an early surgery, and unless they call me back, I'm off for the rest of the day."

"Okay, please make sure the boys do their homework when they get in. I don't know what time I'll be back."

Knowing she had to be at another appointment gave

her a reason to keep her stop short. Her mother answered the door looking surprised to see her.

"Well, I haven't seen you in a dog's age." She stepped aside to allow Mona to enter.

"It's only been a few weeks, Ma."

Her mother sent her a skeptical glance. "And the last time you were here, you told me your marriage was falling apart. You could've called and let me know how things were going, you know."

"And *you* could've called me to see how I was doing."

"Ramona, I know you better than anyone on this planet, and if you're not ready to talk, nobody is going to get two syllables out of you. I figured you'd call me when you had something to say. Come in the kitchen and make a cup of coffee."

She followed her mother into the sunny kitchen at the rear of the renovated 1936 Craftsman bungalow her mother had been awarded in the divorce from her father. Each of them fixed a cup of coffee and took them out onto the screened-in porch overlooking the backyard.

"I came to let you know what I've decided to do and to ask for your help." She cleared her throat, and a shadow of alarm crossed her mother's face. "I told Vic I've stepped down from the charity fundraising, and I'm starting my own business. In order to get the money I need to finance the start-up, I'm selling my car." The older woman gasped and seemed too startled to speak. "Before you say anything, I know what you're thinking. Asking Vic for the money is out of the question, since he already considers me clingy and dependent."

"Did he actually say that?"

"Yes, that's what my husband thinks of me, so all of the beauty treatments, Pilates, breast lift and tummy tuck were for nothing."

She gaped at her daughter. "I can't believe that."

"Believe it, Ma. He said I need to create my own life, and he's right. Making him the center of my existence was a huge mistake. Now it's time for me to focus on Mona."

"What in the world do you know about business?" She ran a hand through the stylish haircut Mona had convinced her to get several months ago.

"Well, my degree was in business administration, even though I graduated a long time ago. I was a good student."

"Yes, you were, but what kind of business are you thinking of starting?"

"My own fashion line. In fact, I'm on my way to see Jamila in a few minutes to talk to her about possibly collaborating with me. I need her expertise in order to get this thing off the ground." She hesitated briefly. "And a friend of mine is trying to hook me up with a celebrity who has her own successful line. She could give me help on how I need to go about doing this."

"How did Vic feel about you selling the Bentley? After all, it was a birthday gift from him."

Mona rolled her eyes, annoyed at her mother's obvious concern for Vic rather than her own daughter. "He wasn't thrilled, but he said it's my car to do with as I please, so I'm doing as I please. I'm taking it to the dealer while the price he gave me is still good, and I'm buying an Audi SUV."

Her mother tapped her fingers on the arm of the wicker sofa. "I hope you're not making a mistake, Ramona. What if Vic wakes up one morning and realizes he misses you representing him in the medical community?"

"That'll be his fault."

"He never said anything to you about how he felt

before now?"

"No, in fact, the conversation we had this morning is the first real talk we've had in a year," she said, intentionally leaving out any mention of Rayvon. "It was nice."

"I hope you know what you're doing, because going all independent on him after he's had you at his beck and call for years might just backfire."

"He said he thinks I should be more independent, and I want to show him I'm capable of standing in my own power."

"Whatever that means."

The way her mother rolled her eyes annoyed her. "You know what it means, Ma. You just never taught me how to do it."

Her mother stiffened and crossed her arms. "It always comes back to how I raised you, doesn't it?"

"Ma, you could've taught me how to be more than just pretty. I'm thirty-six years old, and I feel so useless."

"Can you imagine how bad it would be to feel useless *and* ugly?" her mother asked with indignation in her voice. "Anyway, you said you came to ask for my help. What kind of help?"

"Getting this business off the ground is going to take a lot of time and energy, and most likely there will be times when I'll need to leave the boys. Maite and Mrs. Stafford always watch them, but I don't want to overburden them. I know you're not crazy about babysitting, but the boys aren't little anymore. All they need is someone in the vicinity to make sure they don't burn the house down and they stay off the Internet porn sites."

"They watch porn?" Mona laughed at her dismayed expression.

"No, Ma, but if you don't monitor kids these days when they disappear into cyberspace, you'd be surprised at what they can find. Besides, they're boys, and boys are overly-curious. I wouldn't need you often. I just want to know if I can count on you."

"I guess I could handle them every now and then, as long as I don't have to play tag with them or any other ridiculous thing."

"Kids don't play tag anymore. If they do, it's on a screen, so don't worry." Mona chuckled then checked her phone. "I have to hit the road. Jamila is waiting for me. Thanks, Ma." She placed a kiss on her mother's cheek.

After she pursed her lips. "Girl, I hope you know what you're doing."

After she left Decatur, Mona drove into Atlanta to her Jamila Anderson's studio in the Ellsworth Industrial area. Normally, Jamila came to her, and this was Mona's first time visiting her actual place of business. The small office suite in the middle of the fabric warehouses and decorator showrooms was a combination of living room, dressing room, and beauty salon. Several racks of clothes lined the walls of the two rooms.

She and Jamila sat at the desk in an uncluttered corner, and Jamila listened attentively while she explained her business idea. She asked all kinds of questions, some of which Mona couldn't answer. She felt as though she were in a class where the professor raced through the information, and she was struggling to take notes as fast as she could. They ended by making a tentative plan to sit down with the attorney, as soon as Mona chose one.

Chapter Eleven

Long after she left, Vic still mulled over what Mona had said. Seeing her new-found determination about something that excited her pleased him. He felt bad about being so harsh with her, but it seemed to be exactly what she needed. Her declaration of the end of her relationship with Patterson eased his mind a little, but he called McClendon nevertheless.

"I want you to continue surveillance for another month," he told the investigator. "And I want to know every single place she goes. She'll probably stop at a few places she's never been before. Some of them I already know about. That being said, did you get pictures of her visit to the Ritz Carlton on Sunday night?"

"When I realized she was there with you, I assumed there was no reason to continue."

Vic sighed. "Too bad. I left Sunday night, and Patterson met her there a little while later. She says he left, and she stayed over until Monday morning."

"Damn. I'm sorry, Vic. I just assumed…"

"Don't worry about it. I already know what went down. She says she asked him there to tell him they couldn't see each other anymore. That's the reason I want a really close eye on her now."

"I'll put one of my assistants on her right away."

"If she does meet with him again, I don't want to wait until I get the report to find out. I want you to call me right away."

"Will do."

For the remainder of the week, Vic and Mona didn't see much of each other. She said goodbye to the Bentley, and had the dealer deposit the money directly into her account. From there she picked up her new Audi. Amazingly, Trey and Julian both said they loved the new vehicle because of the built-in DVD player and Wi-Fi connectivity, which she didn't have in the Bentley even though it was a much more expensive car.

He had to go out of town overnight for a meeting and, when he returned, he had to deal with an issue with one of his surgeons, two in-house meetings, a couple of surgeries and reams of paperwork. So far, there had been no evidence of new cases of the CRE infection, and he was confident they had conquered the beast.

On Saturday morning, he caught Mona on her way out with the boys in tow. "What are you guys up to today?" he asked eyeing their overnight bags at the front door.

"They're hanging out with my mother until tomorrow afternoon. I have a lot of running around to do, and I'm not sure what time I'll be done."

Vic's eyes rounded. "Cee Cee is babysitting? How did that happen?"

"Once I convinced her she didn't need to run around and play tag with them, she agreed."

"Play tag?" Trey asked looking bewildered.

"She still thinks of you and your brother as being five years old," she answered her son before turning back to Vic. "I made sure they have all of their electronics, and she promised to take them to a movie."

"Wow, maybe the world really is coming to an end." He grinned at his sons. "Don't give your grandmother a hard time, okay?" The boys mumbled their agreement and headed to the car with their bags. "Tonight is the Black Tie Affair for the 100 Black Men. I'm taking Nick with me to introduce him around. We'll be in late."

"Is your tux clean?"

"Yeah," he answered, appreciating her concern. It had been a while since she'd shown any interest. "We sent it to the dry cleaner after that awards dinner, remember?"

"Right. Well, have a good time, and tell Nick I said hi."

"I will. What are you doing today?"

"Jamila is taking me to see what a workroom is like."

He sent her a quizzical look. "Then you can explain it to me. I hope it all works out. Maybe tomorrow we can go out for breakfast, and you can tell me all about it before you have to get the boys."

She seemed too startled by his suggestion to offer a response, so she just smiled.

Vic picked Nick up at his apartment. He smiled as his brother came down the sidewalk to the car. As the baby of the family, the older brothers often made the mistake of not acknowledging that he was a grown man who had survived college and medical school and was now an intern preparing to do his residency. At this point in his career, his life was all about putting in the hours and proving himself capable of putting what he'd learned in school into practice in the real world. When he'd been involved with his former girlfriend, they did everything as a couple. Cherilyn had become a part of the family, and it was strange to see Nick alone.

"Looking good, man," Vic greeted him when he

opened the car door and got into the passenger seat.

"Thanks for getting me the monkey suit." Nick tugged at his collar. "My budget couldn't stand the hit right now."

"You know I remember those days. As Mona always says, I was broker than MC Hammer."

"So, what should I expect tonight?"

"The Black Tie Affair is to support the educational programs of the organization, which helps kids prepare for the SAT and other things. They also mentor children and give scholarships."

"Definitely worthwhile." Nick gazed out the car window. "When I hear some of the stories my friends tell about trying to scrounge up tuition, scholarships and grants, I have to be thankful Daddy helped us the way he did. Some guys I knew were in school full time and working a full-time job. I don't know how they did it without flunking out."

"I know that's right, and I want to be able do the same for Trey and Julian when the time comes."

"How are they doing? I haven't seen them since the barbeque."

"J is always the same. As long as he's fed and his chargers are working, he's a happy guy." Vic chuckled. "Trey's another story. He's not even thirteen yet, and he's already sweating the girls."

"No shit!"

"And the one he's sweating right now is a little white girl. He came to me a couple of weeks ago to ask if it was okay for him to like her."

"What'd you tell him?"

"I tried my best to be straight with him. After all, she's a girl, and the general rules apply, but the racial issue brings its own rules. I had to give him a PG-13 version of the, *don't touch and be careful in public* talk. You should've seen his face when I mentioned kissing her. It was all I could do not to laugh. Right now, he's not thinking about sex, but we both know that's just around the corner."

Nick barked out a laugh. "For sure, man. Has he taken her out?"

"No, man! He's too young to date, but they did go to the mall with a bunch of their friends to hang out."

Nick snickered. "I know it sounds like something Mama would say, but it seems like he was just playing with Fisher-Price toys a couple of days ago."

"How do you think it makes *me* feel?"

"Do you and Mona plan to have any more?"

Vic's head spun around to face Nick. "Why would you ask?"

"Most women want a girl sooner or later."

He exhaled. "We need to be sure we're on solid ground before doing anything like that. Right now adding a baby to the mix would be irresponsible."

"I'm sorry, man. I'd hoped things were getting better."

"They are a little, I think."

"Is she still *socializing* with Rayvon Patterson?"

"Nice way of putting it. I'm not really sure there was anything between them, but I gave her an ultimatum. All I can do is wait and see." He told Nick about her business idea and then steered the conversation to another topic. "Has Daddy said anything about how Mama's birthday party is coming along? I haven't had time to check in with him."

"The last time we talked, he said something about roping Adanna into helping him with the arrangements."

"Poor Adanna. When he gets finished running her

around, she'll be ready to move back to Nigeria." The brothers shared a laugh and rode for a few minutes listening to the soft jazz coming from the radio.

When they reached 200 Peachtree Street where the event was being held, the ballroom was filling with men dressed like penguins and women decked out in gowns that shined, sparkled and swooshed as they walked.

"Let's get a drink, and then we can mingle." Vic headed toward the bar. The bartender filled their orders, and they began their tour of the room. Nick made polite small talk with the people to whom Vic introduced him. All of a sudden Vic saw his face blanch. "What? What's the matter, man?" He froze where he stood and followed his brother's line of vision. His jaw dropped when he saw Cherilyn on the arm of a man he recognized as a doctor from another hospital.

"Who is he?" he asked in a cool, disapproving tone. "Do you know him?"

"Yeah, he's on staff at Southern Christian. I didn't know they were seeing each other, though," Vic said apologetically.

"Introduce me."

"What?"

"I want to meet him."

A warning voice whispered in Vic's head. "Uh, maybe you should wait until you calm down first," he muttered uneasily.

"I'm calm. Do it," Nick insisted.

"All right. Don't show out, man."

Nick glared at him, and Vic led him toward the couple. "Derrick! How're you doing, man?" He and Vic shook hands.

"I'm doing great, Vic. This is—"

"Cherilyn Vernon," Vic said, finishing his sentence. "It's been a while. How are you, Cher?"

"This is my brother, Nick. He's a first-year surgical intern at Metropolitan. This is Derrick Hilliard, one of the best surgeons at SC, and you and Cherilyn already know each other."

The other man's gaze jumped from her face to Vic's. "You two know each other?"

Nick and Derrick shook hands then Nick took Cherilyn's hand. "It's good to…" he hesitated for a long moment as though he'd lost his train of thought, "see you again. How've you been?" Vic warily observed the polite interaction and didn't quite understand why his brother momentarily hesitated.

Color rose in her cheeks and she stuttered. "I–I'm doing great, Nick. How are you?"

Vic hoped Derrick had missed the way his brother's gaze ran from her bare shoulders, over the form fitting gown that showed off her gravity-defying breasts, down to her strappy stilettos. Cherilyn had never looked so beautiful. Nick was the only one of his brothers who had an attraction to full-figured women. She reminded Vic of Jill Scott–big tits, tiny waist, big hips but tight and fit.

"I'm good. Vic decided it was time for me to get out and start meeting more people in the community. I'm glad I took him up on the offer."

"Have you decided on a specialty yet?" Derrick asked, still not seeming to pick up on the tension between his date and Nick.

"I'm considering men's medicine. It's a growing field. Pardon the pun."

Derrick smiled. "True. I wish you the best. It looks like the program is getting ready to start, so we'd better find our seats. It's good seeing you again, Vic. Nice meeting you, man." He slipped an arm around Cherilyn's waist and turned her toward the tables facing the dais. Nick watched the couple across the room with an expression of disbelief.

Vic swallowed the remaining liquid in his glass. "Whoa. That was uncomfortable." His brother appeared shaken. "You all right?"

"Did you see the ring?"

"What ring?"

"It looked like an engagement ring. A big one."

"You think? It's only been six months since you two broke up."

"Exactly." Nick's gaze followed the couple across the room with laser-like intensity. "What can you tell me about him?"

"We need to find seats. Let's talk about this later." Vic's plan to engage his brother in conversations with the more influential members of the organization was squashed. Throughout the addresses given from the stage, Nick appeared to be totally disconnected and stared across the room to where his former girlfriend sat with her new man. As soon as the dinner and program ended, Vic suggested, "Why don't we go get a drink somewhere?"

Nick ran a hand over his short, wavy hair and blew out a heavy sigh. "Yeah, okay. I don't feel like going home yet."

Vic left the car in the building garage, and they walked down Peachtree Street to the nearest spot in the area still open. He didn't much care for chain restaurants, but it had a bar, and that was all they needed.

"Running into Cher obviously upset you. I didn't realize

you still had feelings for her," Vic said, once they settled at the bar and ordered their drinks.

"This is the first time I've seen her with someone else."

"I'm sorry, man. I know how that hurts, believe me."

"She can't marry that guy. I won't let her," he said with the sense of conviction that was part of his character. "We'd been together for two years, and she wanted to get married, but I wasn't ready. I was still in school, and more responsibility scared the shit out of me. Now here she is already engaged to someone else?"

"Don't do anything crazy. We can't have you ending up behind bars like Greg."

They both laughed at the recent memory of their brother getting arrested for having sex in public.

"I'm not going to stalk her or anything, if that's what you mean. What can you tell me about this Hilliard dude?"

"I don't know him well. We've talked a few times at some meetings and parties, but from what I know, he seems like a stand-up guy."

"What's his specialty?"

"Neuro."

Nick grunted. The neurosurgeons were generally considered surgical royalty, as though the ability to operate on the human brain made them some kind of super race. This alone gave him reason to dislike Cherilyn's companion. "What do you suggest I do? To get her back, I mean."

"You're asking the wrong one. It's all I can do to handle my own woman. They're difficult. The way they think is completely opposite of the way we think, and they expect us to understand. But when you love one of them, you work like hell to try to understand. That's where I'm at right now. Maybe you should talk to one of your other brothers about this."

After one final drink, Vic called for a car. He and Nick had both ingested too much alcohol over the course of the evening, and driving back home was out of the question.

After the talk with her mother, doubt crept in and had Mona once again wondering if everything she was doing was a mistake. While the initial details for her startup garnered most of her attention, she couldn't ignore the pull she felt to call Rhani. A couple of hours passed before she reached for her phone and pressed her lips together in a tight line before she had the nerve to push the button.

"Rhani Drake-Stafford," she answered.

"Hi, Rhani. This is Ramona, Vic's wife. Did I get you at a bad time?"

"Hi, Mona! No, I'm just doing some paperwork, and I need to take a break before my head explodes. What's new, girl?"

She sighed. "A lot. This is more of a professional call than a friendly one."

"Mona, you know I'm no longer a licensed therapist, right?"

"I know. It doesn't matter. I need to talk to someone I can trust to not run back and tell the family."

"As long as you understand, I'd be glad to listen. Are you and Vic still going through?"

"It's going to take a minute to give you the details. Are you sure you have time? I can call you back later."

"It's fine, Mona. Go ahead, and don't leave anything

out."

Ramona took the next fifteen minutes to explain everything that had occurred since she and Rhani had seen each other on July Fourth. She ended with her decision to start the business and her sale of the car.

"Girl, you weren't kidding when you said a lot has happened. I hope you don't mind, but I always made notes in my client sessions so I wouldn't interrupt them and so I could ask questions. I have several questions for you."

"Okay. I'll tell you anything you want to know."

"You said Vic's distance started after he took the Chief of Surgery position. Prior to that, how did you two spend your time together?"

"We went out to dinner with friends, and took at least two week-long vacations each year—one with the boys and one just the two of us. Sometimes, when he wasn't on call, we just stayed home and watched movies. It didn't seem so important back then, but looking back, I realize it was major."

"I want you to be perfectly honest with me. Was there any physical attraction between you and Ray?"

Mona bit her lip. "Yes, there was, but other than that one kiss, we never acted on it. He was always a gentleman. I think what he really wanted was a friend, since he's new to Atlanta and doesn't really know anyone here."

"You said you told him you were married when you first met. Think back to that night, who would you say was the aggressor?"

A few moments passed before she answered. "I guess I was. I gave him my card and told him to call me."

"At that point, what did you want from him?"

"I don't really know. I suppose just having a male

companion for the night, but when he called me five minutes later, I was flattered. Vic let me go to these events alone so many times, and I was tired of it."

"Now that you know Vic had you followed, how do you feel?"

"At first I was so angry I wanted to scratch his eyes out, but when he said I'd given him no choice, I understood how he felt. All he knew was I hadn't told him where I was going and who I was meeting. I was being purposely secretive to make him jealous."

"Have you two sat down and had a serious talk about everything?"

"Not really, but he did wish me good luck with what I have to do for the business and suggested we go out for breakfast tomorrow, so I can tell him about it. We haven't gone out for breakfast in years."

"That's a good sign, Mona. When you do talk, you need to reassure him of how much you love him. I know the men in this family all seem so self-confident, but they're still just men who want to be loved. It's more than likely Vic *was* jealous, and he went to the extreme because he loves you. He wants to be certain you're still his. If he didn't care, he would've gone right to his lawyer."

These words reached deep into Mona's soul. "I never thought of it that way. Rhani, I need to ask you something else. How is your program going, and how does it feel to be in charge?"

"I've been the boss before, but it was just me and my assistant. This is different. I'm running an entire program, and it's expanding by the month. I've made connections with some schools that have referred several girls to me. It's so exciting."

"Are you ever afraid you might fail?"

"I'm running a non-profit, so it's not like I have income goals. My funding comes from private and government grants, which is used to cover the rent, supplies, utilities, speaker fees and my salary. So far, so good."

"Greg is so proud of you. When I called to get your cell number, he said, 'My wife is one awesome woman.' I want Vic to feel that way about me instead of a parasite."

"Vic doesn't think of you that way. In my opinion, he's always seemed proud of you."

Mona gave a cynical laugh. "Vic is only proud of my appearance. Otherwise, he thinks I'm a twit."

"Oh, Mona, that's not true."

"We could debate this all day, but I know what he said, and I heard *how* he said it."

"Are you starting this business for the right reasons? You should only be doing it because it's your heart's desire, not just to prove a point to your husband. Otherwise, you won't be able to see it through."

"It's the only thing I ever wanted to do, but I never gave it serious thought before, because I was tied up with all the charity work."

"Speaking of money, how did he take you selling the car?"

"Better than I expected. He was disappointed but didn't seem mad. He said that's why he put the title in my name."

"Hmm. I guess Vic really is the serious brother. Greg would've caught a case." Rhani laughed. "So what's your next step?"

"To get a small business lawyer who can"

"I mean with Vic. There's more you need to do besides getting your business up and running, Mona."

The question stumped her. "I guess I was going to see how breakfast goes tomorrow."

"You could do that, or you could be more proactive."

"What do you suggest?"

"It's not my place. You know your husband. Be creative. It doesn't need to be a big gesture, just something that resonates with him." Mona noticed how Rhani didn't give her any answers, but prompted her to search for them herself.

"Right." Mona agreed and had ideas already whizzing through her mind. "Thank you, Rhani."

"If you need to talk some more, just call me. If I'm tied up, leave a message, and I promise to get back to you as soon as I can."

"I'll let you know how it went."

She was in bed but still awake reading when the slam of a car door outside drew her to the window where she saw Vic getting out of a car she didn't recognize.

"Did Nick get a new car?" she asked once he came upstairs.

His deep laugh tickled her senses. She didn't hear it often. "Nick is too broke to buy a bicycle. We both had a few too many drinks, so I called for a car."

He'd never done that before. "You left your car in the city?"

"It's just a car, baby." He untied his bowtie and tossed it onto his dresser then removed his shoes.

If he meant that as a dig, it hit the target, but she ignored it. "Okay. How was the event?"

Vic rubbed his head and let out a rush of air from puffed cheeks. "It was good until Cherilyn showed up with

Derrick Hilliard wearing a big diamond on her left hand."

"What!" She scooted to a sit with her back against the headboard. "So soon?"

He unzipped his pants, kicked them off into a pile beside the bed. His jacket and shirt followed. "Yeah, and Nick didn't take it well at all. He didn't get ugly or anything, but the night went downhill from there. I suggested we leave and go somewhere for a drink so he could vent."

"He still has feelings for her."

"I was as shocked as you are," he said with a slight slur before he flopped down onto the side of the bed. "He asked me to tell him everything I knew about Derrick. What bothered me was when he said he couldn't let her marry him."

She squinted. "What did he mean by that?"

"He swears he's not going to stalk her, but I get the distinct feeling he's about to start a campaign to get her back."

"I hope Nick doesn't do anything he'll regret. From what I know of Derrick, he seems like a nice man."

"Nicer than my brother?"

"I'm not saying that, but maybe there's something about him Cherilyn didn't see in Nick."

"You mean like an already-successful medical career rather than being a poverty-stricken intern?"

She twitched at the edge in his voice. "No, Vic, that's *not* what I meant. You know I love Nick, but maybe Derrick treats her differently than Nick did. Or perhaps they just click with each other."

"True." He fell back onto the pillow and turned to her with a dopey, alcohol-induced smile. "We clicked from the first minute we laid eyes on each other. Remember?"

"How could I forget?"

Vic angled his body toward hers then ran his foot up one of her legs. Her body instantly warmed at his touch. With the exception of the episode in the guest room recently, he hadn't gotten this close in…she couldn't even recall.

"You were wearing this flowered…thing that showed your leg right up to…your hip. You looked so damn good, I almost lost it."

Mona closed her eyes, and visions of that day fifteen years ago appeared. An involuntary smile came to her face. She hadn't been in the yard for more than ten minutes before Vic had persuaded their host to introduce them. The two of them spent the entire evening together, and the rest, as the saying goes, was history.

"You don't…wear things like that…anymore."

"I *am* fifteen years older, you know."

"But your legs can still stop traffic, and you're…still mine."

Mona's jaw dropped, and when she looked down at him, his eyes had closed and his head lolled to the side.

Amazing what alcohol made people reveal.

In the morning, she woke before him, so she took a shower and applied her makeup at the vanity table. He dragged into the bathroom and came up behind her.

"Why didn't you wake me?"

"You were pretty glazed last night. I thought you might want to sleep for a while." She dusted her face with a finishing powder to keep down the shine, a necessity in August weather. "We have plenty of time. I didn't tell my mother what time I'd be picking the boys up."

"Good. I don't think I could rush if I tried. Thank God,

I don't have to go in to work today."

"How did that happen anyway?"

He met her questioning gaze. "I've decided not to go in unless it's absolutely necessary," he said nonchalantly as though it was an afterthought. "I can do my paperwork at home."

She left the bathroom wearing a smile and went into her closet to find something to wear.

A half hour later, he came downstairs dressed in jeans and a t-shirt and surprised her by asking, "Are you going to drive me in your new car?"

"Sure, then we can go see if yours is still where you left it."

Vic got ready to step out the front door, until she said, "It's in the garage." His eyebrows rose, but he didn't comment.

"Nice," he said after he got into the passenger seat and studied the interior of the car for a few minutes. "I never imagined you behind the wheel of an SUV, though."

"It's kind of necessary. I'll probably have to transport equipment and supplies for the business."

"Good thinking."

He didn't need to know the suggestion had come from Ray. "Where are we going?"

"Do you feel like driving up to Peachtree Battle?"

She grinned, knowing they were headed to the spot they used to frequent. "We can pick up your car on the way."

"Sounds like a plan." Vic turned up the volume on the Bang & Olufsen sound system. She knew he wouldn't admit it, but the stereo sounded better than the Naim system in the Bentley. He quickly turned it down and pressed a hand to his forehead. "I need coffee," he groaned. "Can you *please* cruise through Starbucks before we get on the highway?"

Mona turned in the direction of the caffeine addicts' haven and ordered his coffee the way he liked it. He sipped slowly and rested his head back on the headrest while she got them to their destination. She took the interstate to the exit nearest the garage where he'd left the Benz last night. Thankfully, it was still there.

When he exited the car and said, "I'll meet you at the restaurant," Mona had the curious sensation that they were on a date.

Vic arrived right behind her after the ten-minute drive up Peachtree Street. The hostess at *Another Broken Egg* seated them at a table. The eatery was known for its handmade biscuit beignets and gourmet omelettes. Vic requested a carafe of coffee. They placed their orders, and he poured some of the steaming brew for each of them. She knew from the intensity in his eyes when he peered at her over his cup that he had something serious to say, so she waited until he spoke.

"The other night at the hotel I gave you an ultimatum. At the time, I thought it was the only way to handle our...situation, but I should've asked what you want to see happen with us. I need you to be straight with me."

For once no anger lingered between them. This was her chance to open her heart to him.

Chapter Twelve

Vic had promised himself no matter what Mona said, he wouldn't lash out at her. He hadn't allowed himself to hear what was really behind her words before, but now he was ready to listen. She looked into his eyes and all he saw was calmness and confidence.

"I love you, Vic. I've loved you ever since the day we met, and I've never stopped loving you." She glanced down at his hands resting on the tabletop then reached out and gently caressed his fingers. "You asked me what I needed, and when I thought about it, I realized it was actually simple. What I need is for you to share your day with me when you get some time and to ask me about mine. I need us to spend time together away from the house like we're doing right now. Most of all, I need you to realize I have a brain, and I want to use it." She threaded her fingers through his. "I need you to make love to me the way we used to. I feel as though I'm starving when you don't hold me or touch me. No man could ever live up to you, Vic, and I've never wanted anyone other than you."

He squeezed her hand, and desire flared in her eyes. "Let's go home."

"But what about the boys? I should call my mother."

"Let Cee Cee enjoy her time with them. I want to enjoy some time with my wife."

"You call her. She never disagrees with anything you say."

He smiled and put the call on speaker. "So, I guess you're still alive," he said with a chuckle when his mother-in-law answered.

"Good morning, Vic. These boys aren't giving me any problems. They are so polite and well-behaved."

"Thanks to their mother. I'm calling to ask a favor. I want Mona to go somewhere with me, and it'll probably take a couple of hours. Did you have any plans for this afternoon, or can Trey and Julian stay a little while longer?"

"I was just about to call Ramona and let her know we're going to the movies at twelve-fifteen, than out to lunch afterwards. We probably won't be back until close to four o'clock, so you two just take your time."

He winked at Mona. "Thanks, Ma. If there's any problem just call one of our cell numbers, okay?"

"There won't be any problems, Vic. I'll see you later on."

He and Mona rushed through a delicious breakfast that should have been enjoyed slowly, but they were on a mission now, and it couldn't be helped. Vic had the heavier foot, so he arrived back at the house first. He parked in the driveway in the rear of the house, and waited for her to pull in beside him.

She rolled the window down and asked, "What's the matter?"

"Nothing. I want to watch you swim."

"Now? Are you kidding?"

"No. I loved seeing you doing laps the other day."

Her eyes rounded. "You were watching me?"

"From the kitchen window."

"I did my hair and makeup already this morning, and

we just ate," she whined in protest. "You're just going to sit there and watch me?"

He closed the distance between them, cupped the back of her head in one hand and put the other to her waist. "I don't ask you for much, baby. Do this for me."

She seemed to read what he was feeling when she gazed up into his eyes. The tension in her body eased beneath his hands. "I'll be down as soon as I change."

While she was upstairs, Vic went into the house, turned on the sound system and set the speakers to play on the patio. He poured two tall glasses of sparkling water with ice and set them on one of the umbrella tables in the shade. They kept the pool supplies in an outdoor closet, and he grabbed a couple of beach towels. Even though he didn't use the pool often, he loved the privacy the heavy shrubbery gave the entire pool area. Stereo speakers nestled among the bushes provided surround sound.

The more he thought about what Mona had said during breakfast, the more he wanted to make this morning all about focusing on her. The neglect she'd felt was his doing, and he'd unwittingly turned a blind eye to her to focus on his job. If he didn't want to lose her, he had to make it his goal to show her that she was still Number One in his life and how much he still desired her.

Mona finally came out the door from the kitchen wearing a black one-piece bathing suit cut high on her hips that made her legs appear even longer. She'd pulled her hair up into a knot at the top of her head, and her face was cleansed of the makeup. She walked to the table, raised her oversized sunglasses and peered at him. He handed her the glass of sparkling water. She took a long swallow and placed her shades on the table. "Are you really going to just sit here and watch me swim?"

"For the time being." He let his gaze openly run down

her body, and she shifted from one foot to the other as though his scrutiny made her nervous. "Go ahead. Show me what you've got."

Vic wanted to laugh at the way she frowned, but he hid it until she turned her back and walked to the edge of the pool. She dove off the side, and he moved to a chaise closer to the water. He kicked off his shoes and lay back with his hands clasped behind his head. Her graceful limbs moving through the water mesmerized him. Damn, she was beautiful. Of course, that wasn't her only positive trait, but having such an attractive wife would make any man proud. He rose from the chaise, removed his phone from his pants pocket and stood at the edge of the pool. As she made a return lap, he caught her eye and began to strip off his clothes. The t-shirt hit the tile first then his hands rushed to unzip his pants. He stepped out of them leaving him in only a pair of black boxer briefs. Mona stopped swimming and focused her intent gaze on his every move. When he hooked his thumbs inside the elastic of his briefs and pulled them down, her hand flew to her mouth.

He launched into the water with his erection leading the way, thankful it was warm from two weeks of ninety degree temperatures. Mona continued to stare with an open mouth. It took a lot to render her speechless, and his masculine pride soared at her expression.

"Vic, what are you thinking?!"

"I'm thinking about making love to my wife in this nice warm water."

She glanced around as though they were running from the cops. "You were standing naked in the middle of our back yard!"

Vic moved closer to where she stood in waist-high water near the steps. "That's right, and you're getting ready to join me."

She grabbed his wrists when he reached for the straps of her suit. "What if someone is watching us?" She retreated until he had backed her against the pool wall.

"Baby, nobody can see into the yard. Maite's gone for the weekend, so it's just us. You used to be the fearless one." He continued toward her, but there was no aggression in the way he approached her like there was the night in the guest room. "Remember the time we made love in my parents' pool while they were away on vacation? If I recall correctly, you didn't have a problem with it then."

"We were stupid college kids who didn't give a second thought to anything."

"Maybe we don't need to give anything a second thought now." He pressed his body against hers, wrapped his arms around her waist and lowered his head until their lips met. The last thing he wanted to do was to rush, so he let his lips linger on hers for a moment before he ran his tongue around the outline of her mouth. Her body relaxed in his embrace, and she opened just enough to take in the tip of his tongue. He took advantage of the invitation and plunged deeper while his hands worked the straps of her bathing suit over her shoulders and down her arms.

"We can't do this," she protested weakly.

"Yes, we can. I can make love to *my* wife in *my* pool on *my* property anytime I want." The thought someone could possibly be watching them just made Vic more eager. It only took a couple of seconds to pull her suit down to her waist. Her bare breasts were perkier thanks to his brother, Charles' surgical skills. He dipped his head and her nipple pebbled between his lips. Mona stretched her arms out to both sides on the pool's edge to keep her balance. Her head dropped back and she surrendered. Everything faded into the background except the delicious sensation of the soft mound between his lips. She uttered a moan when one of his hands dipped below the water and teased the folds between her taut thighs until her hips moved in tandem with his hand. To position himself between her legs, he clasped his hands under her booty and lifted her. Her legs tightened around him and he slid his erection up and down the spot that made her lock her hands behind his neck and writhe uncontrollably against him. In response, she moved her hips to get him to slip inside her. Their rhythm sloshed the warm water over the side of the pool.

"No, not yet," he said between ragged breaths.

They needed to get more comfortable. Vic tread through the water holding her in position then eased her down onto the steps. Mona grabbed the metal railing and rested her back on the steps. Her legs opened wide inviting him in. Before he entered the heaven he craved, he snatched off the elastic tie holding her hair on top of her head. He needed to run his fingers through her thick hair when they made love.

She grabbed his shoulders and tried to pull him closer, but he backed away so his eyes could take her in. There wasn't a more erotic picture to a man than his woman offering herself to him. But even more beautiful was seeing his wife in all her natural glory, free of all the trappings expected of her. Her skin was bare and flawless, and her hair spread behind her head like a peacock's plume.

"I've never seen you look more beautiful," he said, running a hand down her cheek. "I love you natural, without all the makeup." He moved forward, hemming her in with his palms pressed into the steps on either side of her body. Urgency vibrated through his whole body, and he plunged into her with his tongue and his lusty erection.

The animalistic sound that came from her throat let him know she no longer cared if the whole neighborhood was watching. Her nails dug into his shoulders, and her hips matched his movement. The buoyancy of the water only added to the sensuality of the moment. He stroked until she sounded as though she was just about to give in to the ecstasy. He abruptly withdrew, took her hand and led her up the stairs back to the armless chaise, both of them walking on passion-weakened legs. When they reached the lounge, he fell back onto it and pulled her on top of him. She instinctively scooted down so she could corral his bobbing erection between her palms. Her hands twisted and squeezed him as he disappeared between her lips. *Damn, she'd become a virtuoso at this over the years.* And she knew his body as well as he knew hers. The minute he started to groan and work his hips, she momentarily released him and stood. To help her, he fisted himself so she could lower onto him. Mona's hair fell forward and curtained her face as she bounced and rotated her hips like she was doing a hula dance. It didn't take long for them to hit that high. Good thing the pool furniture was sturdy or it would've ended up destroyed by their hedonistic hijinks, and as they often did in the past, they climaxed together.

Mona collapsed on top of him with a throaty laugh completely spent. "I almost forgot how good we are at this," she said, once she caught her breath.

Vic smoothed her wet hair back from her face. "That's my fault, and I'm sorry for making you forget. It won't happen again."

"You promise?"

He took her face between his hands and brushed a gentle kiss across her forehead. "I promise."

The moment was ruined when the opening riff of Michael Jackson's *Working Day and Night* sounded from his phone. It was his customized ringtone for the hospital. Vic dropped his head back and closed his eyes for a couple of seconds.

"Answer it. You can't let it ring."

After a moment's hesitation, he reluctantly reached over

to the table and answered. "Stafford."

"Dr. Stafford, this is Khloe in Dr. Sternhagen's office. He asked me to call you, because he needs every available surgeon immediately."

"Okay. What is it?"

Mona stood and lifted one leg so he could get up.

"There's been a building collapse downtown on Spring Street. Dozens are severely injured. Some of the victims have been taken to Grady, but the majority of them are being brought to us. How soon can you be here?"

He was already looking around for his drawers and his pants. At least they'd been in the water, so he didn't need to shower. "Give me twenty minutes. I'm leaving now."

Mona handed him his clothes. "I'm sorry, baby. This looks like it might be an overnighter. Building collapse with multiple traumas." His appreciative gaze caressed her nude body. "You outdid yourself, girl." He smiled as he pulled on his underwear and jeans then left a penetrating kiss on her mouth. "I love you."

The hospital called in every available surgeon to deal with more than a dozen people admitted from the building collapse. The surgeries Vic performed were intricate and required his full concentration. The entire twelve hours he spent at the hospital, he talked to himself in order to keep his focus on the job at hand even though his thoughts remained at home in the pool.

He'd left the house feeling as though his mind and body had been supercharged. What just happened between Mona and him had been a long time coming. During the past two years, when they'd made love, often they were just going through the motions. And sometimes they just didn't bother because they were tired or angry or just plain disinterested. Today was the complete opposite. Even though Mona was worried about someone seeing them in the pool, she'd been so responsive, and it aroused him even more. What occurred to him as he was elbow deep in a bowel resection was that he'd given her something to respond to. He'd started out with an apology, and he hadn't come home expecting her to be lying there with her legs spread just because he thought he deserved it. Their honest conversation during breakfast at the restaurant opened the door to this reunion of sorts. Vic knew he needed to do more if he wanted their marriage to return to the way it used to be. Maybe he could arrange a surprise vacation for the two of them, but only after they took Trey and Julian somewhere special first. After he went home and caught a few hours' sleep, he planned to place a call to the travel agent they'd used in the past.

Mona watched Vic rush to the car pulling his t-shirt over his head. Suddenly she felt exposed and self-conscious, even though no one else was around. She wrapped her body in one of the beach towels he'd put on the table and her head in the other and returned to the chaise. Afterglow was better with the one with whom you'd just made love, but solitary afterglow was better than nothing.

Vic had literally shocked her pants off when he stripped down to his golden skin and dove into the pool with her. It had been more than a decade since they'd been skinny dipping together. Back then, it had only been naked swimming. What they had just done was wonderful. So wonderful she almost didn't get an attitude when the hospital called. Almost.

The only thing she could do to overcome her resentment toward the entity that paid their bills was to close her eyes and replay their interlude. She'd almost forgotten what an attentive, passionate lover Vic was. This morning was different, though. He wanted to show her how much he wanted their marriage to work. He'd let himself relax long enough to let his guard down, and he'd stepped outside of the box in which he'd put himself for the past couple of years. And she adored him for it.

When he stood over her in all his naked six-foot-two glory, she could barely contain herself. He was so handsome, and his long, slender fingers weren't just gifted at surgery.

He still loves me. Mona indulged in the realization.

Eventually, she got up and went into the house to change and go pick up the boys at her mother's house. As it was, she hadn't watched her grandsons in years. It wasn't a good idea for them to wear out their welcome. Mona called to make sure they were back from lunch and the movies. As she got dressed, she stared at her image in the mirror. Vic had told her she looked beautiful, and for once Mona liked what she saw. She pulled her hair back into a ponytail, redressed in the jeans and t-shirt she'd worn to breakfast, armed the security system and drove to Decatur feeling relaxed and content. Her positive self-esteem fizzled as soon as her mother came to the door.

"My Lord, Ramona, you look like something the cat dragged in!"

"Well, I feel wonderful." She ignored the criticism and brushed past the older woman and walked back toward the kitchen.

"You could've at least put on some make-up, if you weren't going to do your hair."

"There is nothing wrong with my hair, Ma. It's called a ponytail."

Cee Cee looked her up and down with a frown. "Yes, and it should only be worn by horses. I thought you said you and Vic were having a night out. I hope and pray you didn't go out like that."

"Where are the boys?" Mona asked, hoping to deter her mother's critical observation.

"Outside on the back porch playing their games. You didn't answer me, Ramona. Did you go out with him looking—"

She crossed kitchen and opened the back door to the porch. "Hey guys. Do you have everything packed up?"

"Hi, Mom," Julian answered. "Our stuff is in the living room."

"Okay, say goodbye to Grandma and thank her for letting you invade her space, then take your bags out to the car. I'll be there in a few minutes."

Her sons re-entered the house, hugged their grandmother and left out the front door dragging their duffel bags behind them. Once they were outside, Mona turned to her mother and spoke with quiet but desperate firmness. "Ma, we went swimming this morning. It didn't make sense to put on full makeup to get into the pool."

"There is such a thing as waterproof makeup," the older woman groused.

"You know what? I've been listening to all of your ridiculous ideas on how I should look for as long as I can remember, and I'm sick and tired of it."

Her mother's jaw dropped. "Well, I'm not the one who came here moaning and crying about her husband losing interest in her. I would think you'd be trying to do everything in your power to keep him interested."

Mona stepped closer. "This is really something coming from a woman with no man at all." Cee Cee jerked as though she'd been slapped. "You're wrong. Vic and I went out for breakfast this morning. I got up and did my hair and makeup like I always do. After we ate, he said he wanted to come back home and watch me swim. I'll spare you the details, but he made love to me for the first time in months–in the pool. And he said he loves me without all the makeup, that I've never looked so beautiful. Thanks for watching the boys." She turned on her heel and strode out the front door leaving her mother wide-eyed and speechless.

The next two weeks whizzed by in a blur as Mona stepped into new territory. Vic had always had his own office, and she didn't want to share, so she worked on creating her own space. She emptied the guest bedroom of everything except one comfortable chair and a lamp and replaced them with a desk, art table and file cabinet. One wall now held a large white board and the other was covered with corkboard where she could hang photos and drawings. When she felt satisfied with the room, she made a trip to the office supply store for drawing pencils, sketchbooks and the run-of-the-mill supplies she needed. The next day, she visited the attorney Jamila recommended and set up the business incorporation.

That night, after Vic got in from being at the hospital for eighteen hours, he crawled into bed beside her. "What have you been up to?"

"I had an appointment with a lawyer who's going to do my incorporation, and Jamila took me to visit two workrooms. It was fascinating."

He scooted closer, put an arm around her waist and pulled her back against his body. "What are they?"

Thrilled because he wanted to know about what she'd been up to, Mona opened her mouth and the words came out in a torrent. "First we went to a workroom in Norcross, then she took me to the Factory Girls[3]. It's a fashion incubator focused on high-level apparel designers based in the Southeast. They provide studio space, access to pattern makers, sample makers and production, all *right here* in Atlanta. Their goal is to grow the local fashion design industry, by creating a place for local talent to flourish." His chest vibrated against her back. "Are you laughing at me?"

"No. It's nice to hear you so excited about something. Go on, baby. Finish telling me about it."

She rolled over to face him and continued. "They not only work with designers, but they give classes, lectures, interactive discussions, and workshops for the fashion community. And you know what?"

"What," he said with a chuckle.

"I signed up to take a class on the legal steps to take to protect the business and to make sure my products are consumer ready. It's supposed to teach the difference between trademarks, copyrights and patents and what steps to take to make sure my line is consumer ready in terms of marketing, social media advertising, advertising with bloggers and label laws, FTC stuff and recent case rulings."

He hooked a finger under her chin and raised her head so he could look into her eyes. "Wow. Seeing you like this is hot."

Mona laughed. "Huh?"

"It is. You've never been so fired up about anything since we've been married. I like it. So what else did you do?"

"After that, we went to meet with a couple of artists, since I can't even draw stick people." The grin on his face sent warmth flowing through her. It wasn't the heat of arousal, but a sweet, cozy feeling like drinking warm cocoa after coming in from the cold. His breathing slowed, and she realized he was fast asleep. This time she didn't mind, because he'd listened to her.

Her dream really started to begin to take shape when she received a call from a woman who identified herself as LaLa Anthony's assistant. She said her boss had recently had a conversation with Rayvon Patterson in which he told her about Ramona's business idea and asked if she could help. When she said LaLa was willing to do a video chat with her, Mona thought she'd misunderstood her, and asked her to repeat herself. The woman then proceeded to rattle off a few dates when the TV star/fashion designer would be available. Once Ramona recovered her ability to speak, she repeatedly thanked the assistant and gave her a date a week out.

"This is *really* happening," she said aloud to herself. "Ray kept his word." It amazed her that he was willing to help her after she'd kicked him to the curb. He cared about her, and made the soft spot she had for him even softer. What could she do to show her appreciation without Vic going off the deep end? She'd have to take some time to think about it.

Making a lunch date with Daphine was the next thing on her To Do list. It was time to tell her friend what was going on in her life. Ramona called her, and they agreed to meet the next day. Before they ended the call, Daphine asked, "What's going on? I haven't heard from you in ages. You had me all up in my feelings, as Tia always says." She chuckled, referring to her thirteen-year-old daughter.

"I'm sorry, girl. Everything has been crazy in my house lately. I'll tell you all about it tomorrow. I promise."

"You'd better. I'll meet you at Strip at one o'clock."

Immediately after she hung up, she called Jamila to tell her about the video chat with LaLa Anthony. "Since you're my stylist, I need you to be on the call with me. I think she'll understand, because her stylist is her business partner."

"When is it?"

"Next Thursday at two o'clock. Can you make it?"

"Do you mind telling me how in the world you got an appointment with Madame Carmelo?"

Ramona bit her lip and hesitated for a moment. "A friend of mine knows her. He set it up."

"Rayvon Patterson?"

"Yes, as a matter of fact, it was. Why?"

"I never heard you mention any celebrity connections before."

"Because I don't have any. He did it as a favor, and I'm so grateful."

"Oh, cool. I'll be there on Thursday."

The next day, she joined Daphine at Strip in Atlantic Station and revealed her news.

"That's fantastic!"

"Yes, it is, especially since Vic has ordered me to stay away from Ray."

Daphine slapped a hand to her chest. "He did?"

"Yes, ma'am. I guess I'd better start from the beginning."

"Please."

While they ate, Ramona told her friend all that had been going on between her and Vic, right up to selling the Bentley, their pool rendezvous and her conversation with her mother.

When she finished, Daphine sat open-mouthed. "My God, Mona! You weren't kidding. I had no idea. How do you feel about Vic making a demand like that?"

"He was being unfair, because I knew there was nothing between Ray and me. You know Vic. He's all or nothing, but I'm convinced now that he loves me, so I'm willing to go along with his conditions."

"Marv and I have had our problems in the past, so I understand, but anyone can see from the way Vic looks at you that he still loves you."

"Most of Vic's adoring looks didn't have anything to do with who I *am*, just how I *look*. I hated to admit it to myself, but it's true. I want him to be proud of me for more than the outer stuff. The problem was I hadn't given him much to admire."

"Not true, Ramona! You're a great mother, and you've built a stellar reputation in the medical community for your charity work."

"You know what I mean. I look at his brothers' wives, and they all have their own careers or businesses. I have nothing of my own to brag about, but it won't be for long. I'm getting ready to start my own fashion line, and guess what?" Daphine stared at her with expectation. "Carmelo Anthony's wife, LaLa, has agreed to give me some coaching."

"Are you serious?"

She told Daphine about the phone call with the famous fashionista's assistant. "I've talked to my mother about helping me out with the boys when I'm busy. Now I guess I need to tell my mother-in-law."

"Well, that shouldn't be a problem. She adores you. I know you'll have her support."

"I hope so, because I'm going to need everyone's support in order to get this business off the ground. Maite is willing to do some overtime, but that costs us more money. My mother said she's willing to help out with the boys, only I'm not so sure I can count on her."

"Why not?"

"She thinks this whole idea is ridiculous. My working messes with her vision of my being the pampered wife, which was *her* dream, not mine."

Daphine's face broke into a genuine smile. "If no one else is proud, I am. Do you need an assistant?"

"Give me a break, girl. That would only cut into your shopping and salon visits. Besides, I would have to fire you for not showing up for work, because you're in the middle of a mani/pedi." Both women laughed knowing how true it was.

"You're probably right. You can count on me to help with the boys if you need it. I just don't know how they'd feel about spending time with my girls."

"I can't speak for Julian, but Trey will probably love it. I didn't tell you about the little girl he's all cross-eyed over right now." Ramona filled Daphine in about Megan while they finished lunch and promised to get together again soon.

Ramona called her mother-in-law when she got in the car. "Hi, Mama. It's Mona. Are you busy?"

"Not right now. Adanna is coming by later to go over some foundation business. How are you?"

"Better. That's why I'm calling. I wanted to stop by and talk to you. What time is Adanna supposed to be there?"

"About five. You sound like you're in the car. Can you come now?"

Vic's mother was the final person she needed to talk to. Ramona hoped and prayed she would support her the way she did her other daughters-in-law. Lillian Stafford was open-minded and encouraged the women who'd married her sons to pursue their own dreams. "I'm on my way."

Lillian Stafford opened the door looking cool and stylish in a white Capri outfit that complemented the gray in her hair. "Let's go into the kitchen."

Mona followed her to the table where a pitcher of freshly-made lemonade sat waiting. Her mother-in-law's kitchen table was the heart of her house. She thought of the many conversations they'd had over the years in this same spot. This one somehow seemed more significant to Ramona than all the others. Beyond knowing she had her husband's mother's support, she needed her approval. Ever since she and Vic had started dating, Mama had provided the listening ear Mona didn't get from her own mother. She amazed Mona with the wisdom she shared and how she stayed on top of what was going on in the world, the community and her family. She never failed to give sound advice whenever any of her daughters-in-law needed it, and they all loved her dearly.

"You sounded like something was on your mind," she said, pouring Ramona a glass of cold lemonade and sliding it across the table. "How are things with you and Vic?"

"Vic and I are doing better, but a lot has been going on between us." She spent the next few minutes bringing her mother-in-law up to date on the whole Rayvon issue, her stepping down from the fundraising and even what Vic told her about the woman in Chicago. She skipped the part about their pool adventure and merely said with a smile, "And things have been a whole lot more romantic lately."

"I'm disappointed to hear about these temptations both of you experienced, but I understand why they happened. I'm just thankful neither of you gave in completely. Vic loves you, Mona, and he values what you two have built together. What surprises me is his attitude about you *not having anything to do*." She smirked. "He never mentioned being unhappy with you staying at home before."

"Mama, I think we're both at different stages in our lives. Vic wants more than a stay-at-home mom for a wife. I want more than to just be a medical widow. We're realizing we have to come to terms with our new expectations of each other."

"Marriages change and grow, Ramona, and those changes aren't usually easy. In fact, they're never easy, but if we're in tune with our husband or wife, we can weather the storms and come out stronger." She patted Mona's hand. "I'm proud of you for being committed to Vic and not giving up because it got hard. And I believe you were born to be a fashion maven, girl."

"Thank you, Mama. I'm scared, but I'm excited at the same time. It's a big step for me, and I want Vic to see me make a go of this. I don't know what might happen if I fail."

"You're not going to fail. Now tell me what I can do to help you."

"That's the reason I'm here. You've always helped us out with the boys, but now that I'll have these new responsibilities, I might need to call on you more often. Of course, Maite is available in an emergency, but I'd have to pay her overtime. And my mother said she can pitch in every now and then."

Lillian's eyes widened slightly. "Really? That's good. She needs to get to know the boys better now that they're getting older. They're great kids."

"Yeah, they are." Before she left, she told her mother-in-law about Trey's crush and the upcoming chat with LaLa Anthony. She found she was feeling more confident about becoming a businesswoman.

Chapter Thirteen

Normally, Vic wasn't a pessimistic person, and since he and Mona had been getting along so well, he kept trying to shake the feeling that things between them had become too good too soon. What was wrong with him? At the moment, she was engrossed in her work and seemed elated with the whole process. They were communicating better. Their sex life had been resurrected from the dead, and he'd cut back his hours at the hospital by doing a good portion of his administrative work at home. The CRE infection on the surgical floor had been resolved. The boys were doing well in school and both of them appeared to be happy with his increased presence. So, why did he have this nagging feeling it was all going to come crashing down around him?

The last three reports from the investigator showed nothing out of the ordinary in Mona's daily schedule. He chided the negative little devil sitting on his shoulder suggesting his positive attitude was premature and the other shoe was about to drop.

One afternoon, while he was going over some patient files, his cell phone rang. When he saw Superior Investigations on the display, his throat tightened. Why would McClendon be calling him after all these weeks?

"Stafford."

"Vic, Doug McClendon. Are you free to talk?"

"Yes." A warning alarm sounded in his head. "What's up?"

"You asked me to let you know immediately if your wife had any more personal contact with Rayvon Patterson."

His heart hammered, and a lump that felt like the size of a cantaloupe formed in his throat. "I did."

"Well, she just met him at McCormick & Schmick's in CNN Center."

It took a minute for him to take in what he'd just heard, and the shock rendered him briefly immobile. He took off his glasses and rubbed his eyes before he could speak. "What?"

"I'm sorry, but you said you wanted to know."

"No, you did the right thing." A suffocating sensation tightened Vic's throat, and he swallowed hard. "How long has she been there?"

"About ten minutes. I assume she's staying for lunch, or she would've exited the building by now."

You're probably right. Thanks for the warning."

McClendon cleared his throat. "Vic, don't do anything rash, especially out in public."

Vic barely heard his advice. His mind was overcome with emotion. "I…I'll get back to you." He ended the call without saying goodbye.

Mona had lied to him again. If she wanted to continue her relationship with Patterson, why couldn't she be woman enough to admit it? She didn't need to deceive him. All along, he'd suspected she had been more influenced by his wealth than she was willing to confess.

He buzzed Shondell and struggled to keep his voice normal. "Do I have anything on my calendar this afternoon?"

"Just a follow-up with Dr. Carroll and Dr. Wiley at three o'clock."

"Okay, I'm going out for about an hour."

He grabbed his keys, stalked past her desk and headed for the garage with single-minded purpose. Within the confines of his car, he silently asked himself why he was going to confront Mona and her… The thought of what Rayvon Patterson really was to his wife made him sick. Was it his money, his youth, his body or all three? Whatever it was, she couldn't seem to resist him. It had always been that way. The athletes always pulled the women, no matter how dumb or how ugly they might be. Mona was the only woman he ever loved, and even with all of their recent conflict, he still loved her more than his own life. But if she no longer loved him, they needed to move on, and he had no other choice but to end their marriage. He refused to live a lie.

The sound of the engine racing snapped him back to the present, and he eased his foot off of the accelerator. He needed to keep his wits about him, so he didn't go into the restaurant acting like a maniac. It was a typical Friday in downtown Atlanta. At one-fifteen, the downtown streets were clogged with employees out to spend the first part of their paychecks on a good lunch or a little shopping. And none of them cared that he was in a hurry.

He didn't even know what he would do when he got there, but he couldn't stop himself. Suddenly he wondered what might happen if Patterson decided to get physical. Vic couldn't worry that Rayvon was more than twenty years younger than him and in admirable condition; he needed to confront them together, even if it ended with him getting his ass whipped. Mona probably assumed he wouldn't have the nerve to meet Patterson face to face.

Marc had always been the most physical one among his brothers. Not that he was aggressive, but he was never one to back down from a fight. Vic remembered several times his younger brother had been sentenced to punishment for getting into a street brawl when he was in high school. Greg had been the motor mouth and a quick thinker who usually talked his way out of conflicts.

He parked in the deck opposite CNN Center and bounded across the street dodging the cars blaring their horns at him. When he reached the front doors of the restaurant, he slowed his pace and tried to calm his breathless rage.

"I'm meeting Ray Patterson," he told the hostess once he entered.

She checked the reservation list. "I'm sorry, sir, I don't see a Patterson. He might not have made a reservation, but you can look around and see if you spot him."

He managed a weak smile. "Thanks."

A few seconds later, he saw Mona sitting across from Patterson at a table in the center of the room. He watched them for a moment while they appeared to be studying the menu before he slowly approached. She was the first to look up and see him standing above them and seemed too startled to say anything. Patterson finally glanced his way with one raised eyebrow, obviously wondering who he was. Before he could speak, Vic bent down and said to Mona, "I guess this meeting is important enough to you to put your marriage on the line."

She immediately tried to explain. "Vic, this is business. Ray got an invitation to a huge fashion event, and he wanted me to—"

"He could've FedEx'd it to you."

"Vic, please listen. He thought—"

"That's real nice and everything, but I don't care what he thought." He faced Patterson, still keeping his voice low and controlled. "You used this as a reason to stay in touch with Mona. I don't know who the aggressor is in this little game—you or her—but I want you both to know it's the *last* time."

Patterson, who hadn't moved a single one of his impressive muscles, finally spoke. "You're wrong, man. I meant no disrespect."

"Yeah, whatever." Vic threw up his hand. "If I find out you've seen each other again, I won't be responsible for what happens."

Mona jumped up from her chair. "Are you threatening us?"

"Oh, so now it's *us*?" He moved closer so they were face to face. "*Us* used to be you and me. Sit down, Mona."

She glared at him with her lips parted as though she were in shock. "Vic, I didn't mean it that way."

"I. Said. Sit. Down." Vic bent down so he could look Patterson in the eye, and his voice hardened. "My wife apparently believes I'm not a violent man, because I've never carried a gun or gotten into a street fight, but she's mistaken. I know dozens of way to kill a man without ever pulling a trigger or throwing a punch. Don't try me." He grabbed Mona by the forearm and jerked her from her seat, but not before she snatched up the papers she and Patterson had been reading from the table. "Stay away from my wife." Vic ground the words out between his teeth.

Patrons seated near them momentarily stopped eating and gaped as he pulled her between the tables toward the front door.

"Vic, you're hurting me," she protested under her breath as she stumbled along and tried to keep up with him in her stilettos.

"Where's your car?"

"Ow! In the deck across the street." She tried to yank from his grasp, but he kept a tight hold on her upper arm while he waited for the light to change.

"Give me your keys."

"Why? I can drive myself home."

She shrunk back at the way he glared at her then reached into her purse and handed him the keys. Vic hit the button on the key fob and opened the driver's side door.

"Get in."

He kept the key in his hand as he went around the car and entered on the other side. The air held a touch of early fall briskness Atlantans welcomed, so he put the key into the ignition, reached across her and rolled down the windows without starting the engine. His heart was still pounding; he dropped his head back on the headrest, closed his eyes and inhaled deeply, hoping to reduce his heart rate. Mona didn't make a peep during the few minutes it took for his head to clear. Without opening his eyes, he asked, "Do you want to be with him?"

"No, Vic. I thought I made it clear before."

He raised his head and looked at her. "I thought you did too, but you insist on seeing him when I asked you not to."

"Ray called and said he wanted to give me this information."

"You said that already. Why couldn't you tell him to overnight it to you?"

"I don't know. I guess I was so excited about the chance to be part of this fashion expo, I wanted to get my hands on it right away."

"Are you sure that's all you wanted to get your hands on? What would've gone down if I hadn't shown up?"

"I would've had lunch, taken my papers and gone home, Vic. Ray has a girlfriend. He's not interested in me."

He uttered a scornful laugh. "He's a baller. He probably has several girlfriends. You're just one of many."

"And if he does, it's none of my business. All I wanted was the information on the expo. It's an event for black designers put on in conjunction with the National Black Chamber of Commerce, and it would give my line some great exposure. Don't be mad at me for wanting to get ahead."

"I understand how you feel, but as your husband, I'm asking you not to see him in person again for *any* reason. I've given you every chance to make this right. You say you love me, but you refuse to do what I ask. If you refuse, you're saying you don't respect me or care about my feelings. That would leave me with only one option–to call Cam and have him file for a legal separation."

The finality in Vic's voice scared her to death. Vic hadn't made a scene. He'd been so calm in the restaurant, and his voice so controlled, it was lethal. The way he'd threatened Ray left no doubt in her mind that he had reached his breaking point.

"I didn't intend to disrespect you. When he told me about the expo, I got so excited, I wasn't thinking about anything but getting the information from Ray so I could register for the event before the deadline. It would be such a great opportunity for Reverie.

Her eyes widened when he suddenly started to laugh. "For the past couple of years you've been ticked off, because I was doing everything in my power to excel at my job. Now it looks like we've changed places." His admission was dredged from a place beyond logic and reason.

Even though she felt the stab of guilt at causing yet another blow-up between them, she had to smile at his reaction. "It seems that way, but the point is, you're jealous."

Vic raised his head from the seat and turned to her with a rueful smile. "You're damn straight I'm jealous."

Finally hearing him say it gave Mona a twisted sense of satisfaction. She regretted him feeling dishonored, but a tiny part of her basked in the knowledge of her power. "I've never seen you be so…territorial." She gazed into his eyes. "That was so hot."

His gaze clung to hers, analyzing her for a long moment. Suddenly, he threw his head back and let out a loud peal of laughter. "I never had any reason to be territorial with you. But I want you to understand I'm not giving you up to anyone. Oh, hell. Nobody on this planet makes me as crazy as you do. I love you, woman." He reached across her, started the ignition, hit the control for the air and rolled up the windows. She uttered a small gasp when he forcefully pulled her to him and took her mouth with a savage intensity. His hand slid between her legs and ran up her thigh until he touched her most sensitive spot.

"What are you doing?" she murmured against his mouth.

"What does it feel like I'm doing?"

They were in the front seat in broad daylight, so they couldn't do anything too obvious, but when she opened her thighs, he seemed to put their location out of his mind. He pulled the crotch of her panties to the side and let his fingers, which had been trained to do other precise and delicate work, tease her until she moaned in delight. Her hips matched the rhythm of his hand, and he increased the pace until she cried out in ecstasy. In the midst of their outdoor orgy, a man walked past and stopped in his tracks. He backtracked two steps and ogled them for a couple of seconds before he laughed and went to his car.

Mona saw their voyeur for a brief moment when she opened her eyes, but when he moved on, she reached for Vic's waistband, worked the button free and pulled the zipper down. He made a passionate sound then stunned her by lowering the back of his seat. When she dipped her head and took him between her lips, his body went stiff, and he gave a loud, lustful groan then threaded his trembling fingers into her hair. Mona couldn't believe how he seemed to completely forget where they were. He would never have done anything like this before. The possibility of being seen was too great. He'd changed so much in the past few months; it was almost hard to believe. Vic closed his eyes and let her pleasure him. His long legs stretched out in front of him as his hips worked to her rhythm. Without taking her attention from the task at hand, she reached into the console and grabbed a handful of napkins just as he exploded in release.

"Now *that* was hot," he murmured before they collapsed in laughter and she cleaned him up. "What time is it?"

She glanced at the clock on the dash. "Two-seventeen."

"I have a three o'clock meeting," he said, looking as though he didn't want to move.

She laughed, knowing he was temporarily incapacitated. "I guess you'd better get back then."

Chapter Fourteen

*T*hree days after the restaurant confrontation in CNN Center, Vic came home from the hospital after another twelve-hour shift to find Mona's car missing from the driveway. "Hi, Maite," he greeted the housekeeper who was busy in the kitchen chopping vegetables on the cutting board.

"Hello, Mr. Vic. Have you had lunch yet?"

"No. I didn't bother to eat at the hospital."

"Let me make you a sandwich before you go upstairs."

"Thanks. Did Mona say where she was going?"

"Yes, she said she was meeting Mrs. Weber for lunch."

He crossed the room to where Maite always put the mail on the kitchen counter. A non-standard-size envelope addressed to Dr. and Mrs. Victor Stafford caught his eye. He picked it up, opened it, and what he read sent heat up the back of his neck.

With a roof over our heads and floors under our feet
The Patterson's move is finally complete!
You are cordially invited to our open house party.

Saturday, October twenty-fourth

8:00 PM

490 West Paces Ferry Road, Atlanta, GA

No gifts please.

Vic glared at the writing then pounded his fist on the counter.

Maite jumped. "Is everything all right?"

He glared at the fancy script on the invitation. "I don't know." While he waited for her to finish preparing his sandwich, he scratched his jaw and silently asked himself why Patterson would send this to his home addressed to both Mona and him after their face-off just a few days ago? Was it a taunt? This was the house where the investigator had taken photos of the hotshot baller and his wife. The house they had picked out together. What message was he sending, and did Mona already know about it?

Maite warily handed him a bottle of water and a plate holding a turkey sandwich garnished with lettuce, tomato and a handful of chips on the side. He took the plate and the invitation with him up to the bedroom. When Mona returned he would ask her about it. What he needed right now was some sleep. After he ate, he tucked the envelope into the night table, covered himself with a throw and sank back into the pillows on the bed.

Sometime later, the soothing sensation of soft hands caressing his back woke him. At first he thought he was dreaming, but then he opened his eyes and saw Mona sitting beside him. He couldn't remember the last time she'd awakened him that way.

"Hey," he said, smiling up at her until the last thought he'd had before he'd drifted off to sleep returned. His smile faded. "What time is it?"

"Almost seven o'clock. Are you going to eat dinner?"

"I feel like I just ate lunch. Maite made me a sandwich before I crashed." He sat up and rubbed his eyes then reached into the night table and handed her the envelope. "Can you explain this to me?"

She took it and removed the card from the envelope with a curious squint. "What is it?"

"You tell me."

He studied her expression as she read. "I guess Ray got his closing arranged. That's nice."

"Nice? Why is he sending this to you after what happened the other day?"

"If I'm not mistaken," Mona picked up the envelope and flipped it over. "It's addressed to both of us, Vic."

"Why?"

Her shoulders drooped. "I guess he's trying to say there are no hard feelings."

"Hard feelings? Why the hell should there be any hard feelings on his part. He's the one who's been out of line."

"Honey, look at this rationally. If he wanted to see me, why would he have invited you? He's proud of his new house, and he wants everyone to meet his family."

"You knew he had a family?" Vic jumped up and stalked across the room. "I guess it didn't matter, because he knew *you* had one."

"Vic, calm down. His *family* is his mother and four brothers and sisters. They are coming to live with him."

He stopped pacing and felt a little foolish now, but he wasn't going to admit it. "I don't care who's coming to live with him. I'm not going to celebrate in a house you chose with him."

"You know you're being ridiculous, right? He only asked me to go with him so he could have another person's opinion. It's always been his dream to be able to put his family into a house. From what I understand, they always lived in an apartment in the hood."

"Well, that's a touching story, but it doesn't have anything to do with youor me. RSVP that we won't be there."

She looked at him with fire in her eyes. "Can't you put your jealousy aside just for one night? He's trying to show you there is and never was anything between us."

Her insistence only fueled his anger, and he'd heard enough. "I'm not talking about this anymore. Neither of us is going."

Mona refused to let it end there. "You're being petty and childish. It's no different than Daphine or Ava inviting us to a party. You wouldn't have a problem with that. There's no more going on between Ray and me than there is between Daphine and me! He's being the bigger man by inviting you in the first place."

Those words set off a storm inside him. In his mind, Rayvon Patterson *was* the bigger man–younger, fitter and richer. He couldn't seem to stop those three words from echoing in his head, and hearing her say them squashed every positive emotion he'd had in the past twenty-four hours. He snatched the card from her hand. "I'll respond to this myself."

"I'm trying to get you to see you've created something in your mind that doesn't exist, but you still refuse to believe me." Her voice choked with tears before she rushed from the room.

Vic sank down on the side of the bed and dropped his head in his hands. Was he being petty? Didn't he have a right to protect his marriage? The way she insisted on defending Patterson set him off. She was so mad now; talking to her about taking a vacation was out of the question. At this point, he wasn't sure he even wanted to go.

He reined in his emotions and had a sudden moment of clarity. Why was he insisting on holding it against her when he'd done the same thing? The kiss with Heather in the bar in Chicago had been flattering yet meaningless. He needed to come clean with Mona about his own indiscretion. By the time he left the bedroom, she was on the phone in her new office. Sounds from the boys' rooms drew him down the hall. They were in Trey's room playing Arkham Knight on the PlayStation.

"What's up, guys?"

"Hey, Dad," both of his sons responded without looking away from the screen.

Remembering Mona's chastening about his lack of involvement with the boys, he asked, "Can I play?"

"Sure!" Julian's face brightened as he scooted over to make room for his father on the bed.

Trey chuckled. "Do you even know how to play this?"

"No, but you can show me, can't you?"

His oldest son smiled. "Okay. It's all about Batman's combat and detective skills. It uses his arsenal of gadgets, the Batmobile for transportation and battle, and you can even do side missions away from the main story."

Vic listened attentively as Trey explained the goals and objectives of the game then tried his hand at it while the boys rolled around on the bed laughing.

"Come on, give me a break. This is my first time!"

They schooled him on the fine points of the game. Vic liked strategy, and he actually had fun playing. An hour passed, and when he looked up, Mona was standing in the doorway watching them.

"I'm done, guys. Thanks for teaching me." He glanced up at her from where he was reclined on the bed. "Let's go in your office for a minute." She followed him down the hall, and he closed the door once they were inside. "You did a nice job in here. It looks good," he said scanning the room before he sat on the sofa.

"Thanks. There are still a few things I need, but I'll get around to it later." She crossed her arms and waited for him to say something.

"I didn't mean to go off on you like I did. Give me some time to think about going to this party, okay?"

She offered him a weak smile. "Okay. Thanks"

"Since we're going for complete honesty these days, I think I should tell you something about my last trip to Chicago."

Her eyes narrowed. "Go ahead."

"I've been too hard on you, and I need to confess something." He reached for her hand and pulled her to sit beside him. "Remember when I said you weren't the only one who caught somebody's eye the weekend of the fundraising ball?" She gave him a wary nod. "There was an incident during my trip to Chicago."

She pinned him with a suspicious gaze. "What happened?"

"One night most of my colleagues wanted to go out on the town, and I wasn't in the mood, so I decided to stay at the hotel. I was still sitting at the bar when I got into a conversation with a woman." Mona straightened and gave him her full attention. "We started talking and I asked her if she was staying for dinner, and when she said yes, I asked her to join me. It was completely innocent. I just wanted someone to talk to." She watched him with a keenly observant eye. "We ate, and during dessert she got a little flirty, and she kissed me."

"She kissed you?"

He couldn't look her in the face. "Yes."

"Did you kiss her back?"

His mouth twisted. "Yes."

"And that was it?"

He met her questioning gaze. "That was it. I told her I was married, and I never saw her again."

"Why did you kiss her back?"

He stared at her in confusion. "Why?" He paused for a long moment. "I guess I was flattered that another woman was interested." He shrugged. "I don't know."

"Vic, women have always been interested in you. Maybe you've never paid much attention, but I've had to deal with it since the day we started dating. It's funny how when the situation is reversed you have a hard time dealing with it."

He frowned. "You're not angry?"

"No. If you say nothing happened, I believe you, but now you know how it feels to have someone else show an interest in you, especially when things aren't right at home. It looks like we're both susceptible to attention from the opposite sex. If we don't want this to happen again to either of us, maybe we'd better pay attention to what's made us both so vulnerable."

"I have, and you were right. My mind had been so consumed with work for the past two years; I forgot I had work to do at home. We need to get away and spend some time alone together."

Mona flipped her hair over her shoulder and nodded but didn't respond. A tremor touched her lips as though she were holding back a smile. "You mean a vacation?"

"Uh huh, but I think we should take the boys somewhere first, so they don't feel neglected."

Now a wide, open smile spread over her face. He

should've been pleased, but the fact that his own wife felt grateful because he was willing to take time away from his daily routine to devote to her made him feel lower than pond scum. How had he gotten so far away from the love of his lifea woman most men would kill to have? "Do you have any idea where you'd want to go or what the boys might like?"

"I'd have to ask them, but I've always wanted to go to the Fiji islands."

"Wow." He chuckled and reached out to smooth the hair cascading over her shoulder. "I thought you were going to say L.A. or Miami or someplace, but you were never a woman to think small, were you?"

"Never."

"Okay, I'll see what I can find out. Just remember Mama's birthday party is October seventeenth."

"Ooh, I almost forgot. Did your father decide on the gift from the family?"

"I haven't heard from him. Guess I'd better call in case he wants five grand from each of his sons." They both laughed. "Will you talk to the boys to see what they have in mind?"

"You should do it. They need to know it was your idea."

"I'll ask them now." He pressed a slow, thoughtful kiss on her mouth then his lips left hers to nibble at her earlobe. "You're a wise woman, Mrs. Stafford."

Early the next morning Ramona sat at her desk feeling more hopeful than she had in ages. Even with Vic's revelation of his tête-á-tête with the woman in Chicago, she knew in her heart he meant business about working on their marriage. He'd already started coming home earlier and bringing his paperwork with him instead of staying late at the hospital, and he was actually talking about taking a vacation. A positive mood was exactly what she needed in order to contemplate the tasks on her plate for the next twenty-four hours.

The video chat with LaLa Anthony was scheduled for the next afternoon. In a few hours, Jamila was coming by to help her compose specific questions. All kinds of thoughts swirled in her head, the first of which was what should she wear? She had considered buying an item from LaLa's Fifth and Mercer collection, but then thought it would be tantamount to brown nosing. Looking fashionable was a given; only she didn't want to appear as if she were trying too hard. Just the thought of having a one-on-one conversation with the reality TV star put her nerves on edge. It had been bad enough the day when Jamila started firing questions at her, and she hadn't had the answers. She didn't want to look unprepared and ridiculous.

"I want to make it clear at the outset that starting the clothing line is something I'm considering and haven't yet invested any money into," she told Jamila when she arrived. "I don't want LaLa to think I'm just jumping into this off the top of my head."

"Good. She should know where you're at, so she can know how to advise you."

Her stylist helped her prepare a brief opening statement. "I also want her to know just how grateful I am she agreed to do the chat."

"Where do you plan to sit?" Jamila asked. Mona's confused expression must've answered the question. "I've been told when you do a video chat, your background should be clutter-free and not distracting." She glanced around the room. "How about over here? The light from the window is good and the only thing in the background is that beautiful lamp."

"Whatever you say. You're the stylist."

They spent an hour devising questions then went into Ramona's closet to choose an outfit for her to wear. Jamila recommended she dress casually and keep her makeup to a minimum.

When two o'clock rolled around the following afternoon, the two women were seated in front of the laptop waiting for the video chat ring to sound.

"If I need to say something to you, I'll hit the mute button." The program rang, Ramona took a deep breath before she clicked in and waited for a picture to appear. LaLa's assistant made sure everything was working then she introduced her boss.

"Ramona? My husband told me about his conversation with Rayvon, and how much he wanted me to talk with you about your business idea. I'm glad to tell you whatever I can," the lovely Latina said with the same open smile Ramona had seen so many times on television.

"First of all, I can't thank you enough for doing this. When Ray said he'd called your husband, I was shocked."

She raised her perfect eyebrows. "You must be really special to him."

"Oh, no. We're just friends," Ramona insisted.

"Well, he thinks highly of you. We only have ninety minutes, so I guess we'd better get started."

"Is it okay with you if I save this to my RealPlayer so I can refer back to it later?"

"Sure. Could you send me a copy?"

"You bet."

Ramona introduced Jamila, and the three women launched into a spirited discussion. Whenever it seemed as though she was floundering, Jamila stepped in. LaLa was encouraging and upbeat, just the way she appeared to be on TV. An hour and a half later, after Mona thanked LaLa repeatedly, they ended the chat. She couldn't wait to show the video to Vic when he got home, and she wanted to pinch herself to make sure she wasn't dreaming.

As soon as Jamila left, her lingering excitement gave way to the ever present fear that she might be making a huge mistake. What if she didn't do well? After all, LaLa was a celebrity who was married to a celebrity. Women wanted to buy her designs just because of who she was. *Nobody knows who I am.* She'd never had to face any real challenges in her life. What would Vic think about her if she failed? The main points the famous Mrs. Anthony had stressed were to do her research, to be economical but not cheap when it came to expenses, not to rush, and to find the right manufacturer to create the garments. She had her work cut out for her. LaLa's warnings and Jamila's sound advice convinced her to buy a full service development package with The Factory Girls which included Pattern making, Fitting, Sample Making, Consulting, Marking & Grading, Small Run Production, Day Passes to Workroom Facilities and Brand Consulting. For the time being, she planned to concentrate on taking as many classes as she could.

October arrived in a flash while Mona was busy commuting back and forth into Atlanta for classes and seminars. Even though she knew it would be fabulous, she wasn't really looking forward to her mother-in-law's sixty-fifth birthday party on the weekend. The last time they were all together, she'd made a fool of herself on the dance floor and had set off the gossip mill within the family. At least this time she and Vic were speaking. Actually, they were communicating in every way imaginable. She couldn't recall him being so horny since their honeymoon. It seemed to her that he was finding reasons to come home early now, and she loved it. He hadn't mentioned Ray's open house, so she hadn't either.

When she, Vic and the boys stepped into the Grand Atrium of 200 Peachtree on Saturday night dressed in their evening finery, he said, "You look gorgeous, baby." He was all smiles as they greeted the rest of the family at the tables set up at the head of the room. All of his brothers and their wives were already there. Greg and Rhani had flown in the night before and so had Mark, Gianne and ChiChi. They all greeted each other with hugs. Nick arrived alone a few minutes later.

When their parents arrived, and his father escorted their unsuspecting mother into the room, everyone shouted, "Surprise!" and launched into singing Happy Birthday To You. She appeared to jump six inches off the ground then reached into her purse for a tissue to dab at the tears threatening to ruin her makeup.

"You said we were going to dinner, Victor!"

"We are. We're just having it with a couple of hundred family and friends."

One by one her sons, their wives and her grandchildren hugged her.

"Happy birthday, Mama!" Vic kissed his mother on the cheek.

"I'm thrilled to see you two looking so happy together," she whispered in Mona's ear when she embraced her.

"Thanks, Mama. We're doing much better, but tonight I don't want to talk about us. This night is all about you."

"Do you believe this crowd? I think Victor invited everyone we've ever met since we got married forty-seven years ago!" She laughed, and gazed around at the breathtaking room with its thirty-foot ceilings, majestic chandeliers and stained glass windows. Mona could see how tickled she was about the over-the-top celebration. "You all can sit here once you get yourselves something to eat. The children are at this table," she waved her jewel-clad hand toward a table behind them. "Daddy went all out and used the house caterer for a Southern Charm menu. Whatever that is."

Her father-in-law appeared out of nowhere. "That's right. You'd better eat up before the dancing starts."

They took Trey and Julian across the marble floor to the catering stations where they loaded up their plates with fried chicken, macaroni and cheese, shrimp and grits and biscuits with honey butter. The boys conveniently skipped the broccolini with garlic butter and fried green tomatoes, but made sure they got slices of the mint chocolate cake.

She and Vic had to laugh when their sons' eyes widened at the next station where the chef was assembling what were called, Mason Jar Stacks—sweet potato biscuits, bourbon BBQ pulled pork, and firecracker coleslaw garnished with fried okra, the perfect mix of southern ingredients in eight-oz. mason jars.

Mona's stomach growled at the sight of so much food, since she'd been too busy getting everyone ready to eat lunch. "I'm going to have to make two trips," she whispered to Vic.

"Tell you what we'll do," Vic said with a wink. "You get everything you want. I'll get everything I want on my plate, and we can share."

They filled their plates and joined the family at the head tables. Mona noticed her mother and father-in-law watching them as she and Vic ate from each other's plates. She was certain they were wondering what was responsible for the change in their relationship. Vic returned to the buffet for dessert. They devoured the sweet confections, and then the brothers got into a huddle at one of the tables. She, Gianne, Adanna, Rhani and Cydney gathered at another table and shared the latest news while they ate. Getting to see her long distance sisters-in-law was always a pleasure.

"Doesn't Mama look spectacular tonight?" Adanna commented. "I hope I look that good at sixty-five."

Cydney chuckled. "Heck, I wish I looked that good now. So, what's going on with everybody?"

"Well, I received another clean bill of health from my oncologist," Gianne said with a wide smile.

"Oh, that's wonderful!" Jesse's wife, Cydney, said. "I'm *not* pregnant for once, and that's always good news." All of the women howled. She and Jesse had three children under the age of five.

Adanna's cheeks puffed into a big smile. "We have some news, but I think Charles wants to tell everyone later." She turned to Rhani, Greg's wife and the newest sister-in-law. "How is your non-profit coming along?"

"It's getting better every month. We have almost eighty girls in the program, and I got some additional funding from a couple of unexpected sources, and I hired two additional staff members. I've even been able to take them on a field trip to a teen conference in Philadelphia."

Listening to all of this interesting news, Mona couldn't hold it any longer. She twisted her hands beneath the table then blurted out, "I've decided to start my own business. The only ones who know are Vic, Mama and my mother."

Cydney's eyes lit with interest. "Seriously? What kind of business, and how are you going to find time with all your charity work?"

"I've given up the charity work, and I'm creating my own fashion line. I've already started taking classes at a fashion incubator, and my stylist is going to help me design the clothes."

The hush that came over the table had her feeling some kind of way. You would've thought she'd just confessed to a murder.

Finally, Gianne broke the uneasy silence. "Isn't it really expensive?"

"Yes. I sold the Bentley in order to get my seed money."

A collective gasp momentarily stopped the conversation again.

"I wanted to do this all on my own, and not ask Vic for the money."

Rhani sent her an approving smile. "Where are you going to sell the clothing? My best friend owns a boutique in Manhattan. I know she would be interested in taking a look at what you come up with."

"Thank you, but I haven't even decided on the particulars yet. It's going to be a while before I get any pieces into production, because I have a lot to learn first."

Cydney, the only stay-at-home mom in the group, frowned. "What does Vic think about it?"

"Vic thinks it's fantastic," his deep voice said from behind them. "And I'm counting on all of you ladies buying everything she creates. I was sent over here to break up this hen party. Daddy said the music is getting ready to start. It's party time."

The DJ switched from the mellow jazz he'd been playing during the meal, cranked up the volume and opened with the hot Latin rhythm of Pitbull and Chris Brown's *Fun*. Greg literally snatched Rhani from her seat and pulled her onto the dance floor. Everyone in the ballroom turned to watch them kick off the party with a sexy salsa. By the second verse, the floor was packed.

Vic took Mona's hand and raised her from her chair. "May I have the first dance?"

Mona splayed a hand across her chest. She loved to dance, but Vic had always been on the opposite end of the spectrum from Greg and Nick, the family hoofers. "Where is my husband and what have you done with him? You hate to dance."

"Hey, I never claimed to be a dancer, but I *can* keep the beat."

Mona's lips parted and she felt almost giddy as Vic did a lazy side-to-side two-step reminiscent of the move Will Smith taught to Kevin James in *Hitch*. She grinned throughout the entire song. He was doing everything in his power to show her that he was putting her needs first, and the knowledge made her heart sing with delight. He spun her around then pulled her against him so they were pelvis to pelvis swaying together to the beat. The rest of the family stared in apparent shock.

Dancing and laughter filled the room until it was time for the family to present their gift to the guest of honor. They sat Lillian on the stage in a chair surrounded by her sons, daughters-in-law and grandchildren. Her father-in-law made a big production of presenting her with their combined gift of a two-week trip to Italy, Spain and Morocco, something she'd dreamed about for decades.

"Honey, Charles and Adanna have a special gift for you," Dr. Stafford announced after she thanked her family and the guests who had filled one of the large round tables with cheerfully-wrapped gifts.

Their twin son and his wife came to the microphone, and Charles said, "Mama, we wanted to let you know Adanna and I won't be going to Nigeria this spring like we planned, because we have to take care of the gift we have for you. We won't be able to give it to you for about seven months, though." He pressed a hand to Adanna's abdomen.

It took a few seconds for his words to register with his mother, but when they did she jumped up and shouted. "You're having a baby!" She swept Adanna into her arms and they jumped up and down like two little girls.

Cheers filled the room. The men on the stage all slapped Charles on the back or gave him some dap. He and Adanna had been instrumental in helping Marc and Gianne adopt their daughter, ChiChi, who was abandoned at the hospital where Adanna had worked and he volunteered in Nigeria. Until now they'd had no children of their own. The only childless couple among them was the newlyweds, Greg and Rhani, who seemed content with their status at the moment.

In typical Stafford style, the music played, the liquor flowed, and the party rolled on until everyone was either too exhausted from dancing or too drunk to stand. Her in-laws made sure taxis and Uber cars transported those who couldn't drive safely back to their homes. Mona and Vic were among the casualties.

Chapter Fifteen

A short five hours later, the sun poured through the bedroom windows, and Vic fumbled around on the night table for the remote that controlled the Roman shades. Neither he nor Mona had had the presence of mind to close them when they'd stumbled in earlier. Thankful he didn't have to go into the hospital today; he closed his eyes and let the now dark room invite him back into slumber.

Sometime later, Mona turned over and groaned. "Oh, my God. Whatever made us drink so much last night?"

"I don't know about you," he said slowly, trying to form each word without it hurting his head, "but I was having a good time." He stretched and ran a hand over her bare booty. The boys had gone home from the party with Jesse and Cyd. He and Mona took an Uber car home. For the next hour, they had unsteady, slaphappy sex and, for the first time in more than a year, she'd fallen asleep in his arms. Mona looked beautifully disheveled with her hair partially covering her face. He smoothed it back and tucked it behind her ears.

"I can't remember the last time I had so much fun." She pressed a hand to her forehead. "But my head hurts."

"Mine too."

She groaned. "Mama isn't expecting us at church, is she?"

"Marc and Greg are staying at the house. They can go with her. I can't. I guess we need to repent and rehydrate. If you're game, I know someone who can fix us up."

"What are you talking about?"

"IV infusion. A doctor I know who used to work at the hospital opened an infusion clinic. From what I've heard, it's very effective."

"What's in it?"

"The one for hangovers is a saline solution with electrolyte replacement and a choice of nausea, heartburn or anti-inflammatory medication."

She cringed. "Ugh, you know how I feel about needles."

"I know, but it's supposed to be a spa-like atmosphere," he said, hoping it would convince her. "Come on."

She hesitated for a few seconds. "I guess I'm not good for anything else today. All right." The fact that he was trying to convince her to do something together was enough to make her agree to anything—even an intravenous puncture.

Vic called and made the appointment then they showered and changed clothes. An hour later, after a taxi dropped them at his car in the 200 Peachtree garage, they arrived at the clinic. One of the clinic staff offered them beverages, seated them in massage chairs in a calming green Asian-inspired infusion room and covered them with blankets.

"Vic Stafford. It's been a while. How're you doing… other than being hung over, I mean," the owner said with a chuckle as he entered the room a few minutes into their rehydration. He and Vic had worked together at the hospital for a couple of years.

"Mike Goodman." Vic reached his free arm out to shake the hand of his former colleague. "Just recovering from my mother's sixty-fifth birthday celebration last night. Otherwise I'm doing great. This is my wife, Ramona."

"It's my pleasure, Ramona." He smiled and shook her hand. "I heard you were promoted to Chief of Surgery a little while back. How's it going?"

Vic gave her a fleeting glance. "You know, a lot of paperwork and a lot of politics, but I still get into the OR pretty regularly."

"I can't imagine you being an administrator, knowing how much you love to cut. Do you ever regret taking the job?"

He looked at Mona once again. "Sometimes. Looks like you're doing well."

"Very well." Dr. Goodman grinned. "I figured why not jump on the bandwagon while the infusion craze is all the rage. I'm still in private practice, though. You need to have something that doesn't rest on the whims of the general public."

"Right." Vic agreed. "Well, I wish you the best, man."

He asked what they wanted to watch on the big screen TV and turned to the jazz music channel at Vic's request before he left the room.

"Would you ever do something like this?" Mona asked after Dr. Goodman left.

"No. I don't have an entrepreneurial bone in my body."

"I could see you in private practice like Charles used to be."

"You'd like that, wouldn't you, me not having to answer to the hospital?"

She sighed. "It would be different."

This was his chance to bring up the subject they had

both been avoiding. "Speaking of different, I've given some thought to the invitation. If you want to go to Patterson's open house, we can."

Her head swiveled toward him and her eyes narrowed. "Are you sure you're not still drunk?"

Vic laughed. "I'm quite sober now. You can reply for both of us. I put the invitation on your desk."

"Thank you." They exchanged a smile. "I meant to ask you last night about what's going on with Nick. He looked so lost without Cherilyn. He loves to dance, and I think I only saw him on floor once, and that was with Mama."

"I think when we ran into her at the 100 Black Men Affair something broke in him. He was so emphatic about me introducing him to Derrick, I was nervous about what he might do. He handled it well, though. Nick needs to meet another woman."

"But it sounds like he's not interested in meeting anyone else. He wants Cherilyn back."

"Well, I hope he doesn't intend to get into a battle with Derrick. I don't know him well, but he doesn't seem like the type of man to give up on what he wants. He's gone far in his field for someone so young, and you don't make those kinds of accomplishments by lying down and letting people run over you."

"You should talk to Nick. He's never been serious about anyone before."

"He didn't ask for my opinion, baby."

"Men! You're his oldest brother, and he idolizes you, Vic."

"I'm not getting all up in his business unless he asks."

The nurse came in to unhook them from their IVs. "How are you feeling?"

Vic grinned at her. "Now that you mention it, I'm actually feeling much better. Tell Mike the next time I have another serious lapse in judgment, I'll be back."

"How about you, Mrs. Stafford?"

Ramona pushed herself out of the recliner and stood. "Not one hundred percent yet, but I felt like death warmed over when we got here."

"You should feel increasingly better in the next hour or so. Just stick to drinking water for the rest of the day."

Before they returned home, she and Vic drove to Jesse's house to get the boys. His brother opened the door and appeared shocked.

"I expected to see you two on your hands and knees this morning. You were both pretty lit when you left last night, but you look like you've recovered."

He and Mona laughed. "We just finished getting an IV infusion."

Jesse's green eyes widened. "You did it yourself?"

"No, fool! We went to a hydration station. Do you remember Mike Goodman? He opened a clinic in Buckhead."

"I've heard about that. It really works, huh?"

"Yeah. It's just lactated ringers with added antioxidants, vitamins and something for nausea. Worked like a charm."

"I hope Trey and Julian weren't any trouble," Mona said, looking around for her sons.

"No. They were cool. They're in the family room. Cyd's in the kitchen."

"Let me go thank her. I'll be right back." Mona headed down the hall toward the back of the house, which was almost an exact replica of her in-laws' house.

As soon as she was out of sight, Jesse said, "There was a big difference in the way you and Mona acted last night than the way you were at the barbeque."

Vic's smile deepened into laughter. "We're in a better place now."

A momentary look of discomfort crossed Jesse's face. "The Rayvon Patterson issue is settled?"

"There really wasn't an issue. It was mostly in my mind."

"Good…I guess." The deep lines between Jesse's brows contradicted his words.

"Thanks for recommending McClendon. He was thorough, and what he presented me didn't prove anything to my satisfaction. We'll be all right. You'll see."

"I hope you're right."

A week later, the hired valets outside of Patterson's Buckhead mansion on the most prestigious street in the city opened the car door for Mona. Vic stepped out of the car and forced down his irrational resentment as he glanced up at the house. Whether Mona would admit it or not, he knew she was impressed with Patterson's ability to buy a home that made their two-million dollar house look like budget real estate.

The front doors opened to a gold gilded stairway leading to the second floor from the foyer. A girl who appeared to be about Trey's age met them with a prepared speech. "Hi, my name is Leshanique. I'm Rayvon's sister. Welcome to our open house. Can I have your name, please?"

"Hello, Leshanique," Mona said with a warm smile. "We are Vic and Ramona Stafford."

The young teen ran her index finger down a list and

finally said, "Oh, here you are. Come on in. Rayvon is walkin' around somewhere. You can look at the house. The party is in the ballroom."

"Thank you, sweetie. You're doing a great job." The girl beamed and then focused her attention on the next guests. "Let's just wander around." She took his hand and strolled into the room to their left. "I guess we'll run into Ray sooner or later."

Later was fine with him. He followed her into a sitting area with a group of ornate velvet and gold furniture arranged in the center of the room. The ottoman in the middle of the chairs reminded him of a fancy marching band bass drum turned on its side. As they made their way through the house, he peered into a cigar room, theater, two gyms, an eight-person steam room, several kitchens, a recording studio, a massage room, a nail and beauty salon. Vic gave a *what's up* nod to faces he recognizedfamous ballers, rappers and even a few movie and TV stars when they glanced in his direction. They were obviously looking at Mona and not him. She looked fantastic tonight in a black jumpsuit that showed off her curves to their best advantage.

He had to hide his fanboy reaction when they turned the corner and saw Patterson talking to Carmelo Anthony, one of his favorite players.

"Ramona!" Patterson called out when he saw her. "I'm glad you made it." His gaze met Vic's, and the two men studied each other for a tense moment before he extended a large hand and clasped Vic's as though nothing negative had ever transpired between them. "Vic, I want you to meet Carmelo Anthony, and this is the lady we hooked up with La."

"It's so nice to meet you." The six-foot-eight forward shook his hand and then Mona's.

"I have to thank you so much for telling your wife

about my business idea," Mona gushed. "We had a Skype chat last week. She's absolutely wonderful!"

"Yeah, I think she is." His round face puffed into a smile. "Glad I could help. Hope your launch goes well."

"Thanks. It'll be a while before I get the company off the ground, but LaLa's input was priceless. Make sure you let her know I said so."

"Will do."

"Which way is the food, Ray?" Mona asked gazing around the enormous rooms.

"Straight ahead and to your right. Did you meet my family?"

"Just your little sister at the front door. She was so cute with her little speech."

"I wrote it up for her, so she wouldn't say anything crazy." He grinned. "I'll catch up with you two in a few. Make yourselves at home."

Vic was trying his best to keep an open mind toward both Patterson and his new digs. He was trying his best to like the house, but in all honesty felt it was a hideous, ostentatious monstrosity he imagined would appeal to someone who'd never had anything.

Poor people often went to the opposite extreme when they came into sudden wealth. He'd once heard Dolly Parton say in an interview that growing up poor she was always led to believe more and bigger was better. So once she became famous, she went "hog wild" with the hair and the tits.

They found the ballroom where a catering staff served the guests from at least a dozen long tables laden with every imaginable item. After they had their plates, he and Mona found seats along the outskirts of the room lined with velvet and satin-covered chairs, which reminded him of different kinds of thrones. He had to admit watching the crowd was entertaining. The guests were a strange combination of young men with gold and diamond grills in sagging jeans showcasing their designer drawers to plump middle-aged women who looked as though they were dressed for Sunday service to buxom young women wearing short, tight dresses leaving nothing to the imagination.

"Interesting crowd," he whispered to her between bites of some kind of delicious beef on a skewer.

She laughed. "Seriously. It's fun, though, don't you think?"

He shrugged. "Better than staying home watching television, I guess." When he looked up, Patterson was heading toward them holding an older woman by the hand and followed by four teens.

"I had to round up the family from their posts, so I could introduce you. This is Ramona, the one I told you helped me pick out the house, and her husband, Vic. This is my mother, Hazel Patterson, my brothers, Ja'Vante and Tyrez, and the twins, Leshan and Leshanique," he said proudly.

"She *is* beautiful," the oldest brother remarked, which made Mona blush and him wonder what Patterson had told them about his wife.

"Thank you," Mona said before they both spoke to each of the family members. "I know you all are so excited to be here with Ray. He told me about his promise to you, and now he's made it come true. I hope you like living in Atlanta. I was born and raised here, and I think it's the best. She turned to Ray. "I see you decided to include all the furnishings."

"Yeah, it was just easier. Besides, I could never buy furniture like this."

Who would want to? Vic thought. It reminded him of what you might see in an old movie about royalty. *Guess it makes him feel like a king.*

When Vic glanced up, he saw the adoring expression on Patterson's face and immediately wanted to put his fist in his face. He had no right looking at his wife that way. Instantly, his suspicions about whether they had been intimate returned.

"What's wrong?" Mona asked when he shook his head to clear the thought.

"Headache. You got any coffee around here, man?"

"We have everything," their host said with a proud smile that set Vic's teeth on edge. "Any of the servers can help you."

Berating himself for being so petty, Vic headed for one of the beverage tables on the opposite side of the room. At six-foot-two, he was taller than the average man, but everything about being here made him feel small, something he'd never experienced. All of his life he'd been the tall, good-looking, talented one. Tonight he felt dwarfed not only by the house but also by the fame and physical stature of many of the guests. It made him angry. The server fixed him a cup of coffee, and he took it outside to check out the pool. With the exception of the theater, this was the only area of the house he really liked. Out here there were no hand-carved ceilings, mosaic floors or elaborate furniture.

While Vic gazed out over the manicured two-acre grounds down the street from the governor's mansion, the reason for the anger boiling in his chest suddenly occurred to him. In all the years he and Mona had been married, nothing had ever challenged his ability to provide for her. But having her make a connection with a man who could give her all of this ate at the essence of who he was. Even if he owned the hospital, he could never offer her the kind of life Patterson lived.

"There you are," her voice brought him out of his contemplation. "I've been looking everywhere for you. Are you ready to go? I've had enough of this."

Surprised, his gaze met hers, and he studied her face. "Really? I'm ready, if you are."

"Yes. This isn't exactly my kind of crowd. If we see Ray on the way out, I'll say goodbye. If not, he certainly won't miss us."

On the way back through the house, they didn't see Patterson, and Vic was glad. He just wanted to get away from the pretentious display of wealth, and he wasn't in the mood to compliment him on the house.

The valet brought the car around, and they were on the way out of Buckhead when he turned to Mona. "So what did you think of all that?"

"You mean the house or the guests?"

"All of it."

"I told Ray from the beginning I thought it wasn't a wise move for him to buy such an expensive house. Being an athlete is such an iffy way to make a living. If he gets injured, there's no way he'd be able to pay a sixty-thousand dollar a month mortgage. All he's looking at is the amount of his contract, not the fact that he'll have this huge mortgage hanging over his head and upkeep fees through the roof."

He gave her a sidelong glance, surprised by her words.

"I also told him I really couldn't comment on the house itself, because it isn't my taste. He didn't realize I was trying to be kind. It would've been mean to say the place is over-the-top and garish, and I don't think he would've understood anyway. He took one look at all the gold and…stuff," she waved her hands around in the air, "and he was hypnotized."

She chuckled. "He doesn't need forty thousand square feet. I mean, his family would be ecstatic to live in a ten thousand square foot house. Personally, I think he made a big mistake, but he wasn't listening to anything I had to say. His mind was made up."

Vic listened and smiled, not so much at what she said but because she didn't like the house.

The next day, they went to church and then joined Vic's parents, Jesse, Cydney and the girls for dinner at The Beautiful. After they got home, Mona made sure Trey and Julian started their homework before she went into her office to watch a few videos recommended as part of the last seminar she'd attended at The Factory Girls. Vic hunkered down in his office to attack the mountain of paperwork he'd brought home from the hospital. Granted, they were both working, but just knowing he'd chosen to do his paperwork at home comforted her. She hadn't understood until now what he'd meant when he said she needed something to do. When she was engrossed in studying, she had no desire to be clingy, as he'd called it. She hadn't even realized a couple of hours had passed until he came up behind her, moved her hair off her neck and planted a kiss there.

"It's seven o'clock. How long do you plan to be in here?"

"I didn't know it was so late. Are you hungry?"

"Uh huh." He grinned. "But we should wait for the boys to go to bed, don't you think?"

"I meant from the kitchen, you perv." She tilted her head back for another kiss. "Maite made up a few things before she left."

"Yeah, I could eat. I'll get Trey and Julian. I need to talk to all of you about something."

"I'll meet you downstairs." She logged off her iPad and wondered what this was all about as she watched him leave the room. This was the first family meeting they'd had in a year. She searched through the refrigerator reading labels on the plastic containers Maite had been so diligent to leave for them. He and the boys came in and sat at the island. "It looks like Maite left us some shrimp pasta salad, chicken and rice and fruit salad. I'll put everything here on the counter, and you can fix your own plates. She took four plates down from the cabinet, removed the tops from the containers and stuck a serving spoon in each.

"Daddy has something to talk to us about," she said once they all had their food.

"I was going through my mail, and I found an invitation to speak at a conference in February. I thought you might want to go with me." His gaze rested on their faces one by one.

Trey wrinkled his nose and didn't look up from his plate.

The always curious Julian asked, "What kind of conference?"

"It's on Interactive Surgery," Vic answered.

He was obviously trying to include them in something, but it sounded to Mona like a quick way to die from boredom. "What would we do while you're at the conference?"

"Oh, I don't know. Considering it is being held at the Wailea Beach Marriott Resort and Spa in Maui, I imagine you could find *something*."

"Hawaii!" Trey shouted. "We're going to Hawaii?"

Vic smirked. "Only if you want to. I'm not going to force you or anything."

"Did I hear you say *spa*?"

"Yes, ma'am. Are you interested?"

"Are you kidding? Of course, I'm interested. Oh, Vic, that would be wonderful!"

"What do you think, J?" Vic asked his youngest son.

"They have volcanoes in Hawaii, right?" Julian asked.

"Sure do."

"Can we go see one?"

"I think it can be arranged. You'll need to take a few days off from school, but I don't think that'll bother you."

"No way, Dad!" Trey responded with uncommon enthusiasm. "That'll be awesome."

In one forward motion, Mona was in his arms. "He's right. That *will* be awesome. Thank you."

He whispered in her ear then swatted her on the booty. "You can thank me later." Thirty seconds later his phone rang. He groaned and answered. "Stafford."

The call cancelled Vic's last words and signaled an end to their family time. "Rinse your plates, and put them into the dishwasher when you're done," she told the boys before she got up from the island. "Put your uniforms out for the morning, and don't forget clean socks and underwear," she added for Julian's benefit. She returned to her office and restarted the last video she'd been watching.

Vic stood in the doorway several minutes later. "Gotta go, baby. I'm counting on you giving me a rain check for that thank you."

"I hope the trip really happens. It would be a shame to disappoint the boys."

"It would be a shame to disappoint my wife. It's going to happen. In fact, I'm getting Shondell to make the arrangements in the morning." He placed a gentle kiss on her mouth and left the room.

The more she thought about what was going on between them, the more she understood how he felt about her being engrossed in something besides him. It wasn't healthy for her to be waiting for him to come home just because she'd never done anything for her own satisfaction. It wasn't that she didn't miss him when he was at the hospital now, but she miraculously didn't notice how long he'd been gone.

The next few months, working with Jamila on her designs and attending classes, seminars, networking sessions and visiting workrooms, filled Mona's every waking hour. The exhilaration of learning and being exposed to a world she had only known from the outside was a high unlike anything she'd ever experienced. She decided the line, which she named *Reverie by Ramona Stafford*, would be sold exclusively online and not in actual storefronts. Her long-range goals were to eventually create a massive collection and ultimately make it into the major retail stores. In the midst of her hectic schedule, the holidays snuck up on her, and Maite was off for the Thanksgiving weekend. Mona convinced Vic to take them to the St. Regis for its famous holiday buffet. She had to do Christmas shopping for Vic and the boys, all of his brothers and their wives and children, her in-laws, and her mother along with Jamila and a little token for the two women who owned The Factory Girls. Their vision of helping aspiring designers create their own companies was changing the way she saw herself. Being around such strong, successful, determined women did wonders for her self-esteem. They made her see she was capable of achieving her dream. Not only was her mind stimulated by what she was learning, but her heart was so involved, the process felt almost like a personal relationship. Her love of fashion had moved to a deeper level.

One night, while she was studying in her office, from the corner of her eye she noticed Vic watching her from the doorway. He was leaning against the frame with his arms folded. When she turned to glance at him, his eyes bathed her in admiration. The only other time she had seen that look in his eyes was as she nursed the boys when they were babies.

"What?"

"Nothing. I just like watching you work." He smiled. "You look like you're enjoying yourself."

"Believe it or not, I am. It's one thing to love fashion, but it's fascinating to learn how the industry works and what it takes to create products that will sell. I'm considering opening a store here in Atlanta once the line is up and running and making a profit. What I had to ask myself is whether I want to be the next Michael Kors, of if I want to run a small business with a roster of private clients?"

"And what's the answer?"

"I think I'd like to be somewhere in the middle. Starting out selling strictly online will give me an idea of what people really like, but I want to create a limited number of items for private clients."

"I haven't told you this, but I am so proud of you, baby.

"And I haven't said how proud I am of you for the way you're making me and the kids a priority in your life again. It means everything to me, Vic, and I know Trey and Julian appreciate seeing you around here more often."

"Trey hasn't said anything, but you know Julian. He came to me the other day and said, 'Dad, I like when you come home from the hospital, even when you're doing work here."

"He's such a sweetheart. I hope that doesn't disappear as he gets older."

"J's a lot like Charles. He has a good heart, and he's not embarrassed about showing it."

As was their custom, the family celebrated Christmas at her in-laws' house. Everyone was able to make it this time, even though they had all just been together for her mother-in-law's birthday party.

In February, she and the boys joined Vic on a flight to Hawaii where he was attending the conference. Mona had never seen her sons so excited, even Trey, who was becoming more like his father every day and had become an expert at maintaining a serious façade.

She and Vic had gone over the conference schedule before they left Atlanta. Besides the two seminars he had to teach, he only attended early workshop sessions so he could join her and the boys for sightseeing and dinner together. They visited the tourist traps and took Julian to see his first volcano. A luau at the hotel topped off their final night on the island. After they strolled through the craft market where they watched people working on handmade items, they ate a buffet dinner on the beach.

"This is *so* good," Mona said to Vic about the meal of purple sweet potatoes cooked in coconut sauce, lava-oven roasted pulled pork, mahi mahi in lemon butter sauce and other delicacies.

"I had a feeling you'd enjoy it," he said, looking pleased with himself. "What do you think, guys?"

Trey treated them to what amounted to a rave from him these days. "It's great."

"Yeah, it's great," Julian mimicked his brother. "Can I get some more of this meat?"

"It's a buffet, man. Knock yourself out."

The boys returned to the buffet for the second time, and as the sun set over the ocean, live drummers began playing. Mona popped both boys on the back of the head when they snickered at the men dancing with sarongs tied around their hips. Trey's attitude changed dramatically when a group of stunning Hawaiian women took the stage and demonstrated to the audience how to do an authentic hula. When they invited the kids to come up to the stage to try, Julian joined in. Trey refused.

"He's getting enough enjoyment from just watching all that hip shaking," Vic said in her ear with a laugh.

More dancers in elaborate headdresses and costumes took the stage followed by another set that performed a narrated historical number. Again, the boys looked embarrassed when a group of male dancer performed in what amounted to loin cloths.

"His butt is showing!" Julian said behind his hand and laughed until the fire twirler grabbed his attention.

Of all the performers, a graceful and agile acrobat who did a dramatic aerial dance on a long piece of fabric suspended from the top of a tree turned out to be Mona's favorite. During her romantic and emotional performance, Mona rested her head on Vic's shoulder and wrapped an arm around his waist. He tucked her under his arm, and his lips slowly descended to meet hers.

The boys cringed and groaned at the public display.

He raised his mouth from hers, ignored his sons' complaints, gazed into her eyes and whispered, "Looks like we're going to make it."

When she looked up, she saw the same love in his eyes

that she'd seen the night he asked her to marry him. "I was just thinking the same thing. It's always been you, Vic. Only you."

Epilogue

The last Saturday night of the following May, the entire family arrived at Le Fais do-do for the Reverie launch party. Vic was so proud of what Mona had accomplished. The party at the lavish venue in the Ellsworth Industrial area, not far from Jamila's studio, was his gift to her. She had chosen the location because of its spacious rooms and their ability to set up a floor plan to suit the event. Planning the party herself became too much for her on top of her other responsibilities, so she hired an event coordinator who carried out every detail of her concept for the launch.

He continued to marvel at how his wife was growing into not only a businesswoman, but also a creative force. She and Jamila had worked tirelessly to bring Mona's dream to fruition. Tonight she looked like she had stepped right out of a Hollywood movie set. Needless to say, she wore one of the most daring dresses from her collection, a short, white, backless number that plunged down to her waist in the front. Her hair was piled high on the top of her head and cascaded over her right cheek in a mass of curls. In his opinion, she would outshine every one of the models she'd hired to walk the runway tonight, and he hadn't even seen them yet.

Most of the guests probably wouldn't know she was nervous, but he noticed how she kept biting her lip and twisting her neck as though it were sore. He caught her arm as she flitted past him for the tenth time. "Relax, baby." He massaged her shoulders then handed her a bottle of spring water. "You've seen to every detail. It's going to be fantastic. Take a deep breath and drink some water. You look fabulous. What do you call this anyway?" He touched the flouncy fabric around her hips.

Mona took his advice and opened the water. "Thanks. It's called a peplum."

"Well, you're definitely the perfect model to show this off."

"That's exactly what Jamila said. It's the reason I decided to wear it tonight. I need to go the family VIP section and say hello to everyone before the guests get here. Come with me." She grabbed his hand.

Vic had rented out the entire facility, and the guests had plenty of space to mix and mingle. Each section designated for the media/fashion bloggers, special guests, and family was manned by someone from the security firm they had contracted for the night.

They crossed the floor to where the family was seated in one of the tented sections, and everyone cheered when they saw Mona approaching. They smothered Mona in kisses and hugs then asked all sorts of questions until she had to beg off to get ready for the doors to officially open. On their way back to where the runway had been set up, she made it a point to greet all of the doctors' wives she'd invited. Even Adanna had ventured out in spite of Charles' fierce objections. She was two days past her due date, but she refused to miss the launch party. He'd requested a comfortable chair for her, and he propped her feet up on another chair he'd moved from one of the tables.

To him it was beginning to look as though every single one of the five hundred invitations she'd sent out had given a positive RSVP.

Mona hired the DJ who provided the music for his mother's birthday party, and she'd instructed him to start the music promptly at eight o'clock when one of the security men opened the doors for the crowd. She had intentionally kept them waiting outside for several minutes, because she felt it would help to drum up excitement.

His mother-in-law circulated among the crowd, boasting about Mona's new venture, even though she had considered it a foolish move when Mona first told her about it.

Before the invitations had gone out, Mona asked how he felt about Patterson and his mother being included on the guest list. Her rationale was since he had been the catalyst for her meeting with LaLa Anthony, it would be bad manners not to include him. Vic really didn't care whether Patterson was invited or not, but just the fact that she asked his opinion before she extended the invitation was enough to show how much things had changed between them.

He saw LaLa and Carmelo before Mona did, and he pushed through the crowd to let her know. She looked shocked when the lovely Mrs. Anthony asked, "Ramona, do you have someone to introduce you?"

"Not really. I was just going to welcome everyone and tell them how the evening is supposed to go."

"I'd like to do that, if you don't mind."

"Mind? I'd be honored. Thank you so much." The way Mona was beaming, Vic knew she was overwhelmed by the offer.

"Just give me a heads up when you're ready for me. Melo and I are going to the bar."

As the power couple walked away, Mona appeared stunned. "I can't believe they actually came, but I really can't believe she's going to do that for me. This is amazing!"

Vic brushed a light kiss on her forehead, so he didn't smear her lipstick. "This is going to be a great night, baby. You're making your mark in the fashion world." He wasn't surprised Mona had been able to pull the event off. She'd organized benefits and balls for her charity work and become an expert at putting together impressive affairs, but she'd never done anything like this for herself. His chest was poked out so far he thought it might burst.

"May I have your attention, please?" Daphine spoke into the mic near the runway. Mona had asked her to do the announcements for her. "The buffet is open for your enjoyment. Help yourselves. The festivities will begin in about thirty minutes." Mona had contracted Jus-So All Inclusive Events, one of the top black caterers in the city, and the spread they provided was more than impressive.

When the time came to open the program, Mona rounded up everyone who'd had a hand in bringing her line into reality–Vic, Jamila, Rosa and Regina, who were the brain-trust behind The Factory Girls, Rayvon and LaLa to the podium. Daphine got everyone's attention then passed the mic to LaLa.

"Good evening. My husband and I are so excited to be here for the official launch of Reverie by Ramona. I was honored when she contacted me to get my thoughts on her idea of starting her own fashion line. She's worked hard to create the pieces, and I know you are all as anxious as I am to see them. Please join me in welcoming the fashion world's newest designer, Ramona Stafford!"

The room exploded with applause and cameras flashed as she took the platform. It had been more than two decades since Mona had been the center of attention, but her pageant training automatically kicked in. She smiled and posed briefly to allow the media to get good shots.

"I'm not going to say a lot, because I want the clothes to speak for themselves, but I would be remiss if I didn't thank those who've contributed to bringing my dream into reality." She turned around, reached for Vic's hand and pulled him forward to stand with her. He had no idea what she was going to say, but when she started to speak, all he could do was smile.

"First, I have to thank my husband, Vic for being the catalyst that started this whole project. Thank you, honey for giving me the kick in the pants I needed." He chuckled when she winked at him. "We also have him to thank for this fabulous party tonight. I love you so much, honey." Mona touched her glossy lips to his then released his hand and reached for Jamila's. "None of this would've been possible without the expertise and creativity of my stylist, Jamila Anderson. She has been my stylist for the past few years, and she's responsible for introducing me to the Atlanta fashion industry. She took me by the hand and showed me where I needed to go and who I needed to know to get this line off the ground. Jamila explained things to me in baby talk when I didn't understand the industry jargon. This is a woman you all need to know. Thank you, girl.

"LaLa Anthony generously gave of her time and knowledge, and I can't even express how much her help has meant to me over the past seven months. I am so honored to have her and Carmelo here to celebrate with us."

She beckoned Rayvon with a manicured index finger. "Last, but not least, I have to publicly thank Rayvon Patterson, the new point guard for our Atlanta Hawks, for introducing me to LaLa. You're a good friend, and you know what they say about the importance of getting the hook-up." Everyone laughed, and she stood on her toes gave him a quick peck on the cheek. Lastly, she brought the two women from The Factory Girls forward, gave their business a glowing recommendation and thanked them for her continuing education on what she needed to make her business a success.

"I'd be remiss if I didn't acknowledge our fabulous sponsors." Mona mentioned each of the companies by name. "They are responsible for the incredible gifts in the welcome goodie bag you received at the door. The show is set to begin in about thirty minutes, so in the meantime, please continue to enjoy this fabulous buffet."

Vic watched his wife move through the room greeting reporters, bloggers and couples from the Atlanta medical community, and he knew this step into a new world had changed her. Mona had always exuded confidence, but tonight the glow she had was different. She seemed self-satisfied in a way he'd never seen, and it looked good on her, and in a strange way made him want her even more.

No one could have imagined how terrified Mona was when she arrived at Le Fais do-do. She'd chosen the site partly because she loved the name. In the Cajun culture, a fais do-do was a big party, where dancing and festivities last long into the night. The venue was able to create just about anything she wanted. It provided over four hundred parking spaces and a stock of impressive furnishings including luxury lounge furniture. She especially appreciated that only one event was scheduled per day which allowed her the option of using the space for up to a total of fourteen hours. She had never been there before, and had seen what an exquisite job they did for the wedding of The Real Housewives of Atlanta's Kandi Burruss on TV.

Being the center of attention wasn't anything new to her. She'd been raised learning how to smile for the camera and speak in front of crowds. Being recognized for something other than her body, face or runway walk was a strange kind of good, but tonight, the fear of failure tormented her. Everyone who was anyone would be filling the chairs lined up on both sides of the runway. What would she do if the audience had a negative reaction to her garments? Or, possibly even worse, what if they had no reaction at all? The thought nearly paralyzed her.

I can't think about this now. There are people waiting to meet me, and I need to be in the right frame of mind.

Mona had done everything she was supposed to do: had a kick-ass web site created by a web designer; hired a party planner; found a great location; secured several high-profile sponsors, and invited the right guests.

As all the experts advised, she'd made sure there was fantastic music, had multiple bars set up, and ordered a sumptuous buffet. Invitations had gone out to fashion bloggers, and press releases were sent to every media outlet in the metro area. To coax more journalists to come to the event, she'd included an extra pair of passes with the press invitation. Allowing journalists to bring their friends was supposed to give them greater incentive to attend, which meant more press.

Mona didn't know of anything more she could do, but it still didn't seem like enough. This was the biggest thing she'd ever done in her life. The pageants, fundraising balls and even her wedding didn't compare. So much of her anxiety centered on the fear that something might go wrong, and Vic would see her fail. Even with all of the important, powerful people on the guest list, he was the only one who mattered.

She left to join Jamila and the models in a room they had designated as the dressing room. Paying an agency to provide models for the night wasn't cheap, but at Jamila's suggestion she had hired six models to each wear four pieces. Mona's body vibrated with a mixture of excitement and fear at the flurry of activity when she opened the door.

The noise level in the room was higher than she expected. Jamila had brought three women who'd created the prototypes and samples at one of the workrooms, two to serve as dressers for the models. The other was a seamstress whose job it was to steam and press the garments, to take care of the last-minute nips and tucks and handle any unexpected garment emergencies like popped buttons or broken zippers. The makeup artist and hair stylist were busy at their stations working on the last models before the show began.

She did a final check of each garment hanging on racks with the appropriate accessories lined up underneath. She had a large photo of each look, and she instructed each of the dressers to be sure each model was dressed exactly like the picture right down to how many buttons should be open or closed. She reminded them that they were responsible for making sure the model was on time for each curtain call. Timing was crucial. The job of re-hanging the items and bagging the accessories back up was assigned to the two dressers so there wasn't a mess backstage and none of her fashions disappeared. At the end of the show, Jamila would take inventory to make sure.

In all of the hustle and bustle, one of the waiters brushed by her carrying a tray and his elbow mussed her hair. Before she knew it, she felt her mother's fingers rearranging it.

"Mom!" she said, waving her away.

"Ramona, there are photographers here, and you don't want to look messy." She reached up and continued to fuss with the loose curls, her eyes darting back and forth as though looking to see if anyone else noticed.

"Please stop it!" She backed away from her mother a couple of steps. "The people here don't care about my hair. They came to see my fashions."

"Don't be ridiculous," her mother insisted.

Mona stepped closer and shot the older woman a withering glance. "Tonight is about what I've been able to do without using my face or my body, Mom. Don't you understand?"

Cee Cee shriveled at the insistence in her daughter's voice. "Fine! I was just trying to help."

"I know." Her voice softened, but her shoulders straightened. "I just want you to realize my days of trying to impress people with my looks are over. They have to take me or leave me as I am. It's time for the show to start. I'll see you when it's over."

She returned to the dressing room, where the noise level had risen several decibels. The two dressers yelled back and forth to each other in Chinese. One of the models seemed like a drama queen who whined and complained about everything from the temperature in the dressing room to there only being spring water and no champagne for them to drink.

"Listen, sweetheart, this is not Fashion Week, and you are not in Paris. Ramona has instructed the caterer to feed every single person working here tonight. Once the show is over, you can eat and drink to your heart's content. Right now you're here to work," Jamila said, firmly putting her in her place.

When Jamila finished, Mona stood in the center of the room and addressed the models. "Ladies, may I have your attention? You all look marvelous. I want to see lots of energy and smiles tonight. None of those snooty, sour haute couture expressions. Engage the audience without being cutesy. Make my garments look good and there will be as much champagne as you can drink. Make me proud, ladies! Okay, five minutes to first looks."

The order in which the models were to come out was posted at the runway entrance. Mona hugged Jamila, took a deep breath and waited for Daphine to announce the commentator for the evening. "All right, ladies, it's show time."

The show went off without a hitch, and judging by the

audience's reaction, her designs were well received. Mona watched from backstage with a sense of pride then closed out the show to cheers and whistles when she walked the runway to showcase her dress, which she considered the signature piece of the line. After she thanked the crowd, Vic presented her with a bouquet of long-stemmed red roses, and she left the platform to schmooze with the bloggers and fashion reporters.

Jamila made sure the models and backstage crew were fed. Later, as the caterer cleared out, the DJ wound down, everyone except the family left the premises; Mona's head was still spinning. The whole night seemed like a dream, and she couldn't wipe the smile from her face. She collapsed on the sofa where the family had congregated, kicked off her shoes and rested her head on Vic's shoulder. "I've never been so tired in my life."

He lowered his head and kissed her forehead. "I know what that feels like, but there's something about being exhausted when you know you're spent because you did your very best. Was it worth it?"

"Every single second." She glanced across at her mother-in-law, who was sitting beside Rhani, the two women who truly believed she and Vic could solve their problems. Both of them wore smiles, and it wasn't just because of the success of the show. Mona smiled back, knowing in her heart that in spite of their stubbornness and mistakes, she and the man she loved were headed for great things together.

Credits

[1]Art Institute of Atlanta - http://bit.ly/1aixxyf

[2]Tony Gaskins, Professional Life Coach, Author, Speaker - www.tonygaskins.com

[3]http://www.factorygirlsatl.com/

[4]http://www.490westpacesferryrd.com/gallery/

A Preview of

I Want You Back

Book Five in the Stafford Brothers series

Coming Winter 2016

Chapter One

Nick Stafford's hands trembled as he straightened his tie. He needed to be at The Estate, a well-known Atlanta wedding venue, early before all the guests arrived. His gift for the bride had to be delivered in person. It was a gift with special meaning to her, and he'd spent hours coming up with the two lines he'd written in the card. He wanted to put it into her hand himself, even though he knew he wasn't supposed to speak to the bride.

Rather than have someone else drive him, he took his own car. The peace and quiet of being alone was necessary for his sanity before the ceremony began. His stomach clenched with anticipation and anxiety, yet he couldn't wait to get there.

Only a handful of cars were in the parking lot of the Buckhead venue, known for its beautiful weddings, when he arrived. Nick parked and entered the eighteenth-century antebellum mansion through the beveled glass double doors and absentmindedly gazed at the artwork lining the walls as he passed through one of the front salons.

"Are you here for the wedding?" a tuxedo-clad man

asked when he saw Nick stop and gaze into the ballroom decorated in white and peach, Cherilyn's favorite color.

"I'm here to deliver a special gift to the bride. Can you tell me what room she's in, please?"

"Sure. The ladies are in the bridal suite upstairs on the right. You'll hear them cackling." He laughed and went on his way.

"Thanks, man." Nick proceeded up the steps, turned to his right and stopped outside a closed door where he could hear the sound of women's voices. He swallowed hard and knocked. A woman he didn't recognize partially opened the door and peeked out.

"May I help you?"

"Yes, I'm here to deliver a gift to Cherilyn Vernon." He struggled to keep his voice from shaking.

"I'll take it," she said with outstretched hands.

"Sorry, I have to give it directly to the bride. You understand, right?"

"I guess." She turned her back to him. "Cherilyn, there's a man here who says he has a gift he can *only* deliver to you."

"Ooh, really?" The bride's voice rose in expectation. "Tell him I'll be right there."

"She's coming. I'd ask you in, but there are ladies getting dressed in here."

Nick held his breath and waited. A few seconds later, a rustling sound preceded the door opening wider. He lost his breath when Cherilyn appeared looking like a vision in a strapless gown with sparkling jewels adorning her ample cleavage. When she saw him, she merely stared, tongue-tied.

"Cher, I know this is inappropriate, but I had to come and bring this to you." She stared down at the box he held out to her. "Please open it."

She still hadn't spoken, but she took the gift from his hand and removed the top. A soft gasp escaped her as she stared down at the elegant white gold pendant of the Eiffel Tower that captured the tower's distinctive beauty. Round diamonds brought the brilliance of the tower's lights to life. He'd taken three-hundred dollars from his already anemic bank account to buy the necklace.

Tears immediately sprung to her eyes. She stepped out into the hall and closed the door behind her. "What does this mean, Nick?"

"It means you're getting ready to make the biggest mistake of your life." His eyes drank in the sensuality of her full-figure in the form-fitting strapless gown. "It means I still love you, and I don't believe you love Derrick. He was just your rebound man. If you don't marry him today, I promise you we'll go to Paris, and I'll marry you beneath the Eiffel Tower just the way you've always dreamed. *Please* don't do this, Cher."

The door suddenly opened, and Cherilyn's mother stared at him open-mouthed. "How dare you come here, Nick! Leave now, or I'll have security escort you off the property."

"I'm sorry, Mrs. Vernon, but I had to speak to her before she did this."

Her nostrils flared. "How dare you!" she repeated with mounting rage. "I'm going to find security."

Cherilyn held up her hand. "No, Mommy. Please close the door. I need to talk to him for a minute. Her mother glowered at her and turned away muttering under her breath. Cherilyn closed the door again.

"You wouldn't return my phone calls, Cher. What other choice did I have? I've called you every day for the past two weeks, and you wouldn't return my calls."

She blinked as though she were bewildered. "Why are you doing this?"

"Because I can't let you marry him. I messed up. I know that, baby." His heart thundered in his chest. "I panicked at the thought of added responsibilities on top of medical school, but I was wrong. If you can look me in my eyes and tell me you don't love me anymore, I'll leave." He knew the answer by the way she averted her gaze from his face.

"I can't do that to Derrick. He's a good man."

"Look at me, Cher. I'm sure he is, but if you still love me, you're doing an awful thing to Derrick by marrying him. Your marriage would be a lie."

A tear cascaded over her cheek. "Please go away, Nick." She shoved the box into his chest. "I can't. We have two-hundred guests waiting upstairs. I can't! You need to go, Nick, please." He pressed the box into her hand once again, and she shut the door in his face.

He stood there for a long moment before he could get his feet to move. As he reluctantly trudged toward the steps back to the first floor, it was as though an unseen force turned him in the direction of the ballroom. If she insisted on going through with the wedding, he needed to see it with his own eyes. It would be the only way he could make his mind understand that it was truly over between them.

A few early birds sat in the white chairs that filled the elegant ballroom, so Nick took a seat in the back to wait for the start of the ceremony. He wanted to be near the door so he could make a quick exit once the wedding ended. He sat at the inside end of the row. The disdain on Mrs. Vernon's face was burned into his mind. Not long ago, he had been one of her favorite people. Now she despised him for breaking with Cher the way he had. If there had been some other way to handle this, he would've done it, but her daughter had completely shut him out after the last night they had been together. The memory of what he'd done to cause their break-up put an ache in his chest every time he replayed it in his mind.

"Do you realize we've been together for more than two years?" *she'd asked him after they finished their dinner of homemade smothered chicken, rice, sautéed spinach and biscuits. Cherilyn was a superb cook, and she wasn't one of those girls who agonized over every bite she put into her mouth for fear of gaining an ounce.*

"Right. We met in January at Ryan's New Year's Eve party. I hadn't been out anywhere for ages, because I was studying for the second phase of my licensing exam."

"Are you happy with our relationship the way it is?" she asked studying him intently.

"Sure I am. Aren't you? I don't think there are two people more compatible than we are."

"That's true, and that's why I feel like we should be thinking about going to the next level."

His eyes widened. Did she mean what he thought she meant? They were already sexually involved, so she obviously wasn't talking about that. "Right now, I think we should stay right where we are. With school and all, this is not the time for me to make any major moves."

She clasped her hands together and stared at them, lowering her lashes quickly. When she lifted her gaze, pain flickered there. "How long do you plan for us to stay where we are?"

"I don't know, baby. Does it matter? I thought we were happy together. I know I am." He smiled, and she returned a blank stare.

Cherilyn spoke calmly, with no lighting of her eyes, no smile of tenderness. "Nick, you know I want to get married. I never made any secret about that. How would it change anything?"

"That's what I want to know. How would getting married change an already great relationship?"

An expression of tired sadness passed over her features, and she sighed. "It would show me that you are serious about us, and I'm not just a place to stop when you want to do your laundry or get a home-cooked meal, or get your rocks off."

He hadn't meant to hurt her, but the damage was already done. "I don't think of you that way, Cher. You're the only woman in my life, and I like it that way."

"But I'm still not good enough for you to marry?"

"You aren't the problem. It's my life at the moment. School is about to kill me, and I still have two years of residency facing me."

"And you don't think having a wife to help you would make your life easier?"

This time he was the one with the blank stare.

She rose from the sofa and clicked off the television. "My mother was so right. What reason would a man have to commit to a woman who's already giving him everything? You should go now, Nick."

"Baby, come on. I'm just trying to be realistic about where I'm at right now."

"Right," she said, standing with her hands on her voluptuous hips. "You're going home, and I'm not playing wifey anymore. Lock the door on your way out."

He gaped at her retreating back as she carried the dishes into the kitchen. "Cher…"

"Good night, Nick."

Looking back on that night, Nick realized everything she'd said was true. Being with her had become so comfortable that he'd taken it for granted. Her sweet nature and sense of humor   calmed him after he'd had a grueling day. And she'd been there for him with the pleasure of her incredible body and her culinary skills. He was ashamed for lying to his family and telling them he and Cherilyn split because he was getting too serious, but if he had told them the truth he would've looked like a fool for so carelessly letting such a wonderful woman get away.

Soft music began to play, and after it played for nearly twenty-five minutes with no appearance of anyone in the bridal party, the low hum of whispers gradually rose as the guests started shooting restless glances over their shoulders. Everyone seemed to realize this delay was more than a bride being fashionably late, and their speculation was confirmed when the groom appeared at the front of the room with the best man at his side.

He appeared visibly shaken. Nick held his breath as Derrick's words came haltingly. "I'm sorry…but…but there's not going to be a wedding today. Please enjoy the food and drink…and please take your gifts with you when you leave. I'm sorry." The best man escorted him through a side door with his arm around the groom's back as though he were holding him up.

Nick rushed out of the doors before he was detected by any guests who knew him. Little did they know he was as shocked by the turn of events as they were; Cherilyn hadn't given him any indication that she was having second thoughts. He'd needed to get away before the groomsmen or Cherilyn's father spotted him. Mr. Vernon liked him when he and Cherilyn were dating, but their breakup had surely changed his opinion. He strode out of the ballroom as fast as he could without drawing attention to himself. Once he closed himself in the car, he took out his phone and sent a text to Cherilyn before he passed through the front fountain garden and left the property. *Can I come by your place? We need to talk ASAP.*

Cherilyn broke down as soon as she closed the door. Her bridesmaids rushed to her aid, helped her sit on one of the white ottomans in the middle of the salon. One of them fanned her with a paper plate from the table with the appetizers that had been provided for the bridal party. Her maid of honor poured her a glass of cold water and pushed it into her hand.

Her mother paced around the room ranting about Nick being an ignorant barbarian, and then she asked, "How could he intrude on your special day like that? What is in the box?" She reached for the gift, but Cherilyn snatched it away and clutched it to her breast.

"It's personal, Mommy," she sobbed, her professionally-applied makeup beginning to run down her cheeks. Another one of her attendants dabbed her face with a tissue.

"Girl, what is wrong with you? You are getting ready to marry a wonderful man, and you're letting that…that *boy* get you all upset. Nick Stafford is your past. Don't let him ruin your future!"

"Your mother is right," another one of the bridesmaids agreed, tipping the water glass up to Cherilyn's lips. "Forget about him. If he'd wanted you, he would've married you when he had the chance."

"That's the problem," she blubbered. "I didn't want to admit it to anyone, but I still love Nick, and he's realized he still loves me."

Her mother stopped pacing and stood in front of her daughter with a red-faced scowl. "How can you be sure that's why he came? Maybe he just resents being beaten out by a better man."

"Stop!" Cherilyn waved them all away. "I need time to

think."

"Baby, you don't have time. Derrick is waiting for you at the altar." Mrs. Vernon pressed a hand to her forehead and grimaced as if she were in pain. "You can't do this to him."

"Would you rather I married him knowing I'm still in love with Nick? That would be starting our marriage out with a lie."

The bridesmaids all stared at each other as though they were at a loss for anything to say.

Shamika, her maid of honor, took her hand. "What do you want us to do, Cher?"

"Go get Derrick, please, and everyone leave us alone for a few minutes. I have to tell him this face to face."

"Tell him what?" her mother asked, looking at her as though she already knew the answer.

She clenched her jaw to kill the sob in her throat. "That I can't marry him."

"Oh, Cherilyn," her mother moaned. "Don't you know how that will hurt him?"

"It would hurt him more to know I married him but was still in love with Nick." She dropped her head into her hands and covered her face. "Somebody go get him, please."

"I'll do it," Mika said, standing and smoothing her gown. Ladies, why don't you go downstairs to the ballroom, so they can have some privacy." She stuffed a wad of tissues into Cherilyn's hand and kissed her cheek. "I'll stay in the hall in case you need me."

Girding herself with resolve, Cherilyn imposed an iron control on herself while she waited for Derrick to come upstairs from one of the wine cellar rooms he and the groomsmen occupied on the lower level. How was she going to say this?

Several minutes later, Derrick stood in the doorway looking suave and handsome, yet his face was clouded with uneasiness. "What's going on, Cher?"

She slid the box Nick had given her underneath the ottoman and stared wordlessly at him, her heart pounding and lower lip trembling as she returned his gaze. "I…I can't…"

"You can't what?"

"I can't go through with the wedding." Her voice was fragile and shaking. So were her hands as she dragged them over her face, further smearing her makeup.

Derrick moved closer and knelt in front of her. "Oh, sweetheart, it's just cold feet." He took her hands, held them between his and gazed into her eyes. "Let me get you a glass of wine. That'll help calm you down."

Cherilyn grabbed his hand as he went to stand. "I'm still in love with Nick."

The tension between them increased with frightening intensity, "And you didn't know that yesterday or last week or last month?" His voice was absolutely emotionless and it chilled her. "How could you?" He pulled the door open with such force it slammed against the adjacent wall and he stormed down the hall.

Mika ran in and pulled Cherilyn into her arms. "What happened?"

"When I told him I wanted to call the wedding off, he thought I just had cold feet." She sniffed and blew her nose into a tissue. "But then I told him how I felt about Nick. Oh, God, Mika, the way he looked at me was so awful! Did I make a horrible mistake?"

"Not if you love Nick," Mika said with a hint of a smile.

"Let me help you out of this dress. Do you want to put on what you wore here?"

"Yes, and could you take me home, please?"

"Sure, honey, but you're still pretty shaky. Maybe you should sit for a few until you calm down. Stand up for a sec." She started unbuttoning the first about twenty buttons at the back of the gown but stopped when Cherilyn's parents entered the room. "I'll go get you a drink," she whispered in her ear.

"Okay. Thanks."

"Oh, Cherilyn, why did you do this?" Her mother moaned.

Her father raised his hand. "Don't." He drew his daughter into a comforting hug. "Are you okay?"

"I don't know, Daddy. I'm so sorry for embarrassing you and Mommy."

"Stop it." He kissed her damp cheek and chuckled. "We would've been more embarrassed if you'd gone through with it and ended up getting divorced six months later."

"Thanks, Daddy. I just want to get away from here. Mika's taking me home. I just need to take off this dress."

Mika returned with a glass of wine and took her into the en suite powder room inside the salon where she washed off Cherilyn's mascara-streaked face then finished unbuttoning the gown and handed her the outfit she had on earlier. "Sit down and sip this. I'll be right back."

Mika eventually exited the bathroom and spoke to Mr. and Mrs. Vernon. "I'm going to take her back to her apartment. Mrs. Vernon, can you please round up the other girls and let them know?" she asked, finding a reason to get her mother out of the room. "Mr. Vernon, will you stay with Cher until I get the limo to come around to the back of the building?" She left the room with her arm hooked through Mrs. Vernon's.

Cherilyn opened the powder room door and peeked out. "Who told everyone the wedding is off?" she asked her father when she saw they were alone.

"Derrick did. The best man went out with him."

"He must hate me."

"I imagine he's pretty angry, but he'll come to see that it's for the best."

"Do you really think so?"

"He will. It might take some time, and meeting another woman, but he will."

"God, I hope so."

"Your mother said Nick came to see you. What did he have to say?"

"He said I was making the biggest mistake of my life and he couldn't let me marry Derrick because he was still in love with me."

"Why did he wait until the last second to tell you in front of all the family and guests?"

"Daddy, he's been calling me and texting me for three months ever since he found out Derrick and I were engaged. I refused to answer him. He said it was his last resort."

Mika returned to the salon looking flushed and sweaty as though she'd been running. "Are you ready? I explained to the driver that we're going back to your apartment then he can return for the rest of the girls. We need to go out through the kitchen so nobody sees us."

"Let's grab all your things and get out of here," Mika said, stuffing the wedding gown and veil back into a garment bag. Cherilyn reached under the ottoman and retrieved the box holding the necklace then picked up her sparkly white shoes and put them inside the bridal money bag, a gift from her bridesmaids.

"I'm so sorry, Daddy." She kissed her father on the cheek and followed Mika down a set of stairs that led to the kitchen where they escaped out a service entrance. Her best friend threw the garment bag into the back seat of the limo and they jumped inside, all the while gazing around the area to see if any guests saw them.

"I knew all along I shouldn't have accepted Derrick's proposal. Nick has always been in the back of my mind," she whispered to Mika so the driver wouldn't hear. "Even though we weren't seeing each other anymore, a piece of my heart still belonged to him. I kept telling myself it didn't matter, but when he showed up here today, I couldn't deny my feelings."

"You're doing the right thing, Cher. I think everybody was shocked when you announced your engagement after dating Derrick for only five months."

"I knew it was too soon, but something inside me just wanted to prove to Nick that another man wanted me."

"You can't marry a man for spite." When she looked up, tears were streaming down Cherilyn's cheeks. "Oh, girl, don't cry. I didn't mean that in an ugly way."

"It's not what you said. I'm just so angry with myself for not listening to my heart in the first place."

"Well, it's over now, and–" Mika's phone rang, and it took her a minute to find her purse amongst all of the items she'd grabbed from the salon. When she clicked into her missed calls, her expression changed into a wide smile. "That was Nick. Should I call him back?"

She was too surprised to do more than nod.

"Hello, Nick. What? We didn't know you stayed for the

ceremony. We're in the limo on the way back to Cher's place. Yes, here she is."

Cherilyn took the phone with a trembling hand. "You were there?"

"Yes," he said in a soft voice. "I had to see if you would go through with it. I'm so glad you didn't. Mika said you're going back to your apartment. Is it all right if I meet you there?"

"Uh, yes. I don't see why not."

"See you in a few minutes."

Cherilyn handed the phone back to Mika. When she dropped her head back into the cushy headrest and closed her eyes, the guilt poured over her. "Am I a horrible person for what I just did to Derrick?"

"You did what you had to do," her best friend since high school tried to reassure her. "Stop beating yourself up, and think about your next step. What's in the box, anyway?"

She glanced down at the tiny gift box still clutched in her hand, and then handed it to Mika with a sigh.

"It's beautiful. Is it real?" Mika asked, examining the sparkling necklace.

"Of course it's real. Nick isn't into fake anything, but that's not the point. It's what the necklace symbolizes."

"What does it mean?"

"He and I used to spend a lot of time sharing our daydreams. One of mine was getting married in Paris standing under the Eiffel Tower. When he gave me the box, he said if I'd marry him, we'll get married there."

"He didn't mean right away, did he?" Mika asked with a questioning frown.

"I don't know. We didn't exactly have time to get into

details."

"You always said Nick didn't have any money. How does he intend to whisk you away to France?"

Cherilyn chuckled. "When the Stafford brothers say they're broke, they don't mean broke the way the rest of us do. He once told me his parents put money in trust for each of them that they couldn't touch until they graduated from college, but I wouldn't expect him to dip into it for a European vacation. I don't even want to think about more wedding plans right now anyway. Just knowing he wants to marry me is enough at the moment."

"If you ask me, you'd better strike while the iron is hot, girl," Mika said with a devious smirk.

The limo pulled up in front of Cherilyn's apartment, their starting point this morning. The driver exited and opened the rear door.

"I'm going to see her inside," Mika informed him. "And I'll be right out." She grabbed the gown and other items off the seat and followed the runaway bride up the steps.

Cherilyn unlocked the door to her apartment and pulled her friend into a long hug. "Everyone should have a best friend like you. Thanks, Mika."

"Are you sure you're going to be all right?"

"Nick is on his way. He should be here any minute. I'll be fine."

"Let me put these things inside." Mika took the armful of items and laid them on the chair next to the door, then kissed her cheek and stood back with a gentle, contemplative look. "Make sure you call me if you intend to get on a plane, you hear me?"

"I promise, but we're not going anywhere. Go ahead,

and get that limo back so he can take the rest of the girls home. Please apologize to them all for me."

Mika turned to head back to the car then stopped midway down the sidewalk. "I mean it, Cher. Don't leave this country without telling me." Nick's Charger pulled up behind the limo, and he jumped out. "I guess I'd better get out of here. Love you, girl."

He climbed the four steps leading up to her door and drew her into his arms. "Thank you for giving me another chance. I won't blow it again."

She felt her knees weaken as his mouth descended onto hers in a kiss that sang through her veins. When he raised his mouth from hers, and gazed into her eyes, it was as though they had never been apart all these months.

"I love you, Cher."

"I love you too. Let's go inside."

Thank you for reading *I'm Losing You*. If you enjoyed **I'm Losing You**, please leave a review wherever you purchased the book and on Goodreads.

Note

Vic and Mona avoided the worst, but I have also written a story about another married couple that wasn't as fortunate. Michael and Dee Reese's marriage took a different turn in *Ain't Nothing Like the Real Thing*. If you think their inspirational story might interest you, a free sample is available for download.

Book List

Have You Seen Her?

Hot Fun in the Summertime

Hollywood Swinging

Ain't Nothing Like the Real Thing

I Can't Get Next to You

Ain't Too Proud to Beg

You Make Me Feel Brand New

A Woman's Worth – Book One in the Stafford Brothers Series

Till You Come Back to Me – Book Two in the Stafford Brothers Series

Don't Stop Till You Get Enough – Book Three in the Stafford Brothers Series

I'm Losing You – Book Four in the Stafford Brothers Series

About the Author

Contemporary women's fiction/romance author Chicki Brown has published nine novels and one novella. Her books have been featured in USAToday. She was the 2014 B.R.A.B. (Building Relationships Around Books) Inspirational Fiction Author and the 2011 SORMAG (Shades of Romance Magazine) Author of the Year. Chicki was also a contributing author to the *Gumbo for the Soul: Men of Honor (Special Cancer Awareness Edition)*. She is currently working on the fourth book in her Stafford brothers series.

Nia Forrester, Beverly Jenkins, Eric Jerome Dickey, Lisa Kleypas, and J.R. Ward are among her favorite authors.

A transplanted New Jersey native who lives in Atlanta, Georgia, Brown still misses the Jersey shore.

Her many homes in cyberspace include:

Blog: http://sisterscribbler.blogspot.com
Twitter: http://twitter.com/@Chicki663
Facebook: http://www.facebook.com/chicki.brown

Pinterest: http://pinterest.com/chicki663/

Suggested Reads

Johnson Family series by Delaney Diamond

Jenkins Family series by Sharon Cooper

Brooks Family series by Iris Bolling

Caldwell Family Series by Synithia Williams

Made in the USA
Columbia, SC
30 October 2021